# *Rumpole and the Age of Miracles*

G·K
Hall
&Cº

Also published in Large Print
from G.K. Hall by John Mortimer:

*Rumpole's Last Case*
*Dunster*

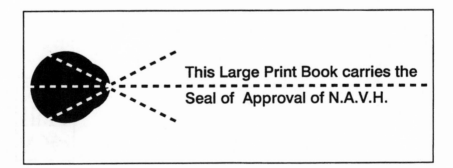

This Large Print Book carries the
Seal of Approval of N.A.V.H.

# Rumpole and the Age of Miracles

## John Mortimer

G.K. Hall & Co.
Thorndike, Maine

Published in 1995 by arrangement with Viking Penguin, a division of Penguin Books USA Inc.

*We Were Dancing* is copyright 1935 by the Estate of Noel Coward and the quotation on page 274 by permission of Michael Imison Playrights Ltd.

G.K. Hall Large Print Paperback Collection.

The text of this Large Print edition is unabridged.
Other aspects of the book may vary from the original edition.

Set in 16 pt. News Plantin.

Printed in the United States on permanent paper.

**Library of Congress Cataloging in Publication Data**

Mortimer, John Clifford, 1923–
    Rumpole and the age of miracles / John Mortimer.
        p.    cm.
    ISBN 0-7838-1188-8 (lg. print : lsc)
    1. Rumpole, Horace (Fictitious character) — Fiction.
2.  Detective and mystery stories, English. 3. Legal stories, English. 4. Large type books. I. Title.
    [PR6025.O7552R775  1995]
    823'.914—dc20                                          94-41448

To Penny

# Contents

Rumpole and the Bubble Reputation     9

Rumpole and the Barrow Boy     58

Rumpole and the Age of Miracles     116

Rumpole and the Tap End     172

Rumpole and the Chambers Party     233

Rumpole and Portia     242

Rumpole and the Quality of Life     295

# Rumpole and the Bubble Reputation

It is now getting on for half a century since I took to crime, and I can honestly say I haven't regretted a single moment of it.

Crime is about life, death and the liberty of the subject; civil law is entirely concerned with that most tedious of all topics, money. Criminal law requires an expert knowledge of bloodstains, policemen's notebooks and the dark flow of human passion, as well as the argot currently in use round the Elephant and Castle. Civil law calls for a close study of such yawn-producing matters as bills of exchange, negotiable instruments and charter parties. It is true, of course, that the most enthralling murder produces only a small and long-delayed Legal Aid cheque, sufficient to buy a couple of dinners at some Sunday supplement eaterie for the learned friends who practise daily in the commercial courts. Give me, however, a sympathetic jury, a blurred thumbprint and a dodgy confession, and you can keep *Mega-Chemicals Ltd* v. *The Sunshine Bank of Florida* with all its fifty days of mammoth refreshers for the well-heeled barristers involved.

There is one drawback, however, to being a criminal hack; the Judges and the learned friends are apt to regard you as though you were the proud possessor of a long line of convictions. How many times have I stood up to address the tribunal on such matters as the importance of intent or the presumption of innocence only to be stared at by the old darling on the Bench as though I were sporting a black mask or carrying a large sack labelled SWAG? Often, as I walk through the Temple on my way down to the Bailey, my place of work, I have seen bowler-hatted commercial or revenue men pass by on the other side and heard them mutter, 'There goes old Rumpole. I wonder if he's doing a murder or a rape this morning?' The sad truth of the matter is that civil law is regarded as the Harrods and crime the Tesco's of the legal profession. And of all the varieties of civil action the most elegant, the smartest, the one which attracts the best barristers like bees to the honey-pot, is undoubtedly the libel action. Star in a libel case on the civilized stage of the High Court of Justice and fame and fortune will be yours, if you haven't got them already.

It's odd, isn't it? Kill a person or beat him over the head and remove his wallet, and all you'll get is an Old Bailey judge and an Old Bailey hack. Cast a well-deserved slur on his moral character, ridicule his nose or belittle his bank balance and you will get a High Court judge and some of the smoothest silks in the business. I can only remember doing one libel action, and after it I asked my clerk, Henry, to find me a nice clean assault or an honest break and entering. Exactly why I did so will become clear to you when I have revealed the full and hitherto unpublished details of *Amelia Nettleship* v. *The Daily Beacon and Maurice Machin.* If, after reading what went on in that particular defamation case, you don't agree that crime presents a fellow with a more honourable alternative, I shall have to think seriously about issuing a writ for libel.

You may be fortunate enough never to have read an allegedly 'historical' novel by that much-publicized authoress Miss Amelia Nettleship. Her books contain virginal heroines and gallant and gentlemanly heroes and thus present an extremely misleading account of our rough island story. She is frequently photographed wearing cotton print dresses, with large spectacles on her still pretty nose, dictating to a secretary and a couple of long-suffering cats in a wistaria-clad Tudor cottage somewhere outside Godalming. In the interviews she gives, Miss Nettleship invariably refers to the evils of the permissive society and the consequences of sex before marriage. I have never, speaking for myself, felt the slightest urge to join the permissive society; the only thing which would tempt me to such a course is hearing Amelia Nettleship denounce it.

Why, you may well ask, should I, whose bed-time reading is usually confined to *The Oxford Book of English Verse* (the Quiller-Couch edition), Archbold's *Criminal Law* and Professor Ackerman's *Causes of Death*, become so intimately acquainted with Amelia Nettleship? Alas, she shares my bed, not in person but in book form, propped up on the bosom of She Who Must Be Obeyed, alias my wife, Hilda, who insists on reading her far into the night. While engrossed in *Lord Stingo's Fancy*, I distinctly heard her sniff, and asked if she had a cold coming on. 'No, Rumpole,' she told me. 'Touching!'

'Oh, I'm sorry.' I moved further down the bed.

'Don't be silly. The book's touching. Very touching. We all thought Lord Stingo was a bit of a rake but he's turned out quite differently.'

'Sounds a sad disappointment.'

'Nonsense! It's ending happily. He swore he'd never marry, but Lady Sophia has made him swallow his words.'

'And if they were written by Amelia Nettleship I'm sure he found them extremely indigestible. Any chance of turning out the light?'

'Not yet. I've got another three chapters to go.'

'Oh, for God's sake! Can't Lord Stingo get on with it?' As I rolled over, I had no idea that I was soon to become legally involved with the authoress who was robbing me of my sleep.

My story starts in Pommeroy's Wine Bar to which I had hurried for medical treatment (my alcohol content had fallen to a dangerous low) at the end of a day's work. As I sipped my large dose of Château Thames Embankment, I saw my learned friend Erskine-Brown, member of our Chambers at Equity Court, alone and palely loitering. 'What can ail you, Claude?' I asked, and he told me it was his practice.

'Still practising?' I raised an eyebrow. 'I thought you might have got the hang of it by now.'

'I used to do a decent class of work,' he told me sadly. 'I once had a brief in a libel action. You were never in a libel, Rumpole?'

'Who cares about the bubble reputation? Give me a decent murder and a few well-placed bloodstains.'

'Now, guess what I've got coming up?' The man was wan with care.

'Another large claret for me, I sincerely hope.'

'Actual bodily harm and affray in the Kitten-A-Go-Go Club, Soho.' Claude is married to the Portia of our Chambers, the handsome Phillida Erskine-Brown, Q.C., and they are blessed with issue rejoicing in the names of Tristan and Isolde. He is, you understand, far more at home in the Royal Opera House than in any Soho Striperama. 'Two unsavoury characters in leather jackets were duelling with broken Coca-Cola bottles.'

'Sounds like my line of country,' I told him.

'Exactly! I'm scraping the bottom of your barrel, Rumpole. I mean, you've got a reputation for sordid cases. I'll have to ask you for a few tips.'

'Visit the *locus in quo*' was my expert advice. 'Go to the scene of the crime. Inspect the geography of the place.'

'The geography of the Kitten-A-Go-Go? Do I have to?'

'Of course. Then you can suggest it was too dark to identify anyone, or the witness couldn't see round a pillar, or . . .'

But at that point we were interrupted by an eager, bespectacled fellow of about Erskine-Brown's age who introduced himself as Ted Spratling from the *Daily Beacon*. 'I was just having an argument with my editor over there, Mr Rumpole,' he said. 'You do libel cases, don't you?'

'Good heavens, yes!' I lied with instant enthusiasm, sniffing a brief. 'The law of defamation is mother's milk to me. I cut my teeth on hatred, ridicule and contempt.' As I was speaking, I saw Claude Erskine-Brown eyeing the journalist like a long-lost brother. 'Slimey Spratling!' he hallooed at last.

'Collywobbles Erskine-Brown!' The hack seemed equally amazed. There was no need to tell me that they were at school together.

'Look, would you join my editor for a glass of Bolly?' Spratling invited me.

'What?'

'Bollinger.'

'I'd love to!' Erskine-Brown was visibly cheered.

'Oh, you too, Colly. Come on, then.'

'Golly, Colly!' I said as we crossed the bar towards a table in the corner. 'Bolly!'

So I was introduced to Mr Maurice — known as 'Morry' — Machin, a large silver-haired person with distant traces of a Scots accent, a blue silk suit and a thick gold ring in which a single diamond winked sullenly. He was surrounded with empty Bolly bottles and a masterful-looking woman whom he introduced as Connie Coughlin, the features editor. Morry himself had, I knew, been for many years at the helm of the tabloid *Daily Beacon*, and had blasted many precious reputations with well-aimed scandal stories and reverberating 'revelations'. 'They say you're a fighter, Mr Rumpole, that you're a terrier, sir, after a legal rabbit,' he started, as Ted Spratling performed the deputy editor's duty of pouring the bubbly.

'I do my best. This is my learned friend, Claude Erskine-Brown, who specializes in affray.'

'I'll remember you, sir, if I get into a scrap.' But the Editor's real business was with me. 'Mr Rumpole, we are thinking of briefing you. We're in a spot of bother over a libel.'

'Tell him,' Claude muttered to me, 'you can't do libel.'

'I never turn down a brief in a libel action.' I spoke with confidence, although Claude continued to mutter, 'You've never been offered a brief in a libel action.'

'I don't care,' I said, 'for little scraps in Soho. Sordid stuff. Give me a libel action, when a reputation is at stake.'

'You think that's important?' Morry looked at me seriously, so I treated him to a taste of *Othello*. 'Good name in man or woman, dear my lord' (I was at my most impressive),

15

'Is the immediate jewel of their souls;
Who steals my purse steals trash;
   'tis something, nothing.
'Twas mine, 'tis his, and has been slave to
      thousands;
But he that filches from me my good name
Robs me of that which not enriches him,
And makes me poor indeed.'


Everyone, except Erskine-Brown, was listening reverently. After I had finished there was a solemn pause. Then Morry clapped three times.

'Is that one of your speeches, Mr Rumpole?'

'Shakespeare's.'

'Ah, yes . . .'

'Your good name, Mr Machin, is something I shall be prepared to defend to the death,' I said.

'Our paper goes in for a certain amount of fearless exposure,' the *Beacon* Editor explained.

'The "*Beacon* Beauties".' Erskine-Brown was smiling. 'I catch sight of it occasionally in the clerk's room.'

'Not that sort of exposure, Collywobbles!' Spratling rebuked his old school-friend. 'We tell the truth about people in the public eye.'

'Who's bonking who and who pays,' Connie from Features explained. 'Our readers love it.'

'I take exception to that, Connie. I really do,' Morry said piously. 'I don't want Mr Rumpole to get the idea that we're running any sort of a cheap scandal-sheet.'

16

'Scandal-sheet? Perish the thought!' I was working hard for my brief.

'You wouldn't have any hesitation in acting for the *Beacon*, would you?' the Editor asked me.

'A barrister is an old taxi plying for hire. That's the fine tradition of our trade,' I explained carefully. 'So it's my sacred duty, Mr Morry Machin, to take on anyone in trouble. However repellent I may happen to find them.'

'Thank you, Mr Rumpole.' Morry was genuinely grateful.

'Think nothing of it.'

'We are dedicated to exposing hypocrisy in our society. Wherever it exists. High or low.' The Editor was looking noble. 'So when we find this female pretending to be such a force for purity and parading her morality before the Great British Public . . .'

'Being all for saving your cherry till the honeymoon,' Connie Coughlin translated gruffly.

'Thank you, Connie. Or, as I would put it, denouncing premarital sex,' Morry said.

'She's even against the *normal* stuff!' Spratling was bewildered.

'Whereas her own private life is extremely steamy. We feel it our duty to tell our public. Show Mr Rumpole the article in question, Ted.'

I don't know if they had expected to meet me in Pommeroy's but the top brass of the *Daily Beacon* had a cutting of the alleged libel at the ready. THE PRIVATE LIFE OF AMELIA NETTLE-SHIP BY BEACON GIRL ON THE SPOT, STELLA

17

JANUARY I read, and then glanced at the story that followed. 'This wouldn't be *the* Amelia Nettleship?' I was beginning to warm to my first libel action. 'The expert bottler of pure historical bilge-water?'

'The lady novelist and hypocrite,' Morry told me. 'Of course I've never met the woman.'

'She robs me of my sleep. I know nothing of her morality, but her prose style depraves and corrupts the English language. We shall need a statement from this Stella January.' I got down to business.

'Oh, Stella left us a couple of months ago,' the Editor told me.

'And went where?'

'God knows. Overseas, perhaps. You know what these girls are.'

'We've got to find her,' I insisted and then cheered him up with 'We shall fight, Mr Machin — Morry. And we shall conquer! Remember, I never plead guilty.'

'There speaks a man who knows damn all about libel.' Claude Erskine-Brown had a final mutter.

It might be as well if I quoted here the words in Miss Stella January's article which were the subject of legal proceedings. They ran as follows: *Miss Amelia Nettleship is a bit of a puzzle. The girls in her historical novels always keep their legs crossed until they've got a ring on their fingers. But her private life is rather different. Whatever lucky young man leads the 43-year-old Amelia to the altar will inherit a torrid past which makes Mae West*

18

*sound like Florence Nightingale. Her home, Holly-hock Cottage, near Godalming, has been the scene of one-night stands and longer liaisons so numerous that the neighbours have given up counting. There is considerably more in her jacuzzi than bath salts. Her latest Casanova, so far unnamed, is said to be a married man who's been seen leaving in the wee small hours.* From the style of this piece of prose you may come to the conclusion that Stella January and Amelia Nettleship deserved each other.

One thing you can say for my learned friend Claude Erskine-Brown is that he takes advice. Having been pointed in the direction of the Kitten-A-Go-Go, he set off obediently to find a cul-de-sac off Wardour Street with his instructing solicitor. He wasn't to know, and it was entirely his bad luck, that Connie Coughlin had dreamt up a feature on London's Square Mile of Sin for the *Daily Beacon* and ordered an ace photographer to comb the sinful purlieus between Oxford Street and Shaftesbury Avenue in search of nefarious goings-on.

Erskine-Brown and a Mr Thrower, his sedate solicitor, found the Kitten-A-Go-Go, paid a sinister-looking myrmidon at the door ten quid each by way of membership and descended to a damp and darkened basement where two young ladies were chewing gum and removing their clothes with as much enthusiasm as they might bring to the task of licking envelopes. Claude took a seat in the front row and tried to commit the geography of the place to memory. It must be said, however, that his eyes were fixed on the plumpest of the disrobing performers when a sudden and unexpected flash preserved his face and more of the stripper for the five million readers of the *Daily Beacon* to enjoy with their breakfast. Not being a particularly observant barrister, Claude left the strip joint with no idea of the ill luck that had befallen him.

Whilst Erskine-Brown was thus exploring the underworld, I was closeted in the Chambers of that elegant Old Etonian civil lawyer Robin Peppiatt, Q.C., who, assisted by his Junior, Dick Garsington, represented the proprietor of the *Beacon*. I was entering the lists in the defence of Morry Machin, and our joint solicitor was an anxious little man called Cuxham, who seemed ready to pay almost any amount of someone else's money to be shot of the whole business. Quite early in our meeting, almost as soon, in fact, as Peppiatt had poured Earl Grey into thin china cups and handed round the *petit' beurres,* it became clear that everyone wanted to do a deal with the other side except my good self and my client, the Editor.

'We should work as a team,' Peppiatt started. 'Of which, as leading Counsel, I am, I suppose, the Captain.'

'Are we playing cricket, old chap?' I ventured to ask him.

'If we were it would be an extremely expensive

game for the *Beacon*.' The Q.C. gave me a toler-ant smile. 'The proprietors have contracted to indemnify the Editor against any libel dam-ages.'

'I insisted on that when I took the job,' Morry told us with considerable satisfaction.

'Very sensible of your client, no doubt, Rumpole. Now, you may not be used to this type of case as you're one of the criminal boys . . .'

'Oh, I know' — I admitted the charge — 'I'm just a juvenile delinquent.'

'But it's obvious to me that we mustn't attempt to justify these serious charges against Miss Nettleship's honour.' The Captain of the team gave his orders and I made bold to ask, 'Wouldn't that be cricket?'

'If we try to prove she's a sort of amateur tart the Jury might bump the damages up to two or three hundred grand,' Peppiatt explained as patiently as he could.

'Or four.' Dick Garsington shook his head sadly. 'Or perhaps half a million.' Mr Cuxham's mind boggled.

'But you've filed a defence alleging that the article's a true bill.' I failed to follow the drift of these faint-hearts.

'That's our bargaining counter.' Peppiatt spoke to me very slowly, as though to a child of limited intelligence.

'Our what?'

'Something to give away. As part of the deal.'

'When we agree terms with the other side we'll

21

abandon all our allegations. Gracefully,' Garsington added.

'We put up our hands?' I contemptuously tipped ash from my small cigar on to Peppiatt's Axminster. Dick Garsington was sent off to get 'an ashtray for Rumpole'.

'Peregrine Landseer's agin us.' Peppiatt seemed to be bringing glad tidings of great joy to all of us. 'I'm lunching with Perry at the Sheridan Club to discuss another matter. I'll just whisper the thought of a quiet little settlement into his ear.'

'Whisper sweet nothings!' I told him. 'I'll not be party to any settlement. I'm determined to defend the good name of my client Mr Maurice Machin as a responsible editor.'

'At our expense?' Peppiatt looked displeased.

'If neccessary. Yes! He wouldn't have published that story unless there was some truth in it. Would you?' I asked Morry, assailed by some doubt.

'Certainly not' — my client assured me — 'as a fair and responsible journalist.'

'The trouble is that there's no evidence that Miss Nettleship has done any of these things.' Clearly Mr Cuxham had long since thrown in the towel.

'Then we must find some! Isn't that what solicitors are for?' I asked, but didn't expect an answer. 'I'm quite unable to believe that anyone who writes so badly hasn't got *some* other vices.'

A few days later I entered the clerk's room

of our Chambers in Equity Court to see our clerk, Henry, seated at his desk looking at the centre pages of the *Daily Beacon*, which Dianne, our fearless but somewhat hit-and-miss typist, was showing him. As I approached, Dianne folded the paper, retreated to her desk and began to type furiously. They both straightened their faces and the smiles of astonishment I had noticed when I came in were replaced by looks of legal seriousness. In fact Henry spoke with almost religious awe when he handed me my brief in *Nettleship* v. *The Daily Beacon and anor.* Not only was a highly satisfactory fee marked on the front but refreshers, that is the sum required to keep a barrister on his feet and talking, had been agreed at no less than five hundred pounds a day.

'You *can* make the case last, can't you, Mr Rumpole?' Henry asked with understandable concern.

'Make it last?' I reassured him. 'I can make it stretch on till the trump of doom! We have serious and lengthy allegations, Henry. Allegations that will take days and days, with any luck. For the first time in a long career at the Bar I begin to see . . .'

'See what, Mr Rumpole?'

'A way of providing for my old age.'

The door then opened to admit Claude Erskine-Brown. Dianne and Henry regarded him with solemn pity, as though he'd had a death in his family.

'Here comes the poor old criminal lawyer,' I

greeted him. 'Any more problems with your affray, Claude?'

'All under control, Rumpole. Thank you very much. Morning, Dianne. Morning, Henry.' Our clerk and secretary returned his greeting in mournful voices. At that point, Erskine-Brown noticed Dianne's copy of the *Beacon*, wondered who the 'Beauty' of that day might be, and picked it up before she could stop him.

'What've you got there? The *Beacon*! A fine crusading paper. Tells the truth without fear or favour.' My refreshers had put me in a remarkably good mood. 'Are you feeling quite well, Claude?'

Erskine-Brown was holding the paper in trembling hands and had gone extremely pale. He looked at me with accusing eyes and managed to say in strangled tones, '*You* told me to go there!'

'For God's sake, Claude! Told you to go where?'

'The *locus in quo!*'

I took the *Beacon* from him and saw the cause of his immediate concern. The *locus in quo* was the Kitten-A-Go-Go, and the blown-up snap on the centre page showed Claude closely inspecting a young lady who was waving her underclothes triumphantly over her head. At that moment, Henry's telephone rang and he announced that Soapy Sam Ballard, our puritanical Head of Chambers, founder member of the Lawyers As Christians Society (L.A.C.) and the Savonarola of Equity Court, wished to see Mr Erskine-Brown in his room without delay. Claude left us with

24

the air of a man climbing up into the dock to receive a stiff but inevitable sentence.

I wasn't, of course, present in the Head of Chambers' room where Claude was hauled up. It was not until months later, when he had recovered a certain calm, that he was able to tell me how the embarrassing meeting went and I reconstruct the occasion for the purpose of this narrative.

'You wanted to see me, Ballard?' Claude started to babble. 'You're looking well. In wonderful form. I don't remember when I've seen you looking so fit.' At that early stage he tried to make his escape from the room. 'Well, nice to chat. I've got a summons, across the road.'

'Just a minute!' Ballard called him back. 'I don't read the *Daily Beacon*.'

'Oh, don't you? Very wise,' Claude congratulated him. Neither do I. Terrible rag. Half-clad beauties on page four and no law reports. So they tell me. Absolutely no reason to bother with the thing!'

'But, coming out of the Temple tube station, Mr Justice Fishwick pushed this in my face.' Soapy Sam lifted the fatal newspaper from his desk. 'It seems he's just remarried and his new wife takes in the *Daily Beacon*.'

'How odd!'

'What's odd?'

'A judge's wife. Reading the *Beacon*.'

'Hugh Fishwick married his cook,' Ballard told him in solemn tones.

'Really? I didn't know. Well, that explains it. But I don't see why he should push it in your face, Ballard.'

'Because he thought I ought to see it.'

'Nothing in that rag that could be of the slightest interest to you, surely?'

'Something is.'

'What?'

'You.'

Ballard held out the paper to Erskine-Brown, who approached it gingerly and took a quick look.

'Oh, really? Good heavens! Is that me?'

'Unless you have a twin brother masquerading as yourself. You feature in an article on London's Square Mile of Sin.'

'It's all a complete misunderstanding!' Claude assured our leader.

'I'm glad to hear it.'

'I can explain everything.'

'I hope so.'

'You see, I got into this affray.'

'You got into what?' Ballard saw even more cause for concern.

'This fight' — Claude wasn't improving his case — 'in the Kitten-A-Go-Go.'

'Perhaps I ought to warn you, Erskine-Brown.' Ballard was being judicial. 'You needn't answer incriminating questions.'

'No, *I* didn't get into a fight.' Claude was clearly rattled. 'Good heavens, no. I'm doing a case, about a fight. An affray. With Coca-Cola bottles. And Rumpole advised me to go to this club.'

'Horace Rumpole is an habitué of this house of ill-repute? At *his* age?' Ballard didn't seem to be in the least surprised to hear it.

'No, not at all. But he said I ought to take a view. Of the scene of the crime. This wretched scandal-sheet puts the whole matter in the wrong light. Entirely.'

There was a long and not entirely friendly pause before Ballard proceeded to judgment. 'If that is so, Erskine-Brown,' he said, 'and I make no further comment while the matter is *sub judice,* you will no doubt be suing the *Daily Beacon* for libel?'

'You think I should?' Claude began to count the cost of such an action.

'It is quite clearly your duty. To protect your own reputation and the reputation of this Chambers.'

'Wouldn't it be rather expensive?' I can imagine Claude gulping, but Ballard was merciless.

'What is money,' he said, 'compared to the hitherto unsullied name of number three, Equity Court?'

Claude's next move was to seek out the friend of his boyhood, 'Slimey' Spratling, whom he finally found jogging across Hyde Park. When he told the *Beacon* deputy editor that he had been advised to issue a writ, the man didn't even stop and Erskine-Brown had to trot along beside him. 'Good news!' Spratling said. 'My editor seems to enjoy libel actions. Glad you liked your pic.'

'Of course I didn't like it. It'll ruin my career.'

27

'Nonsense, Collywobbles.' Spratling was cheerful. 'You'll get briefed by all the clubs. You'll be the strippers' Q.C.'

'However did they get my name?' Claude wondered.

'Oh, I recognized you at once,' Slimey assured him. 'Bit of luck, wasn't it?' Then he ran on, leaving Claude outraged. They had, after all, been to Winchester together.

When I told the helpless Cuxham that the purpose of solicitors is to gather evidence, I did so without much hope of my words stinging him into any form of activity. If evidence against Miss Nettleship were needed, I would have to look elsewhere, so I rang up that great source of knowledge 'Fig' Newton and invited him in for a drink at Pommeroy's.

Ferdinand Isaac Gerald, known to his many admirers as 'Fig' Newton, is undoubtedly the best in the somewhat unreliable band of professional private eyes. I know that Fig is now knocking seventy; that, with his filthy old mackintosh and collapsing hat, he looks like a scarecrow after a bad night; that his lantern jaw, watery eye and the frequently appearing drip on the end of the nose don't make him an immediately attractive figure. Fig may look like a scarecrow but he's a very bloodhound after a clue.

'I'm doing civil work now, Fig,' I told him when we met in Pommeroy's. 'Just got a big brief in a libel action which should provide a bit of comfort for my old age. But my instructing solicitor is someone we would describe, in legal terms, as a bit of a wally. I'd be obliged if you'd do his job for him and send him the bill when we win.'

'What is it that I am required to do, Mr Rumpole?' the great detective asked patiently.

'Keep your eye on a lady.'

'I usually am, Mr Rumpole. Keeping my eye on one lady or another.'

'This one's a novelist. A certain Miss Amelia Nettleship. Do you know her works?'

'Can't say I do, sir.' Fig had once confessed to a secret passion for Jane Austen. 'Are you on to a winner?'

'With a bit of help from you, Fig. Only one drawback here, as in most cases.'

'What's that, sir?'

'The client.' Looking across the bar I had seen the little group from the *Beacon* round the Bollinger. Having business with the Editor, I left Fig Newton to his work and crossed the room. Sitting myself beside my client I refused champagne and told him that I wanted him to do something about my learned friend Claude Erskine-Brown.

'You mean the barrister who goes to funny places in the afternoon? What're you asking me to do, Mr Rumpole?'

'Apologize, of course. Print the facts. Claude Erskine-Brown was in the Kitten-A-Go-Go purely in pursuit of his legal business.'

'I love it!' Morry's smile was wider than ever.

29

'There speaks the great defender. You'd put up any story, wouldn't you, however improbable, to get your client off.'

'It happens to be true.'

'So far as we are concerned' — Morry smiled at me patiently — 'we printed a pic of a gentleman in a pin-striped suit examining the goods on display. No reason to apologize for that, is there, Connie? What's your view, Ted?'

'No reason at all, Morry.' Connie supported him and Spratling agreed.

'So you're going to do nothing about it?' I asked with some anger.

'Nothing we *can* do.'

'Mr Machin.' I examined the man with distaste. 'I told you it was a legal rule that a British barrister is duty-bound to take on any client however repellent.'

'I remember you saying something of the sort.'

'You are stretching my duty to the furthest limits of human endurance.'

'Never mind, Mr Rumpole. I'm sure you'll uphold the best traditions of the Bar!'

When Morry said that I left him. However, as I was wandering away from Pommeroy's towards the Temple station, Gloucester Road, home and beauty, a somewhat breathless Ted Spratling caught up with me and asked me to do my best for Morry. 'He's going through a tough time.' I didn't think the man was entirely displeased by the news he had to impart. 'The Proprietor's going to sack him.'

'Because of this case?'

'Because the circulation's dropping. Tits and bums are going out of fashion. The wives don't like it.'

'Who'll be the next editor?'

'Well, I'm the deputy now . . .' He did his best to sound modest.

'I see. Look' — I decided to enlist an ally — 'would you help me with the case? In strict confidence, I want some sort of a lead to this Stella January. Can you find how her article came in? Get hold of the original. It might have an address. Some sort of clue . . .'

'I'll have a try, Mr Rumpole. Anything I can do to help old Morry.' Never had I heard a man speak with such deep insincerity.

The weather turned nasty, but, in spite of heavy rain, Fig Newton kept close observation for several nights on Hollyhock Cottage, home of Amelia Nettleship, without any particular result. One morning I entered our Chambers early and on my way to my room I heard a curious buzzing sound, as though an angry bee were trapped in the lavatory. Pulling open the door, I detected Erskine-Brown plying a cordless electric razor.

'Claude,' I said, 'you're shaving!'

'Wonderful to see the workings of a keen legal mind.' The man sounded somewhat bitter.

'I'm sorry about all this. But I'm doing my best to help you.'

'Oh, please!' He held up a defensive hand.

31

'Don't try and do anything else to help me. "Visit the scene of the crime," you said. "Inspect the *locus in quo!*" So where has your kind assistance landed me? My name's mud. Ballard's as good as threatened to kick me out of Chambers. I've got to spend my life's savings on a speculative libel action. And my marriage is on the rocks. Wonderful what you can do, Rumpole, with a few words of advice. Your clients must be ever-lastingly grateful.'

'Your marriage, on the rocks, did you say?'

'Oh, yes. Philly was frightfully reasonable about it. As far as she was concerned, she said, she didn't care what I did in the afternoons. But we'd better live apart for a while, for the sake of the children. She didn't want Tristan and Isolde to associate with a father dedicated to the exploitation of women.'

'Oh, Portia!' I felt for the fellow. 'What's happened to the quality of mercy?'

'So, thank you very much, Rumpole. I'm enormously grateful. The next time you've got a few helpful tips to hand out, for God's sake keep them to yourself!'

He switched on the razor again. I looked at it and made an instant deduction. 'You've been sleeping in Chambers. You want to watch that, Claude. Bollard nearly got rid of me for a similar offence.'[*]

* See 'Rumpole and the Old, Old Story' in *Rumpole's Last Case*, Penguin Books, 1987.

'Where do you expect me to go? Phillida's having the locks changed in Islington.'

'Have you no friends?'

'Philly and I have reached the end of the line. I don't exactly want to advertise the fact among my immediate circle. I seem to remember, Rumpole, when you fell out with Hilda you planted yourself on us!' As he said this I scented danger and tried to avoid what I knew was coming.

'Oh. Now. Erskine-Brown. Claude. I was enormously grateful for your hospitality on that occasion.'

'Quite an easy run in on the Underground, is it, from Gloucester Road?' He spoke in a meaningful way.

'Of course. My door is always open. I'd be delighted to put you up, just until this mess is straightened out. But . . .'

'The least you could do, I should have thought, Rumpole.'

'It's not a sacrifice I could ask, old darling, even of my dearest friend. I couldn't ask you to shoulder the burden of daily life with She Who Must Be Obeyed. Now I'm sure you can find a very comfortable little hotel, somewhere cheap and cosy, around the British Museum. I promise you, life is by no means a picnic, in the Gloucester Road.'

Well, that was enough, I thought, to dissuade the most determined visitor from seeking hospitality under the Rumpole roof. I went about my daily business and, when my work was done, I thought I should share some of the good fortune brought with my brief in the libel action with She Who Must Be Obeyed. I lashed out on two bottles of Pommeroy's bubbly, some of the least exhausted flowers to be found outside the tube station and even, such was my reckless mood, lavender water for Hilda.

'All the fruits of the earth,' I told her. 'Or, let's say, the fruits of the first cheque in *Nettleship* v. *The Beacon*, paid in advance. The first of many, if we can spin out the proceedings.'

'You're doing that awful case!' She didn't sound approving.

'That awful case will bring us in five hundred smackers a day in refreshers.'

'Helping that squalid newspaper insult Amelia Nettleship.' She looked at me with contempt.

'A barrister's duty, Hilda, is to take on all comers. However squalid.'

'Nonsense!'

'What?'

'Nonsense. You're only using that as an excuse.'

'Am I?'

'Of course you are. You're doing it because you're jealous of Amelia Nettleship!'

'Oh, I don't think so,' I protested mildly. 'My life has been full of longings, but I've never had the slightest desire to become a lady novelist.'

'You're jealous of her because she's got high principles.' Hilda was sure of it. 'You haven't got high principles, have you, Rumpole?'

'I told you. I will accept any client, however repulsive.'

'That's not a principle, that's just a way of making money from the most terrible people. Like the editor of the *Daily Beacon*. My mind is quite made up, Rumpole. I shall not use a single drop of that corrupt lavender water.'

It was then that I heard a sound from the hallway which made my heart sink. An all-too-familiar voice was singing *'La donna e mobile'* in a light tenor. Then the door opened to admit Erskine-Brown wearing my dressing-gown and very little else. 'Claude telephoned and told me all his troubles.' Hilda looked at the man with sickening sympathy. 'Of course I invited him to stay.'

'You're wearing my dressing-gown!' I put the charge to him at once.

'I had to pack in a hurry.' He looked calmly at the sideboard. 'Thoughtful of you to get in champagne to welcome me, Rumpole.'

'Was the bath all right, Claude?' Hilda sounded deeply concerned.

'Absolutely delightful, thank you, Hilda.'

'What a relief! That geyser can be quite temperamental.'

'Which is your chair, Horace?' Claude had the courtesy to ask.

'I usually sit by the gas fire. Why?'

'Oh, do sit there, Claude,' Hilda urged him and he gracefully agreed to pinch my seat. 'We mustn't let you get cold, must we. After your bath.'

So they sat together by the gas fire and I was allowed to open champagne for both of them. As I listened to the rain outside the window my spirits, I had to admit, had sunk to the lowest of ebbs. And around five o'clock the following morning, Fig Newton, the rain falling from the brim of his hat and the drop falling off his nose, stood watching Hollyhock Cottage. He saw someone — he was too far away to make an identification — come out of the front door and get into a parked car. Then he saw the figure of a woman in a nightdress, no doubt Amelia Nettleship, standing in the lit doorway waving goodbye. The headlights of the car were switched on and it drove away.

When the visitor had gone, and the front door was shut, Fig moved nearer to the cottage. He looked down at the muddy track on which the car had been parked and saw something white. He stooped to pick it up, folded it carefully and put it in his pocket.

On the day that *Nettleship* v. *The Beacon* began its sensational course, I breakfasted with Claude in the kitchen of our so-called 'mansion' flat in the Gloucester Road. I say breakfasted, but Hilda told me that bacon and eggs were off as our self-invited guest preferred a substance, apparently made up of sawdust and bird droppings, which he called muesli. I was a little exhausted, having

36

been kept awake by the amplified sound of grand opera from the spare bedroom, but Claude explained that he always found that a little Wagner settled him down for the night. He then asked for some of the goat's milk that Hilda had got in for him specially. As I coated a bit of toast with Oxford marmalade, the man only had to ask for organic honey to have it instantly supplied by She Who Seemed Anxious to Oblige.

'And what the hell,' I took the liberty of asking, 'is organic honey?'

'The bees only sip from flowers grown without chemical fertilizers,' Claude explained patiently.

'How does the bee know?'

'What?'

'I suppose the other bees tell it. "Don't sip from that, old chap. It's been grown with chemical fertilizers." '

So, ill-fed and feeling like a cuckoo in my own nest, I set off to the Royal Courts of Justice, in the Strand, that imposing turreted château which is the Ritz Hotel of the legal profession, the place where a gentleman is remunerated to the tune of five hundred smackers a day. It is also the place where gentlemen prefer an amicable settlement to the brutal business of fighting their cases.

I finally pitched up, wigged and robed, in front of the Court which would provide the battle-ground for our libel action. I saw the combatants, Morry Machin and the fair Nettleship, standing a considerable distance apart. Peregrine Landseer,

37

Q.C., Counsel for the Plaintiff, and Robin Peppiatt, Q.C., for the Proprietor of the *Beacon*, were
meeting on the central ground for a peace conference, attended by assorted juniors and instructing solicitors.

'After all the publicity, my lady couldn't take
less than fifty thousand.' Landseer, Chairman of
the Bar Council and on the brink of becoming
a judge, was nevertheless driving as hard a bargain
as any second-hand car dealer.

'Forty and a full and grovelling apology.' And
Peppiatt added the bonus. 'We could wrap it up
and lunch together at the Sheridan.'

'It's steak and kidney pud day at the Sheridan,'
Dick Garsington remembered wistfully.

'Forty-five.' Landseer was not so easily
tempted. 'And that's my last word on the subject.'

'Oh, all right,' Peppiatt conceded. 'Forty-five
and a full apology. You happy with that, Mr
Cuxham?'

'Well, sir. If you advise it.' Cuxham clearly
had no stomach for the fight.

'We'll chat to the Editor. I'm sure we're all
going to agree' — Peppiatt gave me a meaningful
look — 'in the end.'

While Landseer went off to sell the deal to
his client, Peppiatt approached my man with 'You
only have to join in the apology, Mr Machin,
and the *Beacon* will pay the costs and the forty-five
grand.'

' "Who steals my purse steals trash," ' I quoted
thoughtfully. ' "But he that filches from me my

38

good name . . ." You're asking my client to sign a statement admitting he printed lies.'

'Oh, for heaven's sake, Rumpole!' Peppiatt was impatient. 'They gave up quoting that in libel actions fifty years ago.'

'Mr Rumpole's right.' Morry nodded wisely. 'My good name — I looked up the quotation — it's the immediate jewel of my soul.'

'Steady on, old darling,' I murmured. 'Let's not go *too* far.' At which moment Peregrine Landseer returned from a somewhat heated discussion with his client to say that there was no shifting her and she was determined to fight for every penny she could get.

'But Perry . . .' Robin Peppiatt lamented, 'the case is going to take two weeks.' At five hundred smackers a day I could only thank God for the stubbornness of Amelia Nettleship.

So we went into Court to fight the case before a jury and Mr Justice Teasdale, a small, highly opinionated and bumptious little person who is unmarried, lives in Surbiton with a Persian cat, and was once an unsuccessful Tory candidate for Weston-super-Mare North. It takes a good deal of talent for a Tory to lose Weston-super-Mare North. Worst of all, he turned out to be a devoted fan of the works of Miss Amelia Nettleship.

'Members of the Jury,' Landseer said in opening the Plaintiff's case, 'Miss Nettleship is the authoress of a number of historical works.'

'Rattling good yarns, Members of the Jury,'

Mr Justice Teasdale chirped up.

'I beg your Lordship's pardon.' Landseer looked startled.

'I said "rattling good yarns", Mr Peregrine Landseer. The sort your wife might pick up without the slightest embarrassment. Unlike so much of the distasteful material one finds between hard covers today.'

'My Lord.' I rose to protest with what courtesy I could muster.

'Yes, Mr Rumbold?'

'Rum*pole,* my Lord.'

'I'm so sorry.' The Judge didn't look in the least apologetic. 'I understand you are something of a stranger to these Courts.'

'Would it not be better to allow the Jury to come to their own conclusions about Miss Amelia Nettleship?' I suggested, ignoring the Teasdale manners.

'Well. Yes. Of course. I quite agree.' The Judge looked serious and then cheered up. 'And when they do they'll find she can put together a rattling good yarn.'

There was a sycophantic murmur of laughter from the Jury, and all I could do was subside and look balefully at the Judge. I felt a pang of nostalgia for the Old Bailey and the wild stampede of the mad Judge Bullingham.

As Peregrine Landseer bored on, telling the Jury what terrible harm the *Beacon* had done to his client's hitherto unblemished reputation, Ted Spratling, the deputy editor, leant forward in the seat behind me and whispered in my ear. 'About that Stella January article,' he said. 'I bought a drink for the systems manager. The copy's still in the system. One rather odd thing.'

'Tell me . . .'

'The logon — that's the identification of the word processor. It came from the Editor's office.'

'You mean it was written there?'

'No one writes things anymore.'

'Of course not. How stupid of me.'

'It looks as if it had been put in from his word processor.'

'That is extremely interesting.'

'If Mr Rum*pole* has quite finished his conversation!' Peregrine Landseer was rebuking me for chattering during his opening speech.

I rose to apologize as humbly as I could. 'My Lord, I can assure my learned friend I was listening to every word of his speech. It's such a rattling good yarn.'

So the morning wore on, being mainly occupied by Landseer's opening. The luncheon adjournment saw me pacing the marble corridors of the Royal Courts of Justice with that great source of information, Fig Newton. He gave me a lengthy account of his observation on Hollyhock Cottage, and when he finally got to the departure of Miss Nettleship's nocturnal visitor, I asked impatiently, 'You got the car number?'

'Alas. No. Visibility was poor and weather conditions appalling.' The sleuth's evidence was here interrupted by a fit of sneezing.

'Oh, Fig!' I was, I confess, disappointed. 'And you didn't see the driver?'

'Alas. No, again.' Fig sneezed apologetically. 'However, when Miss Nettleship had closed the door and extinguished the lights, presumably in order to return to bed, I proceeded to the track in front of the house where the vehicle had been standing. There I retrieved an article which I thought might just possibly have been dropped by the driver in getting in or out of the vehicle.'

'For God's sake, show me!'

The detective gave me his treasure trove, which I stuffed into a pocket just as the Usher came out of Court to tell me that the Judge was back from lunch, Miss Nettleship was entering the witness-box, and the world of libel awaited my attention.

If ever I saw a composed and confident witness, that witness was Amelia Nettleship. Her hair was perfectly done, her black suit was perfectly discreet, her white blouse shone, as did her spectacles. Her features, delicately cut as an intaglio, were attractive, but her beauty was by no means louche or abundant. So spotless did she seem that she might well have preserved her virginity until what must have been, in spite of appearances to the contrary, middle age. When she had finished her evidence-in-chief the Judge thanked her and urged her to go on writing her 'rattling good yarns'. Peppiatt then rose to his feet to ask her a few questions designed to show that her books were still selling in spite of the *Beacon* article. This she denied, saying that sales had dropped off. The thankless task of attacking the fair name of Amelia was left to Rumpole.

'Miss Nettleship,' I started off with my guns blazing, 'are you a truthful woman?'

'I try to be.' She smiled at his Lordship, who nodded encouragement.

'And you call yourself an historical novelist?'

'I try to write books which uphold certain standards of morality.'

'Forget the morality for a moment. Let's concentrate on the history.'

'Very well.'

One of the hardest tasks in preparing for my first libel action was reading through the works of Amelia Nettleship. Now I had to quote from Hilda's favourite. 'May I read you a short passage from an alleged historical novel of yours entitled *Lord Stingo's Fancy*?' I asked as I picked up the book.

'Ah, yes.' The Judge looked as though he were about to enjoy a treat. 'Isn't that the one which ends happily?'

'Happily, all Miss Nettleship's books end, my Lord,' I told him. 'Eventually.' There was a little laughter in Court, and I heard Landseer whisper to his Junior, 'This criminal chap's going to bump up the damages enormously.'

Meanwhile I started quoting from *Lord Stingo's Fancy*. ' "Sophia had first set eyes on Lord Stingo when she was a dewy eighteen-year-old

43

and he had clattered up to her father's castle, exhausted from the Battle of Nazeby," ' I read. ' "Now at the ball to triumphantly celebrate the gorgeous, enthroning coronation of the Merry Monarch King Charles II they were to meet again. Sophia was now in her twenties but, in ways too numerous to completely describe, still an unspoilt girl at heart." You call that a *historical* novel?'

'Certainly,' the witness answered unashamed.

'Haven't you forgotten something?' I put it to her.

'I don't think so. What?'

'Oliver Cromwell.'

'I really don't know what you mean.'

'Clearly, if this Sophia . . . this girl . . . How do you describe her?'

' "Dewy", Mr Rumpole.' The Judge repeated the word with relish.

'Ah, yes. "Dewy". I'm grateful to your Lordship. I had forgotten the full horror of the passage. If this dew-bespattered Sophia had been eighteen at the time of the Battle of Naseby in the reign of Charles I, she would have been thirty-three in the year of Charles II's coronation. Oliver Cromwell came in between.'

'I am an artist, Mr Rumpole.' Miss Nettleship smiled at my pettifogging objections.

'What kind of an artist?' I ventured to ask.

'I think Miss Nettleship means an artist in words,' was how the Judge explained it.

'Are you, Miss Nettleship?' I asked. 'Then you

must have noticed that the short passage I have read to the Jury contains two split infinitives and a tautology.'

'A what, Mr Rumpole?' The Judge looked displeased.

'Using two words that mean the same thing, as in "the enthroning coronation". My Lord, t — a — u . . .' I tried to be helpful.

'I can *spell*, Mr Rumpole.' Teasdale was now testy.

'Then your Lordship has the advantage of the witness. I notice she spells Naseby with a "z".'

'My Lord. I hesitate to interrupt.' At least I was doing well enough to bring Landseer languidly to his feet. 'Perhaps this sort of cross-examination is common enough in the criminal courts, but I cannot see how it can possibly be relevant in an action for libel.'

'Neither can I, Mr Landseer, I must confess.' Of course the Judge agreed.

I did my best to put him right. 'These questions, my Lord, go to the heart of this lady's credibility.' I turned to give the witness my full attention. 'I have to suggest, Miss Nettleship, that as an historical novelist you are a complete fake.'

'My Lord. I have made my point.' Landseer sat down then, looking well pleased, and immediately whispered to his Junior, 'We'll let him go on with that line and they'll give us four hundred thousand.'

'You have no respect for history and very little

for the English language.' I continued to chip away at the spotless novelist.

'I try to tell a story, Mr Rumpole.'

'And your evidence to this Court has been, to use my Lord's vivid expression, "a rattling good yarn"?' Teasdale looked displeased at my question.

'I have sworn to tell the truth.'

'Remember that. Now let us see how much of this article is correct.' I picked up Stella January's offending contribution. 'You do live at Hollyhock Cottage, near Godalming, in the county of Surrey?'

'That is so.'

'You have a jacuzzi?'

'She has *what,* Mr Rumpole?' I had entered a world unknown to a judge addicted to cold showers.

'A sort of bath, my Lord, with a whirlpool attached.'

'I installed one in my converted barn,' Miss Nettleship admitted. 'I find it relaxes me, after a long day's work.'

'You don't twiddle round in there with a close personal friend occasionally?'

'That's worth another ten thousand to us,' Landseer told his Junior, growing happier by the minute. In fact the Jury members were looking at me with some disapproval.

'Certainly not. I do not believe in sex before marriage.'

'And have no experience of it?'

'I was engaged once, Mr Rumpole.'

'Just once?'

'Oh, yes. My fiancé was killed in an air crash ten years ago. I think about him every day, and every day I'm thankful we didn't —' she looked down modestly — 'do anything before we were married. We were tempted, I'm afraid, the night before he died. But we resisted the temptation.'

'Some people would say that's a very moving story,' Judge Teasdale told the Jury after a reverent hush.

'Others might say it's the story of *Sally on the Somme*, only there the fiancé was killed in the war.' I picked up another example of the Nettleship *œuvre*.

'That, Mr Rumpole,' Amelia looked pained, 'is a book that's particularly close to my heart. At least I don't do anything my heroines wouldn't do.'

'He's getting worse all the time,' Robin Peppiatt, the *Beacon* barrister, whispered despairingly to his Junior, Dick Garsington, who came back with 'The damages are going to hit the roof!'

'Miss Nettleship, may I come to the last matter raised in the article?'

'I'm sure the Jury will be grateful that you're reaching the end, Mr Rumpole,' the Judge couldn't resist saying, so I smiled charmingly and told him that I should finish a great deal sooner if I were allowed to proceed without further interruption. Then I began to read Stella January's words aloud to the witness. ' "Her latest Casanova, so far unnamed, is said to be a married man who's been seen leaving in the wee small hours." '

'I read that,' Miss Nettleship remembered.

'You had company last night, didn't you? Until what I suppose might be revoltingly referred to as "the wee small hours"?'

'What are you suggesting?'

'That someone was with you. And when he left at about five thirty in the morning you stood in your nightdress waving goodbye and blowing kisses. Who was it, Miss Nettleship?'

'That is an absolutely uncalled-for suggestion.'

'You called for it when you issued a writ for libel.'

'Do I have to answer?' She turned to the Judge for help. He gave her his most encouraging smile and said that it might save time in the end if she were to answer Mr Rumpole's question.

'That is absolutely untrue!' For the first time Amelia's look of serenity vanished and I got, from the witness-box, a cold stare of hatred. 'Absolutely untrue.' The Judge made a grateful note of her answer. 'Thank you, Miss Nettleship. I think we might continue with this tomorrow morning, if you have any further questions, Mr Rumpole?'

'I have indeed, my Lord.' Of course I had more questions and by the morning I hoped also to have some evidence to back them up.

I was in no hurry to return to the alleged

48

'mansion' flat that night. I rightly suspected that our self-invited guest, Claude Erskine-Brown, would be playing his way through *Die Meistersinger* and giving Hilda a synopsis of the plot as it unfolded. As I reach the last of a man's Seven Ages I am more than ever persuaded that life is too short for Wagner, a man who was never in a hurry when it came to composing an opera. I paid a solitary visit to Pommeroy's well-known watering-hole after Court in the hope of finding the representatives of the *Beacon*; but the only one I found was Connie Coughlin, the features editor, moodily surveying a large gin and tonic. 'No champagne tonight?' I asked as I wandered over to her table, glass in hand.

'I don't think we've got much to celebrate.'

'I wanted to ask you' — I took a seat beside the redoubtable Connie — 'about Miss Stella January. Our girl on the spot. Bright, active kind of reporter, was she?'

'I don't know,' Connie confessed.

'But surely you're the features editor?'

'I never met her.' She said it with the resentment of a woman whose editor had been interfering with her page.

'Any idea how old she was, for instance?'

'Oh, young, I should think.' It was the voice of middle age speaking. 'Morry said she was young. Just starting in the business.'

'And I was going to ask you . . .'

'You're very inquisitive.'

'It's my trade.' I downed what was left of my

claret. '. . . About the love life of Mr Morry Machin.'

'Good God. Whose side are you on, Mr Rumpole?'

'At the moment, on the side of the truth. Did Morry have some sort of a romantic interest in Miss Stella January?'

'Short-lived, I'd say.' Connie clearly had no pity for the girl if she'd been enjoyed and then sacked.

'He's married?'

'Oh, two or three times.' It occurred to me that at some time, during one or other of these marriages, Morry and La Coughlin might have been more than fellow hacks on the *Beacon*. 'Now he seems to have got some sort of steady girl-friend.' She said it with some resentment.

'You know her?'

'Not at all. He keeps her under wraps.'

I looked at her for a moment. A woman, I thought, with a lonely evening in an empty flat before her. Then I thanked her for her help and stood up.

'Who are you going to grill next?' she asked me over the rim of her gin and tonic.

'As a matter of fact,' I told her, 'I've got a date with Miss Stella January.'

Quarter of an hour later I was walking across the huge floor, filled with desks, telephones and word processors, where the *Beacon* was produced, towards the glass-walled office in the corner,

50

where Morry sat with his deputy Ted Spratling, seeing that all the scandal that was fit to print, and a good deal of it that wasn't, got safely between the covers of the *Beacon*. I arrived at his office, pulled open the door and was greeted by Morry, in his shirtsleeves, his feet up on the desk. 'Working late, Mr Rumpole? I hope you can do better for us tomorrow,' he greeted me with amused disapproval.

'I hope so too. I'm looking for Miss Stella January.'

'I told you, she's not here any more. I think she went overseas.'

'I think she's here,' I assured him. He was silent for a moment and then he looked at his deputy. 'Ted, perhaps you'd better leave me to have a word with my learned Counsel.'

'I'll be on the back bench.' Spratling left for the desk on the floor which the editors occupied.

When he had gone, Morry looked up at me and said quietly, 'Now then, Mr Rumpole, sir. How can I help you?'

'Stella certainly wasn't a young woman, was she?' I was sure about that.

'She was only with us a short time. But she was young, yes,' he said vaguely.

'A quotation from her article that Amelia Nettleship "makes Mae West sound like Florence Nightingale". No young woman today's going to have heard of Mae West. Mae West's as remote in history as Messalina and Helen of Troy. That

51

article, I would hazard a guess, was written by a man well into his middle age.'

'Who?'

'You.'

There was another long silence and the Editor did his best to smile. 'Have you been drinking at all this evening?'

I took a seat then on the edge of his desk and lit a small cigar. 'Of course I've been drinking *at all*. You don't imagine I have these brilliant flashes of deduction when I'm perfectly sober, do you?'

'Then hadn't you better go home to bed?'

'So you wrote the article. No argument about that. It's been found in the system with your word processor number on it. Careless, Mr Machin. You clearly have very little talent for time. The puzzling thing is, why you should attack Miss Nettleship when she's such a good friend of yours.'

'Good friend?' He did his best to laugh. 'I told you. I've never even met the woman.'

'It was a lie, like the rest of this pantomime lawsuit. Last night you were with her until past five in the morning. And she said goodbye to you with every sign of affection.'

'What makes you say that?'

'Were you in a hurry? Anyway, this was dropped by the side of your car.' Then I pulled out the present Fig Newton had given me outside Court that day and put it on the desk.

'Anyone can buy the *Beacon.*' Morry glanced at the mud-stained exhibit.

'Not everyone gets the first edition, the one that fell on the Editor's desk at ten o'clock that evening. I would say that's a bit of a rarity around Godalming.'

'Is that all?'

'No. You were watched.'

'Who by?'

'Someone I asked to find out the truth about Miss Nettleship. Now he's turned up the truth about both of you.'

Morry got up then and walked to the door which Ted Spratling had left half open. He shut it carefully and then turned to me. 'I went down to ask her to drop the case.'

'To use a legal expression, pull the other one, it's got bells on it.'

'I don't know what you're suggesting.'

And then, as he stood looking at me, I moved round and sat in the Editor's chair. 'Let me enlighten you.' I was as patient as I could manage. 'I'm suggesting a conspiracy to pervert the course of justice.'

'What's that mean?'

'I told you I'm an old taxi, waiting on the rank, but I'm not prepared to be the get-away driver for a criminal conspiracy.'

'You haven't said anything? To anyone?' He looked older and very frightened.

'Not yet.'

'And you won't.' He tried to sound confident.

'You're my lawyer.'

'Not any longer, Mr Machin. I don't belong to you any more. I'm an ordinary citizen, about to report an attempted crime.' It was then I reached for the telephone. 'I don't think there's any limit on the sentence for conspiracy.'

'What do you mean, "conspiracy"?'

'You're getting sacked by the *Beacon*; perhaps your handshake is a bit less than golden. Sales are down on historical virgins. So your steady girl-friend and you get together to make half a tax-free million.'

'I wish I knew how.' He was doing his best to smile.

'Perfectly simple. You turn yourself into Stella January, the unknown girl reporter, for half an hour and libelled Amelia. She sues the paper and collects. Then you both sail into the sunset and share the proceeds. There's one thing I shan't forgive you for.'

'What's that?'

'The plan called for an Old Bailey hack, a stranger to the civilized world of libel who wouldn't settle, an old war-horse who'd attack La Nettleship and inflame the damages. So you used me, Mr Morry Machin!'

'I thought you'd be accustomed to that.' He stood over me, suddenly looking older. 'Anyway, they told me in Pommeroy's that you never prosecute.'

'No, I don't, do I? But on this occasion, I must say, I'm sorely tempted.' I thought about it and finally pushed away the telephone. 'Since it's a libel action I'll offer you terms of settlement.'

'What sort of terms?'

'The fair Amelia to drop her case. You pay the costs, including the fees of Fig Newton, who's caught a bad cold in the course of these proceedings. Oh, and in the matter of my learned friend Claude Erskine-Brown . . .'

'What's he got to do with it?'

'. . . Print a full and grovelling apology on the front page of the *Beacon*. And get them to pay him a substantial sum by way of damages. And that's my last word on the subject.' I stood up then and moved to the door.

'What's it going to cost me?' was all he could think of saying.

'I have no idea, but I know what it's going to cost me. Two weeks at five hundred a day. A provision for my old age.' I opened the glass door and let in the hum and clatter which were the birth-pangs of the *Daily Beacon*. 'Good-night, Stella,' I said to Mr Morry Machin. And then I left him.

So it came about that next morning's *Beacon* printed a grovelling apology to 'the distinguished barrister Mr Claude Erskine-Brown' which accepted that he went to the Kitten-A-Go-Go Club purely in the interests of legal research and announced that my learned friend's hurt feelings would be soothed by the application of substantial, and tax-free, damages. As a consequence of this,

Mrs Phillida Erskine-Brown rang Chambers, spoke words of forgiveness and love to her husband, and he arranged, in his new-found wealth, to take her to dinner at Le Gavroche. The cuckoo flew from our nest, Hilda and I were left alone in the Gloucester Road, and we never found out how *Die Meistersinger* ended.

In Court my one and only libel action ended in a sudden outburst of peace and goodwill, much to the frustration of Mr Justice Teasdale, who had clearly been preparing a summing-up which would encourage the Jury to make Miss Nettleship rich beyond the dreams of avarice. All the allegations against her were dropped; she had no doubt been persuaded by her lover to ask for no damages at all and the *Beacon*'s Editor accepted the bill for costs with extremely bad grace. This old legal taxi moved off to ply for hire elsewhere, glad to be shot of Mr Morry Machin. 'Is there a little bit of burglary around, Henry?' I asked our clerk, as I have recorded. 'Couldn't you get me a nice little gentle robbery? Something which shows human nature in a better light than civil law?'

'Good heavens!' Hilda exclaimed as we lay reading in the matrimonial bed in Froxbury Mansions. I noticed that there had been a change in her reading matter and she was already well into *On the Make* by Suzy Hutchins. 'This girl's about to go to Paris with a man old enough to be her father.'

'That must happen quite often.'

'But it seems he *is* her father.'

'Well, at least you've gone off the works of Amelia Nettleship.'

'The way she dropped that libel action. The woman's no better than she should be.'

'Which of us is? Any chance of turning out the light?' I asked She Who Must Be Obeyed, but she was too engrossed in the doings of her delinquent heroine to reply.

# Rumpole and the Barrow Boy

In the dog days of life at the Criminal Bar, when my tray in the clerk's room seems to be filled with communications from the Inland Revenue and hardly a brief offers its pink tape to my eager fingers, it's as well to have some more or less constant source of income, some supply of regular customers to fall back on. Such support and comfort has, for many years, been furnished for me by the Timsons, an extended, intricate and perpetually expanding family of South London villians, whose turnover of crime, though never of a sensational or particularly ambitious nature, shows commendable industry. Armed robbery, murder, mayhem or serious fraud are out of the Timsons' league. The most simple breaking and entering, burglary, and the taking and driving away of clapped-out Cortinas are their bread and butter; receiving stolen jewellery their occasional slice of cake. If your telly, your video and your microwave mysteriously leave home while you are away for the weekend, ten to one some Timson has got it and is disposing of it at a knock-down price in the saloon bar of the Needle Arms. Working for the Timsons is not exactly blue chip litigation; it is not much like being retained by I.C.I. or the Chase Manhattan bank. All the same it provides steady and fairly honourable employment and for many years I have been content to act as the Timsons' Attorney-General with Mr Bernard as my solicitor. Many a time, although this is not a fact She Who Must Be Obeyed cares to face up to, we have sat down, in our kitchen in Gloucester Road, to chops and mash bought as a result of the Timsons' endeavours. The pleasant thing about the Timsons was that they were never, to use the favourite expression of contemporary politicians, 'entrepreneurial' and they seemed quite uninterested in 'extending their market share'. They were not, in the smallest degree, 'upwardly mobile'. And then, much to my surprise, a new breed of Timson was born. Out of a docklands comprehensive school, Shepherd's Bush market and the Big Bang on the Stock Exchange, a certain young Nigel Timson came to prominence in the City and was able to introduce me to the world of high finance.

I first heard of Nigel when I was in Brixton prison visiting Fred Timson, the undisputed head of the family, who was awaiting trial as a result of an activity for which he was far too old and not nearly nimble enough — warehouse-breaking by night. Try as I would to discuss the ins and outs of this offence with him, he was only anxious to solicit my help for Nigel.

'Cousin Andy's boy, Mr Rumpole, what went into the City. Works cheek by jowl with lads from Eton and Harrow College.'

'This prodigy is in some sort of trouble?' I asked.

'I'd like to have his trouble. Rides around in a C-reg. Porsche. Girl-friend's the boss's daughter. Luxury flat on the Isle of Dogs. Funny that. Old Andy spent his whole life working his way up from the Isle of Dogs to Shepherd's Bush and now his boy Nigel's gone back to live there. Anyway he wants for nothing; even gets a smashing view of the river from the jacuzzi. And all got on the legit, Mr Rumpole.'

'Then what can I do to help him?' Cousin Andy's boy seemed to need an accountant and not an Old Bailey hack.

'Young Nigel got himself arrested. By the Fraud Squad.'

'So he hasn't entirely let down the honour of the Timsons.'

This was the first I heard of my future client, but later I was able to piece together, in further detail, the history of the rise and fall of Nigel Timson. He was clearly a bright boy at school with a quick head for figures. Released on the world he worked on a cousin's greengrocery barrow, and his instant calculations of the highest price for apples the market would tolerate provided admirable training for his subsequent brilliance in a stockbroker's office. He was an ambitious boy who went to evening classes in computer technology and business studies. When he felt ready he answered an advertisement for a job at the old-established firm of Japhet Jarroway which had just installed roomfuls of new technology to take the temperature of recovering, ailing or simply hypochondriac businesses around the world. Nigel remained, even when he rose rapidly and took out a mortgage on his part of a converted docklands warehouse, the bright and pleasing boy who had always gladdened the hearts of old ladies out to buy half a pound of Granny Smiths. The public-school boys he worked with found him ever ready to come to the help of their faltering mathematics, and Rosie Japhet, only daughter of the firm's Chairman, who occupied the next computer on the dealing floor, fell in love with him. Nigel became the first Timson to relieve the punters of their money in a way which was not only legal but considered, in the strange times in which we live, far more worthy of reward than teaching in schools or nursing the sick. It goes without saying that he received salary and commission which sounded like a prince's ransom to an Old Bailey hack.

The facts of Nigel's arrest came out in the numerous statements obtained by the police. It was his birthday. Bottles of champagne were opened on the floor of the dealing room during a brief lull in business. Nigel's computer was festooned with streamers and birthday cards. His girl-friend, Rosie, presented him with a pigskin Filofax and a pair of boxer shorts decorated with dollar signs. His health was drunk by his closest friends — Rosie and three other young stockbrokers, Hugo Shillingford, Katie Kennet and Mark Marcellus. And then a Kissogram girl equipped with fishnet

61

tights, high heels and a bow in her hair appeared to speak the immortal lines, clearly recollected by those who attended the joyous occasion:

Greetings to you, Nigel,
Whose happy birthday this is.
We wish you all you wish yourself,
That's money dear and kisses.

The Kissogram lady had just implanted her sticky lipstick on Nigel's cheek when two anonymous gentlemen in dark suits and mackintoshes entered to announce that they were members of the Fraud Squad and asked for Nigel Timson. The birthday party took them to be part of the show, hired with the Kissogram to entertain the company, until one of them introduced himself as Detective Sergeant Arbuthnot come to arrest Nigel for certain offences contrary to the Companies Act.

'I think,' Hugo Shillingford said in the ensuing silence, 'that he's seriously serious.'

At the end of the day when I visited Fred Timson in Brixton and had young Nigel commended to my care I was snoozing in front of the gas fire in Froxbury Mansions. Sleep was, in fact, knitting up the ravelled sleeve of care when 'Methought I heard a voice cry, "Sleep no more!" ' It was She Who Must Be Obeyed telling me that I didn't need the gas fire in the middle of March and turning it off with a definitive plop.

There was, I pointed out to her, as I struggled to regain consciousness, a bit of a chill wind blowing. 'I'm not going to let you waste the gas now that I own it.' She had bought ten pounds' worth of shares in British Gas; it was a time when practically everything was being auctioned off on the Stock Exchange. Her investment, she clearly felt, gave her a proprietorial interest in the entire North Sea production. I managed to light a small cigar with freezing fingers, mainly for the purpose of keeping warm. 'Please don't buy the electricity, Hilda,' I begged her, 'or we'll all be stumbling around in the dark.'

'I'm not likely to be buying anything,' Hilda said darkly. 'I went to the bank today to cash a cheque on our joint account.'

'And I hope you went to the little lady at the third window.' I had considerable experience of the Caring Bank. 'She's the most merciful.'

'I went to the Head Cashier, the one with the small moustache. He went to look things up behind the scenes.'

'I should have warned you about that fellow with the moustache, can't keep his nose out of other people's business.'

'As a result, Mr Truscott, the Manager, asked me in for a little talk. It was not a pleasant experience.'

'Oh, I know. Not much of a conversationalist, that Truscott.'

' "We'll cash this one now," ' he said, ' "but tell Mr Rumpole he's scraping the bottom of the barrel." Why're you scraping the bottom of the barrel, Rumpole?'

I gave her a brief rundown on my somewhat precarious financial position; it was the old, old story. The Government didn't believe in spending out too much on Legal Aid and anyway the time it took for me to get paid for any case was about equal to the gestation period of the giant turtle. The small amounts of cash that filtered through to our account in the Caring Bank get frittered away on such luxuries as income tax and sliced bread and washing-powder and Brillo pads and . . .

'Why don't you make fifty thousand pounds a case, Rumpole, like Robin Peppiatt?'

She mentioned the most fashionable Q.C., a smooth talker, who does big commercial and smart libel actions. 'I'm not Robin Peppiatt.' I had to point the hard fact out to her. 'And I'm not a Q.C.'

'Why aren't you?' Hilda remained unsatisfied by my argument. 'Phillida Erskine-Brown's a Q.C.'

'You may not have noticed this,' I did my best to explain. 'But I bear practically no resemblance at all to Mrs Phillida Erskine-Brown. To start with, I'm not a woman.'

'What's being a woman got to do with it?'

'Lawyers feel so awful about the way they've treated women down the ages, not letting them into Chambers, not giving them the key of the loo, they push them into silk gowns as a sort of compensation.'

'What about the Head of your Chambers; why is Samuel Ballard a Q.C.?'

'It is not for us to question the inscrutable ways of Providence,' I told her devoutly.

'He's a silk, Rumpole.'

'In my view, a highly artificial silk.'

'Why don't you do something to get on in the world?'

'Because it's getting rather near the time when I should get off. Probably at the next stop.'

I felt a great temptation to return to sore labour's bath, balm of hurt minds, great nature's second course — sleep. The possibility of asking the Lord Chancellor for a silk gown, entitling me to sit in the front row and to be called a Queen's Counsel, had sometimes crossed my mind, but such a promotion would deprive me of such bread and butter as dealing with the little problems the Timsons might leave in their wake. I was also not at all sure I could find a judge to back my claim, as I had enjoyed differences of opinion, often dramatic, in open Court with most of them.

'I've been thinking about you, Rumpole,' Hilda announced after a prolonged pause for reflection. 'And I've decided that if you don't do something about getting on in the world . . .'

'You want to be upwardly mobile?' I asked her. 'You want us to improve our lifestyle and move to the Isle of Dogs?'

'I want you to pull your socks up, Rumpole.

That's what I want.' I looked down at the woollen tubes concertinaed round my ankles. 'And if you don't, well, you're quite likely to find yourself alone in your old age.'

'Promises, Hilda,' I muttered, and, when asked to repeat myself said, 'I'd miss you, Hilda.'

Further discussion on the Rumpole career was stopped by the fact that Hilda discovered from her *Daily Telegraph* that we were missing the television programme 'City Doings' which, in view of her new holdings in public utilities, She now found essential viewing. As the television screen flickered into life, the distinguished, aquiline features of Sir Christopher Japhet, crowned with beautifully brushed iron-grey hair and surmounting an equally distinguished old-school tie, entered our sitting-room. Sue Bickerstaff, the eager interviewer, was asking him why we heard so much, nowadays, of crime in the City. Was it the after-effect of the Big Bang? Sir Christopher, shaking his head sadly, was very much afraid that the City wasn't what it was when he first joined Seymour Japhet in the firm now known as Japhet Jarroway. He then made a short speech which I can recall, as I had a subsequent use for it.

'In the old days,' Sir Christopher told us, 'a stockbroker's word was his bond. No doubt about it. You had your rules and you'd've no more thought of breaking them than you would've failed to offer your seat to a lady or eaten peas with a knife. Insider dealing? We never heard of insider dealing, and *why*? Not because there

66

were laws against it, but because it just wasn't on. Now we've got a flood of young men working in the City. "Barrow boys", "spivs", I call some of them. "Wide boys". No wonder you get trouble.'

The next item was how to raise money on half paid-up Granny bonds for investment in a Grannyflat, and I was about to tuck in once more to great nature's second course when Hilda asked piercingly, 'Why aren't you *Sir* Horace by now, Rumpole? After all he was *Sir* Christopher and he looked a great deal younger than you.'

Hilda had murdered sleep. 'Do you really want to be a lady?' I asked her.

In due course I defended Fred Timson and, much to my surprise, owing to the failure of the security guard to identify my client as the leader of the posse who escaped after an unsuccessful attack on the warehouse, I got him off. When I went back to Chambers, triumphant from the Bailey, I found our clerk, Henry, reading a glossy publication liberally illustrated with portraits of kangaroos and suntanned bathing beauties. Lifting it from his desk in idle curiosity, I read: *Come to the land of the Koala Bear and the Kookaburra. Sport topless on Bondi and bet your bottom dollar at Surfers Paradise. Watch the crickut at Melbourne and take the family to the footie.* All this led me to ask, as I handed the brochure back to Henry, 'Do I deduce from this that you're planning a holiday in the Antipodes?'

'Not a holiday, Mr Rumpole.' He changed the subject. 'Anyway, your con's upstairs. It's another Timson.'

'Oh yes. So it is.' I remembered young Nigel.

'Don't *you* ever get tired of it, Mr Rumpole?' Our clerk, I thought, looked somewhat stricken. 'Doesn't it ever occur to you, sir, that there must be more to life than saving various members of the Timson family from their just deserts. Don't we all long for a new life, Mr Rumpole, in a new world, perhaps?'

'Henry! Whatever's happened? It's not like a barrister's clerk to feel the call of the wild.'

'I told you, sir. Mr Bernard's upstairs and he's got another Mr Timson with him.' The man avoided my eye. 'You'd better not keep your con waiting, had you?'

So I left Henry to his Australian brochure and went upstairs to meet young Nigel. He was, I knew, charged with a mysterious commercial offence known to the financial cognoscenti as insider dealing. Now I am an acknowledged expert, perhaps *the* acknowledged expert, on bloodstains, gun-shot wounds and disputed typewriting, but insider dealing was a closed book to me. I thought of how I might manipulate my conference so that I could receive instruction without betraying my ignorance. Then I entered my room and the waiting presence of Nigel Timson and Mr Bernard, the Timsons' regular solicitor.

Young Nigel, in his dark blue suit and clean white shirt, looked exactly the kind of personable yet dependable young man with a future every mother would like her daughter to marry. When he spoke he had lost all but a hint of that accent in which he used to call the price of apples in Shepherd's Bush market. I sat down, lit a small cigar, and asked him how his business was doing. A slight shadow fell across those features which I recognized from a couple of generations of Timsons. 'Things aren't what they were with the Big Bang, Mr Rumpole,' Nigel admitted. 'Not since the market's been falling. There's people losing their jobs and their cars and their cottages round Newbury. Everyone's complaining.'

'Less a big bang than a big whimper?'

'The Prosecution will say you needed money.' Mr Bernard brought us sharply to the business in hand.

'Of course, I'm only the marzipan at Japhet Jarroway.' Nigel gave me my first taste of the strange tongue spoken by young, upwardly mobile persons. 'I come above the stodge but definitely under the icing-sugar.'

'So they say you supplemented your income with a bit of insider dealing.' Bernard seemed to be quite *au fait* with this mysterious offence.

'And you know what insider dealing is, I suppose?' I thought it best to challenge Nigel.

'Of course, Mr Rumpole.' He looked at me strangely. 'Don't you?'

'Don't I know what insider dealing is? Of course I do. It might just be helpful, to all of us, if you explained it in your own words.' I sat down to listen and take notes if necessary.

'Explain it to *you?*'

'Yes, please.'

'But you know.'

'I know I know.' I was starting to lose patience. 'But the Jury won't know I know. I just want to hear how you'd explain it to *them*. Regard me as twelve honest citizens with nothing between them except a few shares in British Telecom. Explain what you're supposed to have done.'

'Don't the Prosecution have to do that?' I wasn't getting maximum cooperation from the client.

'Come on, Nigel. We can't leave everything to the Prosecution.'

The boy, being naturally eager to please, began an explanation which I found obscure. 'Well, there's this little fish swimming along.'

'A fish?'

'This little company. Cornucopia Preserves and Jams Ltd.'

'First-class marmalade.' I was on home ground now. 'Adorns our breakfast table in the Gloucester Road.'

'Undervalued stock. Big factory. Lots of old shops on street corners. It seemed W.G.I. was about to make a Dawn Raid.'

'W.G.I.?'

'Worldwide Groceries Incorporated.'

'Of course. Dawn Raid.' The words echoed

down the years. 'Puts me in mind of my old days in the Royal Air Force, ground staff.'

'Takeover bid.' Once again Nigel translated. 'Sudden jump to buy the stock before anyone has quite woken up to it. Well, a week before that happened I bought sixty-eight thousand pounds' worth of Cornucopia shares for a client. And then Cornucopia went soaring up.'

'They say you'd got to know about the Dawn Raid.' Bernard put the prosecution case.

'Which was being planned . . . Where?' This seemed to me, in my extreme ignorance, the vital question.

'In the Corporate Finance department of our firm, Japhet Jarroway.'

'So you could have easily got to know what was afoot,' I assumed.

'No, I couldn't.' Nigel was positive. 'It was in another department, Corporate Finance. Behind a Chinese wall.'

'Behind a what?'

'You know, a wall of silence. Between departments in the same building. We call them Chinese walls.'

'Of course I know,' I lied shamelessly. 'I just wanted to see how you'd explain it for the benefit of the Jury. But not everyone keeps to their side of these imaginary walls?'

'Everyone in our firm does.' Nigel suddenly sounded like a public school prefect explaining what is, and is not, cricket.

'Are you sure?' Was there really honour among

young stockbrokers?

'You'd be out on your ear if you broke the rules.'

'Really?'

'Sir Christopher Japhet is our Chairman. Very keen on the sanctity of the Chinese walls is Sir Christopher.'

'A bit of a Mandarin?'

'You could say that.'

'And this client you bought the shares for?' I remembered one of the more comprehensible passages in my client's statement to the police. 'This Mabel Gloag. You never met her?'

'No. Apparently someone had recommended us. She had a bit of money and I moved it around for her. Then she rang up and said she'd had a legacy. Sixty-eight thousand pounds. She wanted to put it all into Cornucopia.'

'And after the Dawn Raid?'

'I sold her shares. She doubled her money.' A handsome profit, I thought. And the Prosecution would say it was a handsome profit for Nigel, got as the result of information illegally obtained. In all probability they would cast doubt on the very existence of Miss Mabel Gloag.

'What was she like?' I started to cross-examine the client.

'I never met her.'

'You talked on the telephone?'

'Yes. She sounded a nice old lady. It surprised me.'

'What surprised you?'

'I suppose, that she was dealing on the Stock Exchange.' I took another look at my brief, particularly at those points of it I could understand. 'The cheque was sent to her at a P.O. box number in Harrogate, Yorkshire,' I reminded Nigel.

'I suppose that's where she lived. She never gave us an address.'

'But her letters were collected, presumably by someone calling herself Mabel Gloag. And when the transaction was over some anonymous well-wisher paid twenty thousand into your account at the National Wessex in Cheapside.'

'I can only think . . .'

'What?'

'That was Miss Gloag. Showing her gratitude. I never got a chance to thank her.'

'You never heard from her again?'

'No.'

'Had you told her where you banked?'

'That's the strange thing. I never did.' He looked at me then, with the simple faith which all the Timsons happily feel for their regular brief. 'They speak very well of you, Mr Rumpole. They say you can work miracles.'

'Where do they speak well of me? In Brixton prison?'

'Well, I suppose so.'

'They speak well of you there, too. It seems you know Sir Christopher Japhet's daughter.'

'We've been going out together for about six months.'

'I suppose that means staying in together?'

73

'Well, yes. We make up a Dink.'

'Oh, do translate.'

'Double Income No Kids. That's what we call it.'

'How quaint.'

'And now it seems I'm a Yid.'

'Really?'

'Young Indictable Dealer.' He looked at us and his eager anxious-to-please smile died slowly. 'It's not really funny, is it?'

'Not very.'

We were silent for a moment and then he said quietly, 'Knowing my family as you do, you think I must be guilty.'

'I don't think you'll find that Mr Rumpole has ever let the Timson family down,' Mr Bernard rebuked him, and I said, 'That's entirely for the Jury to decide.' That was all I could do then except to tell them both to concentrate on the search for Miss Mabel Gloag, whose exact role seemed to me to be the main point at issue in the case. Bernard told me then he had written several times to the P.O. box number, but it seemed her letters weren't being collected any more.

When they had gone, I sat down to read my brief in detail. For the case of *The Queen* v. *Nigel Timson* I had to start learning a new language. I could forget about tea leaves and shooters. I was in a new world of Dawn Raids and Dinks and Chinese walls. It all made me homesick for the simple days when you just smashed a window, grabbed the money and ran. Times and the Timsons had changed and God knew how I was going to get used to it.

The search for Miss Mabel Gloag, during the next week or two, produced no tangible results. Nigel Timson did find a Harrogate number jotted down on the corner of an old cheque book. That, he told Bernard, was, he was sure, the number Miss Gloag had given him when he was busy when she telephoned him and she had asked to be rung back. Bernard called the number in some excitement, which evaporated when he got through to the Old Yorkshire Grey pub in Harrogate. No one in that establishment admitted to ever having heard of a Mabel Gloag.

All was not sweetness and light among the band of barristers who shared our Chambers in Equity Court. Not only was Henry discontented and apparently planning emigration down under, Claude Erskine-Brown came to me with a peculiar woe. It seemed he nursed a strange ambition to join the club where actors and judges, publishers and journalists, meet to shelter from their wives and enjoy shared reminiscences and nursery food.

'I want to put up for the Sheridan,' he told me.

'Isn't that rather a frivolous ambition for a fellow who can sit through *Tannhäuser* without laughing?'

But Claude was not to be dissuaded. 'I've wanted to belong to the club for years,' he confessed, 'but the trouble is that Ballard's on the committee. He's going to remind them of that unfortunate incident when I was photographed in the Kitten-A-Go-Go.'

'But it was clearly established' — I defended the suffering Claude — 'that you only went there to inspect the scene of the crime.'

'Ballard says members of the Sheridan Club should be like Caesar's wife, above suspicion. And if he decided to blackball, the others on the committee might follow his lead. The blackballs would be all over the place, like . . .'

'Sheep shit?'

'Think of it, Rumpole.'

'Unpleasant, I agree. My God, what did we ever do to get Soapy Sam Ballard wished on us as a Head of Chambers?'

The soundness of that last remark was born out by the behaviour of Soapy Sam at our very next Chambers meeting. When we were all assembled he addressed us in sepulchral tones, so that I thought that at least one of our best solicitor clients had shot himself in the clerk's room. 'I have called you all together,' Ballard told us, 'because I have reason to believe that a crime of major proportions has been committed in Chambers.'

'Someone has nicked the nail-brush from the downstairs loo again?' I remembered the last horror story in our Chambers history.

'I received a fee of fifty pounds for an opinion in a breathalyzer.' Ballard opened his case without condescending to answer my question.

'Come a bit cheap, don't you, Bollard, as one of Her Majesty the Queen's Counsel?' I sounded, I hoped, genuinely concerned at the fellow's rate of reward.

'I signed the receipt, of course. In the usual manner.'

'Hardly worth all the trouble of becoming a Q.C. for that.'

'Do any of you remember how old Pelham Widdershins became a Q.C.?' Uncle Tom, the briefless barrister who is the oldest inhabitant of our Chambers, a friendly figure most often to be seen practising putts along the carpet in the clerk's room, was in reminiscent mood.

'Please, Uncle Tom!' Ballard did his best, but, once started, no one could stop the old fellow's flow.

'Oh, all right, then,' he said. 'I'll tell you. The Lord Chancellor had two lists, don't you see? One for chaps he was going to make Q.C.s, and the other for chaps he was going to ask down for a spot of shooting. Well, he got a bit fuddled, it seems, and mixed the two lists up. Old Widdershins was absolute death to a woodcock but he didn't dare open his mouth in Court. All the same, he was handed a silk gown, and put Q.C. after his name, to everyone's amazement.'

'I still don't understand.' I looked at Ballard in some bewilderment. 'You don't shoot, do you?'

'Perhaps, Rumpole' — Sam was displeased — 'I got silk because I don't regard the criminal law of England solely as a subject for jokes about nail-brushes and suchlike matters. If we might be allowed to return to the subject in hand.'

'Of course. You were telling us about your little breathalyzer.'

'I signed the receipt and gave the cheque to Henry to bank. That cheque, it is my painful duty to tell you, never reached the National Wessex. And I have yet to receive a satisfactory explanation.'

'Eaten by mice?' I tried to make a helpful suggestion, but Ballard wasn't having it.

'I don't think I heard that, Rumpole.'

'No. But perhaps Rumpole's right.' Uncle Tom weighed the evidence carefully. 'There *are* mice in that old cupboard in our clerk's room. Sometimes I get a strange feeling that they've been at the digestive biscuits.'

'I have told Henry that he has to give me a satisfactory account of the matter.'

'What was it? Fifty quid?' I asked. 'He'll probably retire and live on that for the rest of his life.'

'Come to think of it,' said the grey-haired barrister named Hoskins, obsessed with getting his fingers on enough crime to maintain his four hungry daughters, 'I have seen Henry reading a brochure about Australia.'

Ballard was grateful for this and other evidence he took as strong indicators of our clerk's dishonesty. Erskine-Brown contributed the information that Henry now arrived at work in a bright red *Triumph D-reg. sports car,* a clear sign of sin when coupled with the fact that he habitually left this motor holding hands with Dianne, our plucky but not always accurate typist.

'His marriage is on the rocks,' Ballard said severely. 'And when a fellow's marriage is on the rocks he can't be trusted with a cheque.'

'Oh, really?' I tried to sound interested. 'How's your marriage, Ballard?'

'You know perfectly well I'm a bachelor.'

'Then aren't you rather like a life-long vegetarian giving us his recipe for steak and kidney pud?'

'Let us try and keep to the point, shall we? Is it the feeling of the meeting that I tell our clerk, Henry, that he must account for the missing cheque or else . . .'

'Or else what?'

'Or else he will have to look elsewhere for employment. I assume we want to avoid the embarrassment of a prosecution?'

'I support the Head of Chambers.' Erskine-Brown was filled with a sudden enthusiasm for the Ballard cause. 'I think we in Chambers should support each other. I will be behind you in this, Ballard. Just as I expect you to be behind me on another matter.'

'Another matter?' Ballard was puzzled until I enlightened him. 'He means his election to the Sheridan Club.'

'I can't promise you that, Erskine-Brown.' Soapy Sam was at his most judicial. 'Each case,

I feel, must be decided strictly on its merits. Now. How many in favour of an ultimatum to Henry?'

I regret to say that all hands but mine were raised in condemnation. What they all failed to realize was that Henry's comparative prosperity was due to his having the intelligence to be a barrister's clerk and not a barrister. He could sit in comfort taking in ten per cent of our earnings while we slogged out to do breathalyzers on the cheap. However, the vote went overwhelmingly against him. Ballard announced that the resolution was carried and we could all go home by train as he didn't suppose we all had red 'Triumphant' sports cars like our clerk. 'And alas,' he told me, 'my train will be taking me to my bachelor establishment in Waltham Cross. We're not all blessed with the warmth and loving companionship of family life as you are, Rumpole.' Like so many of the pronouncements of our learned Head of Chambers this proved to be misinformed.

When I returned home, travel-worn and weary, having abbreviated my time at the bar in Pommeroy's for the sake of propitiating She Who Must Be Obeyed, no voice challenged me on my entry into the mansion flat with a suspicious 'Is that you, Rumpole?' A cursory inspection of the premises showed me that they were devoid of life — bare, ruined choirs where late sweet Hilda cooked. At last I found, on the living-room mantelpiece, one of those notes, sometimes known as a 'Dear John', familiar to practitioners in divorce cases: *This may bring you to your senses, Rumpole,* she had written, ever economical, on the back of a used envelope. *If I leave you alone you may have time to think seriously about your career. Try not to use too much gas. Hilda.*

I must confess now, and long after the event, that I didn't obey her orders. In fact I turned the gas fire up to a companionable roar, opened the bottle of Château Thames Embankment I had brought home from my brief visit to Pommeroy's and started to knit up the ravelled sleeve of care with my eyes shut.

About an hour later the telephone rang. This time it was Fred Timson who had murdered sleep. I had forgotten that he was now at liberty and he told me that he was anxious to do all he could to help young Nigel. Were we, for instance, in need of an alibi? If so, he could undoubtedly supply any number of witnesses from the Needle Arms to say the lad was in the saloon bar at the time in question.

I told him that it wasn't that sort of a case. What we wanted above all was to find a Miss Mabel Gloag who had a P.O. box address in Harrogate and a telephone number which connected us to the Old Yorkshire Grey pub, where Miss Gloag had never been heard of.

'Right you are, Mr Rumpole. My cousin Den moved up to Yorkshire. I believe he's at liberty at the moment. I'll get him to make a few inquiries relative to the bird in question. Every little helps.

81

The Old Yorkshire Grey, was it?'

'Yes. And she's not a bird, Fred. She's an elderly lady who makes a habit of investing on the Stock Exchange.' At the time I put too little trust in the Timson information service and was soon soaking again in sore labour's bath.

Life continued uneventfully over the next few weeks and I must say I rapidly became used to my solitary existence in the Gloucester Road. I spent little time brooding on the upwardly mobile possibilities of my becoming a Q.C., a title which I have long held stands for 'Queer Customer', and I was able to stay late in Pommeroy's without encountering icy blasts of disapproval on my return home. One night, when Jack Pommeroy was calling 'last orders' in a half-hearted sort of way, I found myself at the bar with our clerk, Henry, who was trying to drown his sorrows.

'Mr Ballard, Q.C., thinks I robbed him of fifty quid, does he?' Henry challenged me as I drew my large Château Fleet Street up alongside his double gin and Dubonnet. 'He wants me out on my ear, does he? He's welcome! That's all I can say. He's very, exceedingly, welcome! He can say what he likes. Because if I'm sacked for thieving, how could I face my wife and the neighbours in Bexley Heath? Quite frankly, Mr Rumpole, a new life beckons. My marriage would be over!'

I bought another round of drinks for us, which Jack agreed to put on the slate until the next Legal Aid cheque came through, and then sought to comfort our clerk by saying, 'Surely, your wife would stand by you?'

'My wife,' Henry shook his head decidedly, 'has gone into public life. She has taken her seat on the Council. She is Chair of the Disabled Toilets Inquiry. She is also Chair of the Senior Citizens Ways and Means and the Equal Opportunities in Catering. These responsibilities keep her out every evening. Do you know what I return home to now, Mr Rumpole? Quite frankly, I return home to cheese on toast.' He drank and I followed his example. Then he asked bitterly, 'Have you any conception of what it's like, Mr Rumpole, to find yourself married to a Chair?'

'You thought you had married a woman, and you find yourself tied to an article of furniture?' I saw his difficulty.

'Oh, too true that, Mr Rumpole. Too very true. And I'll tell you something else . . .'

'Feel free, Henry.'

'Now she's that active in local government nothing can stop her getting "Mayor" eventually. In due course of time, Mr Rumpole, I am likely to serve out my year as her Lady Mayoress.' My heart bled for the fellow as he added, 'Only one way out, quite frankly. Only one means of escape as I reads the situation.'

'What's that?'

'Could my wife appear with a Mayoress sacked from his job in the Temple for petty theft, Mr Rumpole?' he asked rhetorically and I had to admit, 'I suppose that might cause a bit of embarrassment at the function.'

'Too true, Mr Rumpole. Once again, too very true. And to spare her that I would start a new life in the Dandenong Mountains in the State of Victoria.'

'Well, I suppose they have barrister chambers, even in the Dandenong Mountains.' I tried to imagine it.

'I'm not clerking any more. I'm taking up a new career.'

'You want to be a barrister?' Henry, it appeared, was prepared to face a steep drop in salary.

'It is my intention, sir, to go into show business.'

'Much the same thing,' I agreed.

'You may remember I starred in *Private Lives* opposite Miss Osgood from the Old Bailey list office . . .'

'Bit of a hit, weren't you?'

'A rave notice, that's all, in the *Bexley Heath Advertiser*. Well, Dianne . . . Her cousin runs the Commonwealth Inn over in the Dandenongs. She's going as receptionist and I shall be placed in charge of entertainments.'

'You're going to perform, Henry?' Was there no end to the man's desperation?

'From time to time, I might make a personal appearance. I'm working up a nostalgia number. Songs of the war-time years. As my old father used to sing them.'

Songs of the war-time years! Then, as I drank

up and Jack asked if we hadn't got homes, those sad, happy evenings when I fought with the ground staff at R.A.F. Dungeness came back to me. 'Roll out the barrel,' I began to sing softly, 'we'll have a barrel of fun,' and Henry chimed in with 'You Are My Sunshine'. 'Tell you what, you dear old Worship the Lady Mayoress,' I told him, 'how about coming home for a night-cap? I'm leading a lonely bachelor existence now, in the Gloucester Road.'

'A bachelor existence, Mr Rumpole?' Henry was pleased to accept my invitation. 'You gentlemen get all the luck.'

As Henry and I let ourselves in my front door, with a plastic bag of bottles supplied by Jack, who had seemed, at the end, anxious to get rid of us, we were giving a spirited rendering of 'We're Going to Hang Out the Washing on the Siegfried Line'. By the time we had made it to the kitchen and I was finding glasses and plying the corkscrew, we had moved on to a tearful rendering of that moving number, so beautifully given by Dame Vera Lynn, 'There'll be Blue Birds Over the White Cliffs of Dover'.

In fact I was just singing 'Tomorrow when the world is free' and Henry was applying a strange descant to 'And Billy shall go to sleep in his own little bed again', when I noticed a tell-tale and sinister chink of light between the shutters of that hatch Hilda introduced to improve communication between the kitchen and the living-room. At once I scented danger. I moved to the hatch and threw it open. I had been right to feel afraid.

Sitting in the brightly lit living-room were my wife She Who Must Be Obeyed and her old school-friend Dodo Mackintosh. The gas fire was off and they were both looking at the kitchen hatch with the implacable expressions of old-time judges who would wish to know of any reason why sentence of death should not be passed immediately.

Hilda and Dodo Mackintosh went to some academy for young ladies where they had, as Hilda sometimes says, 'the nonsense knocked out of them'. (I always think people are a lot better off with some of the nonsense left in them.) My wife and Dodo were, it seems, the terror of the lacrosse field and they still, given the slightest opportunity, work as a team in the long-running match *She Who Must Be Obeyed* v. *Rumpole*. The manner of my return home had given them an ample opening for a goal. Breakfast the next morning was like a snack with a couple of basilisks and the situation was not made easier for me by the fact that I had a sledgehammer fixed up between the temples and a mouth coated in sawdust. When I asked Hilda, in the politest of tones, whether it was coffee that I saw before me she answered, testily, I thought, 'Of course, it's coffee. What did you have for breakfast when I was away for a few days with my old friend Dodo? Red Biddy, I suppose.'

'I think Hilda came to stay with me' — Dodo came up fast on my left flank — 'to give you a little time to think things over.'

'And I come back and find you carousing with your clerk!' Hilda expressed considerable disgust.

'It rather seemed to me, Hilda, as if they were singing together.' Dodo turned the screw.

'Singing with your clerk! And Daddy wouldn't even take a cup of coffee with his old clerk, Albert. He said it wasn't the done thing.'

'Hilda says it is so terribly important at the Bar to do the done thing, Rumpole.'

'I suppose neither of you ladies has got an aspirin tablet?' I asked to break up the duet.

'I don't think you'll find drugs are the answer, Rumpole.' Hilda gave me one of her sorrowful looks. 'The answer is not to do it in the first place.'

'Yes. But if you've already done the thing. I mean . . .'

'It's so important *now*, isn't it, Hilda?' Dodo asked her friend, 'that Rumpole should only do the done thing. At this moment in his career!'

'Exactly, Dodo!'

'What do you mean, "Exactly, Dodo"?' I was mystified. 'What moment?'

'Now you've applied to the Lord Chancellor to make you a Queen's Counsel.' Dodo supplied the answer. 'I don't suppose it would look quite the thing to have Rumpole, Q.C., singing with his clerk, would it, Hilda?'

'But I haven't asked the Lord Chancellor to

make me a Q.C.!'

'Oh, yes, you have, Rumpole.'

'I can remember last night perfectly clearly. I think. I haven't done anything of the sort.'

'No, Rumpole,' Hilda appalled me by saying. 'I made the application for you.'

'You did *what?*'

'I wrote to the Lord Chancellor. I didn't mince my words. *It's perfectly disgraceful* I told him, *that Rumpole should have been passed over when Samuel Ballard, a younger man, is in a silk gown. I hope,* I put in my letter, *that Rumpole will be called to take his seat in the front row without further delay.*'

'Hilda. You didn't?' I tried to say it hopefully, but all hope was gone.

'Someone has to take your career in hand, Rumpole,' She told me. 'Before it's too late.'

Later that morning, when the sledgehammer had reduced its activities to an occasional thump, the Queen's case against young Nigel Timson opened at the Old Bailey before his Honour, Judge Graves. Graves and my old sparring partner, Judge Bullingham, were as different in their ways as life and death. Where one was bright red with rage, the other had a ghastly pallor. Bullingham went in for the full-frontal glare; Graves preferred the averted eye of disapproval. The atmosphere in Bullingham's Court was often red-hot; in Graves's it seemed that the central-heating was permanently off. A fight with Bullingham could have some of the excitement of the Corrida, with Graves it was like doing battle with creeping paralysis. Not to put too fine a point on it, Judge Gerald Graves was a fellow with about as much of the milk of human kindness as a defunct halibut on a marble slab. As my opponent's opening speech wound on I saw the Judge favouring me with a look of ancient and fish-like contempt. Of course, I thought to myself, he *knows*. Hilda's ill-advised letter urging my claim to a silk gown was no doubt the prime topic of conversation among the Judiciary and the subject of their greatest mirth. 'Rumpole, Q.C.?' they were all saying. 'Of course it would never do.' At that moment a sinister expression crossed the Judge's face; he was, chillingly enough, smiling at the richness of the joke.

Avoiding the Judge's eye, I forced myself to listen to the silken tones of Hector Vellacott, a barrister who smelled of eau de cologne and no doubt owned large portfolios of highly profitable shares. He explained the mysterious offence of insider dealing and the old darlings in the jury box nodded sagely, as though they were the Governors of the Bank of England. 'What the Crown says,' he went on, 'is this. Having got hold of the secret information that Cornucopia Jams was about to be taken over by Worldwide Groceries, this young man, Nigel Timson bought no less than sixty-eight thousand pounds' worth of Cornucopia shares. When the takeover was complete, those shares doubled their value. I say *he* bought them, Members of the Jury. He may be going to tell you that he bought them for a client, a Miss Mabel Gloag. Who is Miss Mabel Gloag, you may well ask? It appears that she had an address, a Post Office box number in Harrogate, to which a cheque was eventually sent. No one has been able to obtain any further information about Miss Gloag.'

Had they not? Before I went into Court that morning I had been accosted by Fred Timson who had appointed himself, as leader of the Timson clan, head of the Find Mabel Gloag Organization. He had with him his cousin Dennis Timson, the ageing villain who had made such a remarkable cock-up of the Penny-Wise Bank robbery, to which I have referred in my previous reminiscences.[*] Dennis, it seemed, had called at the Old Yorkshire Grey in Harrogate where a mate of his was on friendly terms with the landlord.

'Did you find Mabel Gloag?' I had asked.

'Well, to be quite frank with you, Mr Rumpole, no,' Dennis admitted. But as I moved away, disappointed, he added a tidbit of information which I had found of some interest. 'I didn't find her, sir. But this guvnor of the Yorkshire Grey said there was an old girl there who was always talking about the stocks and shares she was buying. She came in in the mornings for a Guinness or two

[*] See 'Rumpole's Last Case' in *Rumpole's Last Case*, Penguin Books, 1987.

and she used the phone to her stockbroker. A Mrs Prescott.'

'Prescott? That's not much help. Anything else known about her?'

'Not really. Respectable old trout, apparently. She'd been a nursemaid to some smart City family. Seems that's where she got her taste for the high finance.'

'Nanny Prescott. Is she still about?'

'Hadn't seen her in the last three months, the guvnor said.'

I remembered this conversation as I sat listening to my learned friend Hector Vellacott cast some understandable doubt on the very existence of Nigel Timson's client. My instructing solicitor was sitting in front of me, and next to him Rosie Japhet had placed herself as a very interested spectator. In the short talk I had had with her I was impressed by her good sense and obvious affection for my client. She was a pretty and intelligent girl who smiled occasional encouragement at her lover in the dock. He looked back at her with all the confidence he could muster. They were both, I thought, very much in love, and they might eventually marry and form a new, even more upwardly mobile, branch of the Timson family, but this happy result might depend on the shadowy figure of Miss Mabel Gloag. With these considerations in mind I leant forward and muttered to Bernard, 'Nanny Prescott. I suppose it's not possible . . .' At the mention of the name, Rosie Japhet turned towards me and whispered eagerly, 'Did you say "Nanny Prescott"?'

'*You* don't know her?' I couldn't believe my luck.

'Well. That was the name of *our* nanny. When we were kids. Mrs Prescott.'

'Mrs? Did she have a Christian name, by any chance?'

' "May Bee". That's what we used to call her.'

'Maybee? Possibly Mabel? You wouldn't have a photograph of this Queen of the Nursery, would you?'

I was rudely interrupted by the Judge telling me that it was customary for Counsel to discuss their cases with their clients and solicitors before coming into Court and not during the opening speech for the Prosecution. 'Thank you, my Lord.' I rose obediently. 'Is my learned friend still opening? Fascinating stuff, of course. I shall be all attention.' I sat, cupped my hand round my ear, and listened eagerly. I didn't particularly like what I heard.

'The sum of twenty thousand pounds was paid into the defendant Timson's bank account after this transaction was completed,' Vellacott was saying. 'Can you doubt, Members of the Jury, that this was the defendant's first dip into his ill-gotten gains, no doubt spent on champagne and his Porsche motor car . . .'

Of course I had to rise then and interrupt. 'My Lord. What this young man chooses to drink . . . Ooch!' — the sledgehammer got in a final blow to the head — 'is entirely irrelevant.'

'Mr Vellacott, will there be evidence as to the defendant's earnings?' the Judge asked, ignoring my existence.

'In a good year, with bonuses, about seventy thousand. That will be Sir Christopher Japhet's evidence.'

'Good heavens.' The Judge looked severely shaken. 'That's more than . . .'

'More than an Old Bailey judge, your Lordship was about to say,' I suggested and was rewarded with a little ripple of laughter from the Jury, a call for silence from the Usher and a few cold words from the Judge.

'It's a considerable sum of money,' he said. 'Particularly if it's added to by the proceeds of illegal dealing.'

The first witness for the Prosecution was Nigel's fellow toiler among the computers, Hugo Shillingford. Hugo was about the same age as the accused, an affable young man who had been taught on the playing fields of Harrow to regard the world, and in particular the small world of stockbroking, as his oyster. He was led gently by Vellacott through his evidence. He was, he said, a friend, but not a close friend, of Nigel Timson, the accused. They worked at nearby desks on the dealing floor of the well-known firm of Japhet Jarroway. Yes, Hugo remembered an evening when he'd gone to the wine bar opposite the office with Timson and some other friends. It was just after the Cornucopia takeover by World-wide Groceries.

'What did Timson say?' Vellacott prepared to play his trump.

'He said he'd just made a big killing in Cornucopia shares. That's all.'

'He'd just made a big killing,' Judge Graves repeated in sepulchral but satisfied tones as he noted down the damning evidence and underlined it with his red pencil.

'Mr Shillingford. You said you weren't a close friend of Nigel Timson's?' I started my cross-examination in the most silken of Rumpole tones.

'Well, I mean, we never went to school together.'

'Ah, yes. My client received his education at a comprehensive and Shepherd's Bush market. He got his financial expertise by fixing the price of Cox's Orange Pippins.' My tones became noticeably less silken. 'Isn't that what you gentlemen on the Stock Exchange sometimes call a "barrow boy"? As distinct from a Harrow boy, of course.' The Jury looked at Nigel with some sympathy and interest. The Judge looked at him with increased distaste.

'Honestly, I didn't know all that about Nigel.' Hugo Shillingford seemed painfully surprised.

'But you knew he hadn't been to a public school?'

'Yes. I knew that.'

'Thank you. Now then, when you heard Nigel say he'd made a killing on Cornucopia shares, did he not add the words "For some little old lady in Harrogate"?'

'I didn't hear that.'

'You didn't hear him say that.' Judge Graves continued to note down evidence adverse to the accused with obvious satisfaction.

'What were you celebrating in the wine bar? Was it *your* birthday on that occasion?' I asked the witness.

'Well, yes. Now I come to think of it.'

'And were you busy juggling?'

'Busy doing what, Mr Rumpole?'

'Juggling, my Lord. With a couple of glasses and a bottle of Dom Perignon.'

'Juggling with Dom Perignon!' His gloomy Honour made it sound as though he had caught Shillingford playing roulette on an altar cloth.

'Well, yes. As a matter of fact I was. I rather think I dropped it.'

'So, at that tragic moment, he might have mentioned the lady in Harrogate?' I suggested. 'When you weren't listening?'

'I suppose he might,' the witness conceded.

'Thank you. Oh, one other matter. There had been rumours of previous insider deals, had there not, around your firm of Japhet Jarroway?'

'My Lord. This can't be relevant.' Vellacott eased himself to his feet and the Judge looked at me as though I were an incompetent white-wig, who still hadn't learnt his trade.

'Whether it's relevant or not, it can't possibly help your client, Mr Rumpole!'

95

'We have seen Detective Inspector Arbuthnot's statement about reports of other suspect deals.' I reminded Graves of the depositions in the case and Vellacott looked particularly saintly as he said, 'I had no intention of putting in that evidence, in fairness to the accused.'

'In fairness to the accused I would like an answer to my question,' I insisted. 'What is it, Mr Hugo Shillingford?'

'There was a lot of talk, yes.' And after a considerable pause I got the answer I wanted. 'There were rumours that someone had been using information from the Corporate Finance department to buy shares.'

'*Someone* was using information.' Judge Graves made another of his notes, underlined it with his red pencil and looked at the young man in the dock, no doubt turning over the appropriate sentence in his mind.

After Hugo Shillingford, we had the Manager of the Cheapside branch of the National Wessex, who said that on the fourteenth of January last, a banker's draft for twenty thousand pounds had been paid into Nigel Timson's account. After further probing by Rumpole it appeared that the draft was on a bank called Transworld Archipelago, trading in the Cayman Islands, and it came as no surprise to discover that the Prosecution had been quite unable to trace the source of the money. 'I suppose, Mr Vellacott,' the Judge suggested, 'you will be asking the Jury to draw certain inferences?' To which dark hint my learned friend agreed, oozing charm and bowing from the waist.

Whilst these stirring events were taking place in Court, Rosie Japhet had gone back to her flat and found an old album of childhood photographs. In it she discovered a snap of her six-year-old self on a bucket and spade holiday in Cornwall. A comfortable-looking Nanny was helping her build a sand-castle. Anxious to help her lover, Rosie detached the photograph and brought it back to Court with no idea of what the consequences would be.

While Rosie Japhet was engaged in collecting evidence, her father Sir Christopher, had entered the witness-box. There he was received with the nearest thing to a smile of welcome that existed in Judge Graves's armoury of expressions, and some untesting questions from my learned friend. He agreed that the Cornucopia takeover bid had been planned behind a Chinese wall in the Corporate Finance department of Japhet Jarroway. Nigel Timson, as a dealer in stocks and shares, had no right to know anything about it, but he had clearly found out somehow because he bought a large number of Cornucopia shares for 'his rather shadowy customer. Miss . . . What was her name?'

'Gloag. Miss Mabel Gloag,' I helped him out with a growl from my seat.

'And then, of course, a large sum was paid into Nigel Timson's bank account,' Sir Christopher went on, without so much as a glance in my direction.

'That twenty thousand pounds' — Vellacott was tightening the screws on his case — 'wasn't part of Timson's wages or a bonus from your firm, was it?'

'Quite definitely not. I have checked that most carefully, of course.'

In the ensuing atmosphere of quiet satisfaction which enveloped the Prosecution and the Bench, I rose to cross-examine. My first shot across the bows, delivered without any preliminary courtesies, was, 'You don't like barrow boys, do you, Sir Christopher?'

'I don't suppose the witness understands that question any more than I do, Mr Rumpole.' His Lordship was at his iciest.

'The witness understands it perfectly well,' I corrected him. 'Didn't you give an interview on the television programme "City Doings"?'

'Yes, I did.'

'And didn't you say that the crime wave in the City was due to the young barrow boys who've got into the Stock Exchange?'

'I said that the old tradition of a gentleman's word being his bond had died out. And I regret it.'

'I'm sure we all regret, Sir Christopher, that the standard of gentlemanly behaviour is declining.' The Judge looked at me in an unfriendly fashion. 'Even in the legal profession. Yes, Mr Rumpole.'

'Young Nigel Timson came to you as an office boy, didn't he?' I returned to the business in hand.

'I believe that is so.'

'And achieved his present position by honest hard work?'

'I believe he was honest.' But Nigel's possible future father-in-law couldn't resist adding, 'To start with.'

'He got to know your daughter extremely well?'

'I think they became quite friendly. Yes.'

'Don't let's mince matters, Sir Christopher. They're living together, aren't they, at a fashionable address in the Isle of Dogs?'

'Mr Rumpole!' Judge Graves's unfriendliness had turned to disgust. 'Has your client instructed you to attack the honour of this gentleman's daughter?'

'My client's honour has been attacked. He's been called dishonest.'

'But what on earth can his relations with Miss Japhet possibly have to do with it?'

'My Lord. May I make a suggestion?' Desperate measures were called for to stem the constant flow of cold water from the Bench. 'May I suggest that your Lordship sits quietly and allows me to develop my defence. Whether I succeed in doing so will be entirely a matter for the Jury!'

God knows what might have happened then had Sir Christopher not switched on his charm to full beam and said, 'Perhaps I can help? My daughter and Nigel Timson are living together, yes.'

'Thank you, Sir Christopher.' The Judge looked at the witness as though he were a good deed in a naughty world. 'That's the frankness I would expect from you, sir. Now perhaps we can pass to something relevant.'

'Certainly.' As ever I was anxious to oblige. 'Have you found out much about Nigel Timson's family?'

'I have made certain inquiries, yes.'

'And have you discovered that many members of the Timson clan have had more criminal convictions than we've had hot dinners?' This received a little laughter from the Jury, and the Usher called for silence. 'And has that led you to regard young Nigel Timson with disfavour?'

It was at this point that Rosie Japhet, her mission accomplished, came back into Court and resumed her seat beside Mr Bernard. She looked up at her father in the box as he said, 'I only want my daughter to be happy, Mr Rumpole.' Rosie opened her handbag then and gave the photograph she had discovered to my instructing solicitor. The cross-examination entered a rougher stage.

'But you don't want her married to a barrow boy, do you?'

There was a pause while Rosie's father thought of the nicest possible way of putting the matter. 'I should prefer my daughter not to marry into the Timson family. If I have to be honest.'

100

'Oh, yes, Sir Christopher. You have to be honest. So is that why you're giving evidence against him on this vague charge of insider dealing?'

'I have given my evidence because it's the truth,' the witness protested, a little too emphatically. The Judge obediently wrote down 'it's the truth' and underlined it, then he said wearily, 'Any other questions, Mr Rumpole?' Hoping, no doubt, to spare the great Sir Christopher Japhet further embarrassment.

'Just a few, my Lord.' It was then I whispered some quick orders to Bernard. The gist was that he was to send a clerk hot-footing it down to Somerset House to trace any relevant information about a Mrs Mabel Prescott, née Gloag. Before the learned judge got restive, I turned back to the witness. 'Sir Christopher. There had been a suspicion of a considerable amount of insider dealing in your firm before the Cornucopia take-over?'

'Unfortunately, yes.'

'And whoever was responsible might have wanted to pin the blame on this young barrow boy, Nigel Timson?'

'I suppose' — he shrugged off the suggestion — 'anything's possible.'

'And it's possible that this "someone" instructed Miss Gloag to buy Cornucopia shares through young Timson. Assuming that this "someone" knew the shares were going to rise?'

'As I said, it's possible.'

'And in order to make things look even worse

for Nigel Timson, this "someone" might have paid twenty thousand pounds anonymously into his bank account?'

'He must have been a very generous "someone" indeed.' This won the witness a little laughter from the Jury and a wintry smile from his Lordship.

'Do you really think so? Out of a profit of sixty-eight thousand pounds?'

'You are suggesting' — Sir Christopher frowned as though seriously trying to follow my drift — 'that this person was responsible for the previous insider deals?'

The opening formalities were over and the time had come to let him have the case for Nigel Timson with both barrels. 'Oh, yes, Sir Christopher. That is precisely what I am suggesting. Have you got a bank account in the Cayman Islands?' And when he looked at the Judge, as though asking for permission not to answer, I fired another volley. 'What's the matter? Have you forgotten how many bank accounts you've collected? Before you commit yourself, may I remind you that we have a law of perjury, which applies even to the evidence of gentlemen.'

Only then did Judge Graves come to the rescue of the City gent. 'I don't need to remind you, Sir Christopher, that you are not bound to answer incriminating questions. That doesn't arise in your case, I'm sure.'

Sir Christopher could see the faces of the Jury. For the first time they were looking at him with a certain amount of doubt and suspicion, and not to have answered then would have been to destroy all his credibility, so he said, as casually as possible, 'Of course, I'm prepared to deal with your question. I have a small account in the Cayman Islands. Yes.'

'At the Transworld Archipelago?'

'I believe that's what the bank's called.' I gave the Jury one of my meaningful looks and changed the subject. 'Your daughter Rosie is a nicely brought up girl, no doubt.'

Rosie looked up at me puzzled, and her father smiled down at her.

'Yes. I hope so.'

'And her formative years were presided over by a devoted nursemaid?'

'We had a nanny.'

'Nanny Prescott?' Sir Christopher stood silent. I pressed on with 'Do you believe that was her name?'

'It was her name, yes.'

'Is that a photograph of Nanny Mabel Prescott?' When the Usher handed him the snap from his daughter's album Sir Christopher had to admit it.

'Can you tell us where Mrs Prescott is now?'

'I have absolutely no idea. I know she had a son in Australia. She may have gone out there.'

'How very convenient. Was there a Mr Prescott?'

'I think she was a widow when she came to us. I really can't remember.'

'We heard that she had a Post Office box number in Harrogate. Did you know she lived there?'

'I seem to remember something about a family in Harrogate.' The witness frowned and then Judge Graves stirred as though rising from the dead. 'Mr Rumpole, may I ask where these questions are leading?'

'I hope, my Lord, to the truth.'

'Which is?'

'That you, Sir Christopher,' I turned on the witness, 'got your old servant, using another name, to place the share order with young Nigel Timson. That you paid the twenty thousand pounds into his bank account. And you did all that because you wanted to cover up your own insider trading. Such a brilliant idea, wasn't it? To blame it all on one of those unspeakable barrow boys, who've let down the honourable traditions of you old City gents.' There followed one of those prolonged courtroom silences which can happen at the turning point of a case, when anyone who has a pin about them might drop it with a resounding crash. At long last, Sir Christopher spoke. 'That is an absolutely outrageous suggestion!' he said.

The day, I think you will agree, had not gone badly for the Defence. What I needed was a little hard evidence to back up my outrageous suggestions. Accordingly I asked the Judge for an adjournment 'out of consideration for the witness', who looked, I thought, drained as a result of our encounter. The old darling on the Bench went up a degree above freezing-point, found my suggestion excellent, and knocked off work until the following morning.

As I came out of Court, not a little flown with triumph, my spirits were somewhat dashed by my clerk, Henry. There had been a call to Chambers from Sir Robert Keith, the Lord Chancellor's chief adviser and right-hand man. Old Keith, Henry told me, wondered if I would care to join him for a drink at the Sheridan Club at six o'clock that evening. It was, it seemed, a matter of some urgency.

Perhaps, at this point, I should fill you in with a rough idea of the way in which humble junior barristers rise to become one of Her Majesty's Counsel, learned in the law. After at least ten years of practice, the aspirant applies to the Lord Chancellor of England for admission to the select band of Q.C.s. He, and occasionally she, must show great respectability, high earnings, and should have a few letters of commendation from friendly judges who are prepared to say he keeps his flies done up and doesn't quarrel overtly with the Judiciary or treat evidence of alleged admissions to the police with unseemly levity. The Lord Chancellor, with Sir Robert Keith at his elbow, goes through the list of applicants and rewards the chosen few with permission to wear a silk gown, long wigs and knee breeches on special occasions, and the right to charge higher fees, do 'bigger' cases, be called 'leading Counsel' and be serviced in Court by a 'junior' barrister, who is often the Q.C.'s senior in age and experience. Many juniors of the old school, Rumpole among them, prefer to hack on in gowns of more plebeian material and not deny themselves the daily bread and butter of petty thefts and indecent exposures. In this way I have been able to carve out a career which, as I hope you may agree, has had its splendour as well as its miseries. It will also be remembered that I achieved my greatest triumph, victory in the Penge Bungalow Murders, as a junior Counsel, alone and without a leader.

My date with Sir Robert Keith, a prospect which caused me to mutter 'Oh, my ears and whiskers' in a distracted manner as I walked up the Strand towards the Sheridan Club, had no doubt been caused by the highly embarrassing fact that She Who Must Be Obeyed, with no prompting at all from my learned self, had written to the Lord Chancellor urging my claim to a silken gown. After a critical looking-over by the hall porter, I was admitted to the Sheridan bar and into the company of a well-nourished, white-haired man with a florid complexion who now treated me to a large club claret and a look of amused sympathy.

'I thought a drink at my club, Rumpole, might be the best way to get over this rather tricky situation.'

'Yes. Well.' I lifted my glass to him. 'Here's mud in your eye.'

'Thank you.' Then he got down to business.

'As you may know, the Lord Chancellor has received an extremely awkward letter from Mrs Rumpole.'

'And Mrs Rumpole can be awkward.'

'She actually suggested we should give you silk! The Lord Chancellor was deeply embarrassed by it.'

'Made him squirm a bit on the woolsack, did it?'

'It's not unprecedented.'

'Oh, I'm glad of that.'

'The wife of a clerk to the Nuneaton magistrates kept writing insisting that her husband should be made Lord Chief Justice of England. Until they certified her.'

He laughed heartily at this. I didn't join him. I had noticed, among a little group of members at the bar, that unlikely club man, Soapy Sam Ballard, Q.C., and I didn't want the Head of our Chambers to overhear any part of my meeting with the Lord Chancellor's right-hand man. Then Keith looked at me seriously. 'Rumpole,' he said, 'you don't want to be a Q.C., do you?'

'Well. Of course it would be an honour.' There had been a moment, coming up the stairs, when I had considered if I might not accept a silk gown if it were to be thrust upon me, so I added, 'And when I look at the learned friends who've got it, I honestly don't see why . . .'

'Why you should bother to join them?' Keith said hopefully.

'I was going to say, why I'm not at least as

good as they are.'

'Some men are natural juniors, Rumpole.' Keith adopted the man-to-man tones which might have gone down a treat in the Mess. 'You are one of the good old non-commissioned officers of the Bailey. Strong in battle. Loud-voiced on the parade ground. But absolutely no criticism of you, of course, never quite officer material. It'll be a relief to the Lord Chancellor to know that you don't really want it, Rumpole.' 'I didn't say that exactly,' I said, but failed to stop his flow. 'Because of course at your age, you know, and given your . . . your type of practice silk is really out of the question. Rumpole, Q.C.? It just can't be done.'

'I see.'

'So you'll break it to your good lady? I know she'll be disappointed. Her father never got silk either. Old Wystan never quite made it.'

There was half a minute's silence whilst we paid tribute to Hilda's father, a perfectly hopeless barrister who almost fainted at the mere mention of bloodstains and was crassly ignorant of the subtler implications of rigor mortis. Then Keith said cheerfully, 'Battling down the Bailey now, are you?'

'Yes, a City fraud. Bit of insider dealing.' I hoped it sounded impressive.

'Jolly good show! You'll want to get along home now. Try and persuade your wife to stop writing letters. Scares the Lord Chancellor to get them. Nice to have had this little chat. Carry on, "Sergeant" Rumpole.'

Taking this as an order to dismiss I rose and made for the door only to be stopped by my Head of Chambers by the bar. 'Rumpole,' he said, in tones of awe and wonder, 'wasn't that Sir Robert Keith from the Lord Chancellor's office?'

'That was old Keith. Yes.' Deeply impressed, Ballard asked permission to buy me another large club claret, and I let him have his way. When it came, he pulled out a wallet and ferreted in it for a five pound note.

'Did Keith mention me at all?'

'You want to know what he said about you?'

'Well, it is interesting to know how one is regarded by the powers that be.' Ballard's search through his wallet had dislodged a pink slip of paper which fluttered to the ground. 'He said absolutely nothing at all about you, Ballard. And what's that you've dropped?'

I stooped with some difficulty and retrieved what turned out, happily as I thought for Henry, to be a cheque for fifty pounds from Snaresbrook & Higgs, Solicitors, in favour of Samuel Ballard.

'That wouldn't be the cheque you're accusing Henry of nicking?' I asked as I handed it back.

Ballard looked at it, gulped and giggled nervously. 'Stupid of me. I must . . . Well, I must've just put it in the back of my wallet and forgotten all about it. Of course I'll tell Henry at once. No doubt he'll be extremely relieved.'

'Making false accusations against your faithful

clerk.' I wasn't going to let the man off lightly. 'What's the Sheridan Club committee going to think of that?' I raised my glass to the light, admired the colour and then took a long and fruity swig. 'Take my advice, old darling. Don't ask anyone to blackball poor old Erskine-Brown.'

'No, no, of course not,' Ballard assured me hastily. 'I've always thought Claude would make a pretty good member here.'

'He might brighten the place up.' I looked around me. 'Bring on the dancing girls, for instance.'

*Mrs Mabel Jane Prescott. Married Arthur Charlton Prescott, Harrogate, the 3rd April 1940. Born the 4th of June 1918, Mabel Jane Gloag.* I was robed and ready, standing outside the Court next morning and reading the results of Bernard's clerk's researches. The landlord of the Yorkshire Grey in Harrogate had, it seemed, identified the photograph, and would be coming to Court later that day. There couldn't, I thought, be a Q.C. in the business who would have taken the risk of cross-examining Sir Christopher as I had done and then been proved right.

'I knew it, Mr Rumpole.' Fred Timson was triumphant. 'I knew as you'd never let the Timsons down.'

'In this case,' I told him, 'I think the Timsons have been saved entirely by their own efforts.'

And now my learned friend Mr Vellacott, for the Prosecution, came padding up to ask, 'Might

I have a word in your shell-like, old boy?' As we wandered away together, he gave me the word with some embarrassment. 'The truth of the matter is, we can't find Sir Christopher Japhet.'

'Oh, you do astonish me!' I feigned amazement. 'Have you looked in the Grand Cayman? Perhaps he's turned himself into an offshore island.'

'Well, Inspector Arbuthnot does seem to think he's done a bunk out of the country. Too quick for us, I'm afraid. We can't go on against Timson. The Judge isn't going to like it.'

'Don't worry, old darling. The shock may bring him back to life.'

I left him then to rejoin my client and tell him the news. Rosie Japhet was standing on her own and, while I was talking to Nigel, she began to move away towards the lifts. He left me to say, 'Rosie, I'm sorry. About your father . . .'

She looked at him for a moment and then said, 'I know. He's gone. You did it to him, didn't you? You and your barrister, and all your family out of various jails!'

She moved away quickly and he called her back. She stopped only for a moment to favour him with a look of complete contempt. 'Oh, for God's sake! Leave me alone,' she said and added, in a voice loud enough for us all to hear, 'Barrow boy!'

My business is saving people from the nick. It is no part of my duty to help them to happy marriages or ensure that the course of true love runs smoothly for them. But I knew then that, by the way I had had to win his case, I had done something for which my client might never forgive me. I went into Court then to hear the Prosecution offer no further evidence and a verdict of not guilty was returned, which Judge Graves swallowed like a cup of cold hemlock. Another case was over.

If I had failed to win the unqualified gratitude of Nigel Timson, my efforts on behalf of Henry were greeted with positive resentment. I went back to our Chambers to be greeted by a clerk bubbling over with resentment. 'You've done it now, haven't you, Mr Rumpole!' he said by way of a greeting.

'Oh, yes, Henry. It was a famous victory.' I tried to strike a cheerful note. 'The chief witness against me made a dash for the nearest airport in the middle of my cross-examination and the Prosecution was left in an embarrassing position without a paddle.'

'No. I mean you've only ruined my life, that's all.'

'Hasn't Mr Ballard told you, Henry? He's found the cheque. There's nothing but good news. Hasn't he apologized?'

'You found the cheque, as I understand it, Mr Rumpole, in his wallet. You made him apologize. Where do you think that leaves me?'

'Leaves *you*. Where . . . ?'

'Lady Mayoress. I've got no way out now.'

'Henry!'

'I'm not ruined any more. I won't have to leave the country. I can't take up a new life in show business in the Dandenong Mountains. Dianne and I won't be travelling to the Southern Hemisphere now, Mr Rumpole. I'm stuck for the rest of my life in Bexley Heath, married to a Chair.'

'Henry, I'm sorry.' It was sincerely meant. I had now got the man's drift.

'Perhaps you'd be so kind as to leave me, Mr Rumpole. I wish to be alone with my dreams. What little is left of them. Close the door quietly, would you, as you go out?'

As you see, it was not a time when Rumpole was leading in the popularity charts. And I had one further person to placate. She Who Must Be Obeyed must be told of my drink with old Keith. I waited for a friendly moment after dinner when I was sporting my old cardigan and bedroom slippers, smoking a small cigar and toasting my toes in front of the unlit gas fire.

'Oh, by the way, Hilda,' I broached the subject. 'I had a chat with old Keith from the Lord Chancellor's office. Matter of fact he asked me for a drink in his club.'

'He didn't.' I could see she was impressed.

'Oh, yes. We had a chat together in the Sheridan.'

'So what is it now? Rumpole, Q.C.?'

'Well, no Hilda.' I hated to disappoint her. 'It's not.'

'*Not?*' I could feel an east wind cutting my

ankles and I started to invent hard. 'Old Keith was talking about your learned father, C. H. Wystan.'

'The man from the Lord Chancellor's office was talking about Daddy?' She was clearly gratified.

'Oh, at length. He said Wystan was such a brilliant lawyer they had decided to make *him* a Q.C. years ago.'

'Daddy, Q.C.?'

'Exactly. But your Daddy went off to a higher court, as old Keith puts it. The Great Appeal Court in the skies.'

'Daddy died,' Hilda had to admit.

'Sadly. So they felt that, as C. H. Wystan had missed it, they could hardly give it to his mere son-in-law. There's some sort of rule, I believe, about too many Q.C.s in the same family.' A silence fell between us and then Hilda looked at me.

'I do understand, Rumpole. After Daddy, it would be a bit of a come-down to give it to you.'

'But the Lord Chancellor sent you his love,' I hastened to assure her. 'From the woolsack. Oh, and he said don't bother to write again.'

'How very charming of him. Such a nice man. And very good legs, I always think, in breeches.' Hilda thought the matter over and then said, with considerable satisfaction, 'C. H. Wystan, Q.C.! One of Her Majesty's Counsel, learned in the law.'

My duty was done. I closed my eyes and once again sought to knit up the ravelled sleeve of care with a little sleep. Hilda awoke me then with an extraordinary suggestion. 'If you're feeling chilly,' she said, 'we might have the gas fire on. Full on, shall we?' After that there was a warm silence and I was after a little of the balm of hurt minds when she switched on 'City Doings' at full blast on the television. She was, it seemed, thinking of buying British Airways.

Oh, well, Hilda had murdered sleep, and therefore Rumpole should sleep no more.

# Rumpole and the Age of Miracles

The age of miracles is not past. I bring these glad tidings to my fellow hacks who trudge the treadmill between the Old Bailey and the Uxbridge Magistrates Court, seeming, at bleak moments, to lose cases by eloquent speeches to the Jury and greatly increase their clients' sentences by their impassioned pleas in mitigation. Life at the Bar may, more often than not, flicker palely between the hum and the drum. A man who has, let us say, won that great classic, the Penge Bungalow Murders, may find himself dealing with some petty matter such as turning back the mileage meters of clapped-out Ford Cortinas or receiving stolen fish. And then, perhaps, you hear a roll of distant thunder, a strange and alluring music is heard about Equity Court, a new star rises over Ludgate Circus, and an unusual and amusing brief drops into your lap. Such a miracle occurred to my good self when I found my services retained for the defence of the Reverend Timothy Donkin, Canon of Lawnchester Cathedral. Although the case did have an element of comedy, it was a deadly serious matter for the good canon. What was at stake for him was, if not his neck, at least his frock.

The matters which arose in the Donkin case were of an ecclesiastical nature, a strange territory

116

to Horace Rumpole whose concerns have been, over a long life-time, largely secular. It is true that my old father was a cleric, so I was, to that extent, a child of the manse; but his increasing doubts about the Thirty-nine Articles were only just balanced by his certainty that he was un-equipped to earn a living in any other profession. So he clung on to his draughty vicarage in East Anglia as a man might to a small raft in stormy seas.

It is also true that, in due course of time, I went up to Keble College, Oxford, where a number of future bishops were educated; but a future bishop makes a somewhat crude companion for a criminal student of tender years and I tended to avoid their brash and beery company. Having scraped a legal fourth (I have always found a knowledge of the law to be a positive disadvantage in a barrister's life), having, as I say, satisfied the examiners (it's libellous to suggest that I did so with the assistance of the names of any of the leading cases on constructive felony scribbled on my cuff), I went into a world where men of the cloth only appear occasionally to protest that the young mugger in the dock is a keen member of the ping-pong team in the Lads' Club, evidence which is always looked on with a scep-tical and fish-like eye by his Honour Judge Roger Bullingham. And so it was for the next half a century until the unlikely figure of Canon Donkin swam into my ken and I was introduced into a world of magic and mystery where miracles were found to be very much alive and kicking.

The dim religious light first made its presence felt when I arrived at my Chambers in Equity Court one morning and was greeted on the stairs by the figure of our clerk, Henry, carrying a clipboard and ticking off names on a list. When I asked him the meaning of this extraordinary behaviour his explanation, given in tones which I thought not nearly apologetic enough, was that he was acting on the instructions of Samuel Ballard, Q.C., our Head of Chambers, who wanted our arrivals and departures noted, presumably so he could calculate precisely how much electric light, soap and lavatory paper we were each using. Ballard is the sort of Head of Chambers who spends a great deal of his time counting the paper clips and adding up the coffee money.

'Soapy Sam Ballard wants us clocked in, does he?' And I asked Henry, 'Where's he gone to earth this morning?'

It seemed that Ballard, Q.C., President of the Lawyers As Christians society (L.A.C.), was in his room and did not wish to be disturbed. When I duly did so, I was surprised to find him on his knees beside his desk, muttering some reverent phrases about having been chosen, unworthy as he was, to do the will of God and promote the true interests of the Church. I was dimly aware that he was not addressing me but some unseen presence and, barging into this conversation with the Almighty, I gave the man a substantial piece of my mind. 'What do you think you're running in Equity Court,' I asked him, 'a Chambers of ladies and gentlemen learned in the law or a maximum-security nick? And if you've just dropped your collar stud, don't expect me to crawl under the desk to help you look for it.'

'Ah, Rumpole.' Ballard climbed to his feet, smiling at me in a pious and soapy manner. 'You interrupted me. I was giving thanks for the honour that's been done to me. Quite undeserved, of course.'

'Of course. What honour?'

'I believe it's the first time in our long history that these chambers have contained a Chancellor.'

'A Chancellor!' I thought that if she had appointed Ballard to the woolsack the Prime Minister must have completely lost her marbles, and I said as much.

It turned out that Ballard's act of thanksgiving was due to a rather lesser distinction. He had been made Chancellor of Lawnchester, a judge of the Ecclesiastical Court in a diocese which contains an unusually beautiful cathedral and, as I was to discover later, an extremely unusual canon.

'You've been made a Grand Inquisitor? If I were you I'd have nothing whatever to do with it,' I warned the man, and he should have heeded my warning.

'It's a post only open to communicating members of the Church of England. It's hardly likely to be offered to someone like you, Rumpole. Oh thou of little faith.' Ballard looked at me in a sad and infuriating sort of way.

'I have a great deal of faith,' I protested.

'Oh, yes?' Now Ballard sounded sceptical. 'In what precisely?'

'The health-giving powers of claret.' I recited my creed. 'The presumption of innocence and not having to clock in in the mornings. Chancellor of the Diocese, eh?' I looked at him with a flicker of interest. 'Are you planning to burn anyone at the stake?'

'Try not to be frivolous, Rumpole. Nowadays the Ecclesiastical Courts deal mainly with ritual and matters of church furnishings.'

'Smells and bells?' I got his drift. 'How many eagles can perch on a lectern? All that sort of paraphernalia. Don't you get a decent chance to unfrock a priest occasionally?'

Ballard looked deeply serious. 'That painful duty,' he intoned, 'has not been asked of the Diocese, as I understand it, for at least twenty-five years.'

'Go to it, Bollard,' I encouraged the fellow as I left him. 'You never know your luck. Tear the frocks off the clergy and leave God-fearing barristers alone.' I seem to have been blessed at that moment, in addition to my many talents, with the gift of prophecy.

Returning after the day's work was done, having paid a brief visit to Pommeroy's Wine Bar, the claret level in my veins having sunk to a dangerous low, I returned *à côté de chez* Rumpole, the alleged mansion flat in the Gloucester Road.

My wife, Hilda, known to me only as She Who Must Be Obeyed, greeted me in the hall, and as I hung up the Rumpole hat I told her briefly of the dark days of the Bollard inquisition. 'Odd,' I said, 'how the more they preach Christianity the less Christian people become.'

'Rumpole!' she whispered in a warning fashion. 'Do be careful. A priest would find that extremely upsetting.'

'Hilda' — I was puzzled — 'have you taken Holy Orders?'

'I'm just trying to tell you we have a visitor.' And she threw open the sitting-room door with something of a flourish. 'It's cousin Esmé's boy, Timmy. He wants to meet you very much indeed.'

Now the ramifications of Hilda's family are complex, and I have gone through life in constant fear of speaking to strangers in case they should turn out to be Hilda's long-lost cousin who would report to her on my behaviour. The relative now revealed to me was hitherto unknown; he was a small, tubby fellow in his forties with an eager expression and a quiff of hair which seemed to stand upright in an inquisitive sort of way, despite all efforts of the comb and brush to keep it in order. He wore that kind of understated dog-collar which consists of a discreet slip of white in place of a tie. 'Uncle Horace' — his voice was high and excitable but now slightly anxious, like a schoolboy who's lost his chewing-gum and fears he may have stuck it, absent-mindedly, on the Headmaster's desk — 'I'm so delighted to

121

see you. It's a relief to me, a considerable relief.'

'Timmy's been made a canon of Lawnchester Cathedral,' Hilda said, and then broke a world record by adding, 'He's quite a big shot now. Aren't you, Timmy?'

'Hilda.' I was lost in wonder. 'Was that a funny?'

The joke, if such it had been, was over and She proposed to get tea for our clerical visitor. Looking at him again I was sure he hadn't simply dropped in to drink Darjeeling and eat digestives with his distant relatives. He had the distinct look, half-apologetic, half-challenging, of a client.

'You're in trouble!' I said as I caught a welcome whiff of business in a lean time. 'What is it? Fiddling the organ fund? Pawning the candlesticks? Choirboys?'

'Rumpole!' Hilda paused on her way to the door to rebuke me. 'Don't be ridiculous!'

'Nothing like that, Uncle Horace, I promise you,' the Canon said, doing his best to smile. 'I suppose it's best described as old-fashioned adultery.' Hilda left us then with a resonant click of her tongue which indicated that Cousin Timmy had sunk in her estimation to something not much better than Rumpole.

When we were alone, Timothy Donkin told me his story. He was not the most popular preacher in his diocese; his views on miracles were, he explained, a little advanced for the good burghers of Lawnchester. It was not that he didn't believe that God could perform miracles. Multiplying loaves and fishes and turning water into wine were the sort of tricks the Almighty could manage in his sleep, but miracles, he felt, were just not in the Deity's style. There was a certain vulgarity, the Canon thought, about miracles; they brought an unwelcome touch of a magic show to God's true work which was to convert the estate agents, bank managers and hard-headed businessmen of Lawnchester to a more compassionate viewpoint. Jesus was, it seemed as he rambled on, best thought of as the Labour candidate for Lawnchester East, and Cousin Timothy had clearly given up assaulting the devil from the pulpit in favour of an all-out attack on the Poll Tax. All this, I ventured to suggest, was of the greatest interest, but hardly relevant to the charge of adultery.

'Well, you see, I'm a married man, Uncle Horace.'

'Makes it much easier to commit adultery.'

'I remember Mother saying that Auntie Hilda had married a barrister with a sense of humour.' Canon Donkin looked at me doubtfully.

'That has been the cross she has had to bear.'

'My wife, Gertrude, is an absolute saint, of course.' The Canon changed the subject.

'Of course.'

'But she's not the tidiest person in the world. And she quite fails to keep the children quiet.'

'You and Saint Gertrude are blessed with issue?'

'Two boys. Twelve and ten. Martin and Erasmus.' I detected a note of weariness and even a certain fear in the Canon's voice. 'It makes it difficult to get sufficient peace and quiet at home. So if I'm composing a difficult sermon . . .'

'You check in to the nearest monastery?' I suggested. Behind the kitchen hatch Hilda was rattling the tea cups with continued disapproval. 'I might join you sometime.'

'As a matter of fact I usually take a room at the Saint Edithna; it's our local Home-from-Home Hotel. I'm not a great one for monasteries and I like to be able to ring for a pot of tea and perhaps a round or two of hot buttered toast in the middle of the afternoon.'

'Pretty good screw you get, then, as a canon?' I was surprised by this account of high living among the clergy.

'The Saint Edithna doesn't charge very much, out of the tourist season,' Cousin Timmy explained. 'Of course I don't stay the night and I do have a little private money. No doubt it gave them the excuse they wanted.'

'Gave who?' I wasn't following the fellow's drift.

'My six accusers, the pillars of respectability, or, should I say, whited sepulchres of my congregation? They made a formal complaint against me to the Bishop.'

'For dropping into your local Home-from-Home?' I knew the chain of hotels from some unhappy nights on circuit. 'Unwise, perhaps, if you're allergic to frozen vegetables and cold claret but not, I should have thought, a criminal offence?'

'They say I had a woman in my room, Uncle Horace.'

This was more my line of country than a theological discussion, however fascinating, on the miraculous manifestations of the Almighty. This was a bit of human frailty I could get my teeth into. I settled in my chair, lit a small cigar and began my cross-examination. '*Who* says?'

'They've got witnesses. A maid says she saw me open the door to a woman.'

'And what do you say about that evidence?'

'I treat it with the contempt it deserves.' This was hardly the sort of answer which rings the bell and wins the prize in Court. I was about to tell the Canon to pull himself together and answer the question when he said something which gave promise of a miraculous change in the hum and the drum of my daily practice. 'Uncle Horace. Do you appear in Ecclesiastical Courts? They're going to charge me with conduct unbecoming a clerk in Holy Orders.'

'There is no Court in heaven or earth,' I told Timmy Donkin firmly, 'where Rumpole isn't ready and willing to appear. On the Day of Judgement, I can assure you, I shall be prepared to get up on my hind legs and put a few impertinent questions to the Prosecution. Why did you pick on me for this ecclesiastical *cause célèbre*? You've got the right man, of course,' I added hastily, before he had a chance to change his mind.

'I just didn't know any other barristers.'

'Oh, I see. Well, thank you very much.' It wasn't the most tactful answer in the world, and further discussion of the Ecclesiastical Trial was prevented by the return of Hilda with the tea. I saw, on the tray in her hands, a complete absence of biscuits. Chocolate-covered digestives, it seemed, were not to be set out for clerics, however closely related, who were charged with conduct both unbecoming and adulterous.

That night, as we lay together in the matrimonial bed, separated by a couple of feet of mattress and the *Daily Telegraph* crossword puzzle, Hilda spoke up with deep feeling. 'It's absolutely disgusting!'

'A rude word' — I was surprised, I must confess — 'in the *Daily Telegraph* crossword?'

'Even the clergy at it!'

'It's *mainly* the clergy at it. From what you read in the *News of the World*.'

'From what *you* read in the *News of the World*, Rumpole. Only you take it.'

'A fellow has to keep up with the law reports, Hilda. As a matter of fact, I quite took to the Reverend Timothy.'

'Oh, I expect you did!' Hilda gave me the retort contemptuous. 'No doubt you're birds of a feather. I've always had my suspicions about that young pupil you go about with.'

She was referring, of course, to Mizz Liz Pro-

126

bert, the intense young barristerette, fruit of the loins of Red Ron Probert, the scourge of the South-East London Council. Mizz Liz is dedicated to a number of causes such as the welfare of one-parent gay and lesbian families in inner-city areas, but she clearly doesn't regard Rumpole as an object of romantic or even charitable interest. It seemed, however, that the alleged infidelities of Canon Donkin had made Hilda feel that all men are betrayers, and even fear that I might play an unaccustomed and unlooked-for role as the Casanova of Equity Court.

'Hilda. You can't be serious!' I made light of her suggestion, but Hilda's new-found jealousy had its part to play, as you will discover, in the miraculous events which surrounded the trial in Lawnchester Cathedral.

'I suppose she'll be helping you in Timothy's case?' Now She was cross-examining me.

'Well, if she's got nothing better to do.'

'Spending afternoons in hotel bedrooms, just for a bit of peace and quiet!' Hilda gave the Canon's defence a full blast of contempt. 'I never heard anything so ridiculous! And I suppose you're going to defend him. You'd never go near a cathedral unless someone had committed adultery; sometimes I think you'd go anywhere for a criminal.'

'The founder of Christianity was tried as a criminal, wasn't He?' I said piously enough to irritate Hilda. 'Sentenced too, from what I can remember.' A silence then fell between us until She

said, 'Anyway, there was always something peculiar about that family.'

'Jesus's family?' I was puzzled.

'Do try not to be blasphemous. The Donkin
family. Bad blood. No doubt came from Arthur
Donkin. Timmy's sister, Wendy, who no one ever
mentions, went to gaol.'

'How do you know that, Hilda?'

'What?'

'I mean, how do you know that if no one ever
mentions her?' It was a question Hilda didn't
care to answer; instead she sighed heavily and
turned out the light.

'Oh. Are we going to sleep now?' I asked politely in the darkness.

'If you can, Rumpole. With *your* conscience.'
She Who Must Be Obeyed still had Mizz Probert
firmly in her sights. I must say my conscience
was perfectly clear. What kept me awake for the
next ten minutes was the thought of Soapy Sam
Ballard, the newly appointed Chancellor of Lawnchester, acting as the Grand Inquisitor and trying
poor cousin Timmy for his frock.

. . . high Heaven rejects the lore
Of nicely calculated less or more;
So deem'd the man who fashioned for the
  sense
These lofty pillars, spread that branching
  roof
Self-poised, and scooped into ten thousand
  cells,

128

Where light and shade repose, where
    music dwells
Lingering — and wandering on as loth
    to die;
Like thoughts whose very sweetness
    yieldeth proof
That they were born for immortality.

So wrote Wordsworth, sublime poet and old sheep of the Lake District, who, although born without a single joke in him, comforts my solitary hours. He was describing quite another building but his lines will do very well for Lawnchester Cathedral. I arrived in the early afternoon of the day before Canon Timmy was due to stand before the Judgement Seat of Samuel Ballard, and found the Cathedral, grey and gold in the sunlight, quiet and dignified in a lake of green grass in the middle of the close. It looked splendidly aloof, after centuries of war, thanksgiving and martyrdom, to the small matter of one of its clergy being guilty or not of conduct unbecoming his cloth.

I went in through the west entrance and wandered for a little under the stone branches of the ceiling, said hello to a few long-gone bishops and canons, sleeping in carved robes and mitres with their skeletons on the floor below them, and then I fell in with a small group, mainly of Americans, who were being shepherded round by a cathedral guide, an elderly man who, I thought, preserved his West Country accent carefully for the benefit of the tourists. As I joined them I heard him telling them that the original church had been built by some ecclesiastical developer called Bishop Sartorious in the year eight hundred and fifty-two, and was dedicated to Saint Edithna. 'Of course,' our guide fixed me with a beady and somewhat disapproving eye, 'you'll know our Saint Edithna, won't you, sir?'

'Not personally,' I assured him.

'She were a real Christian lady in the old Roman town of Lignum Castor, now known as Lawnchester. She were accused of . . . well, you know, naughty carryings-on. It were all lies. What they didn't like was her trying to convert them to Christianity. It were a trumped up charge but they brought in a guilty verdict against her, do you see?' The tourists nodded wisely, as though fully familiar with legal life in Roman Britain, and the guide continued with his rustic impersonation. 'So they stoned our Edithna to death on the site of what is now our Saint Edithna Hotel, part of the well-known Home-from-Home Hotels Limited chain in West Street. Some say that visitors to the hotel have seen the ghost of our saint, others say that she is only visible if you had a good dinner.' It wasn't a wonderful joke, but probably better than any Wordsworth could think of, and the tourists gave him a titter. 'Lady in a white gown, they sees. A wringing of her hands. Her martyrdom is shown in the stone carving in Bishop Sartorious's Chantry. If you would follow me, ladies and gents.'

The party moved off, but I didn't move with

them. Instead I stood transfixed by a vision. In the middle of a sea of empty pews I had seen a familiar figure. He wasn't quite kneeling in prayer but he had adopted that curious crouch with his bottom stuck to the pew and one hand shielding his eyes which is typical of members of the established church at their devotions. I approached quietly and intoned:

'When holy and devout religious men
Are at their beads, 'tis much to draw
    them thence,
So sweet is zealous contemplation.'

'Rumpole?' Claude Erskine-Brown, opera buff and hopeless cross-examiner, old Wykehamist and husband of Phillida Trant that was, the Portia of our Chambers, now Phillida Erskine-Brown, Q.C., asked nervously and without removing the hand from the eyes.

'Everyone in our Chambers seems to be at prayer nowadays.'

'What on earth,' Erskine-Brown now peered up at me, 'are you doing here?'

'Oh, I drop in to West Country cathedrals from time to time, just to charge up the spiritual batteries.' Well, I mean, ask a silly question . . . 'As a matter of fact, I'm pursuing my career, in the Ecclesiastical Courts.'

'You can't do that,' Claude hissed at me in an appalled manner.

'Why ever not?' At this the fellow got up from

131

the floor and rose to his full height, which, as he is tall and willowy, is a good deal higher than mine. 'You have to be a practising member of the Church of England,' he said.

'I'm a member of the Church of England,' I told him, 'practising down the Old Bailey. How did you get in on the act?'

'Ballard was asked to suggest someone to prosecute a cleric on behalf of the Bishop,' Claude explained. 'He happened to know I was a practising member . . .'

'So here you are' — organ music was starting up somewhere in the background — 'practising as hard as possible.'

'It's a case that's excited a great deal of attention in Lawnchester.' Claude sounded as though he had just been briefed in the trial of Joan of Arc.

'I know,' I told him, 'they're after my client's frock.'

'He hasn't got a hope in hell,' Claude told me.

'Hell, in this case, being a trial conducted by you before the Blessed Bollard?'

We were walking together away from the Cathedral through one of those ghastly and soulless areas known as a pedestrian shopping precinct. There were new shops and supermarkets built in livid red brick, somewhere to the east towered a huge concrete multi-storey car park, and a heavy smell of Kentucky fried chicken hung on the summer afternoon. It's a sad thought that, whereas our ancestors will be remembered for the cathedrals they built, we have nothing to offer history but our shopping precincts.

'By the way, Claude,' I wondered, 'don't you feel a little embarrassed at casting the first stone at the Reverend Timmy?'

'I don't understand what you mean.'

'Do you not? Invited any young ladies to the Opera lately, have you?' I was referring to a former occasion on which Claude had the temerity to invite Mizz Liz Probert to a passionate night of Wagner when Mrs Phillida Erskine-Brown was doing a murder in Cardiff.*

'Don't imagine I'm going to enjoy these proceedings,' he assured me in his defence. 'Anyway, Ballard's got to decide the case.'

' "And he took water and washed his hands before the multitude saying, 'I am innocent of the blood of this just person: see ye to it.' " ' I reminded him of a previous Ecclesiastical Trial.

'I do hope you're not going to quote the Bible at me!'

'There is nothing I won't stoop to, Claude. In the ruthless defence of my client.'

We walked on together in thoughtful silence to the Saint Edithna Hotel. I suppose these premises had once housed an old-fashioned provincial inn, a place for Brown Windsor soup, coal fires and fading copies of *Country Life* in the sepulchral Residents Lounge. Home-from-Home Hotels

---

* See 'Rumpole and the Official Secret' in *Rumpole's Last Case*, Penguin Books, 1987.

Limited had done it up and given it all the joys of tinned muzak in the lifts, the Bishop Sartorious Coffee Shop, the Pride of the West Country Carvery and waitresses with black waistcoats, bow-ties and plastic name plates. Some of the original building, the façade and an imposing central staircase, remained. In front of the hotel a luridly painted sign showing the blessed Saint Edithna, a generously built lady in a white nightgown, acting as an easy target for a couple of Roman stone-throwers, reminded visitors that they were sleeping on a scene of ancient injustice.

When we arrived at the open-plan lounge and reception area Claude Erskine-Brown went off to join half a dozen worthy citizens, apparently his clients, seated round a tea table, whilst I did business with the girl at the desk, whose name, as appeared from her label, was Tracy. I had left my luggage with the porter whilst I visited the Cathedral and was now checking in, a process considerably delayed by the invention of the computer. Tracy, frowning but pretty, played repeated tunes on the keyboard of this instrument and then stared at it in complete bewilderment. While I was waiting for her machine to stop bleeping, a tall, studious-looking fellow inquired for me at the desk. He turned out to be Frank Marlin of Marlin, Marlin & Spikings, my instructing solicitors. I lost no time in asking him about the group treating Erskine-Brown to toasted tea cake on the other side of the lounge.

'Those are our six accusers. Of course, you

know Ecclesiastical Law, Mr Rumpole.'

'Of course. My regular bedtime reading. Just remind me, will you?'

'A case of conduct unbecoming against a priest has to be brought by six of his parishioners. They have to put up the money for the trial, in the first instance.'

'Then they must be dead keen on unfrocking the Canon.'

'Oh, I think they are.'

Marlin then gave me a brief run-down on our accusers. There was a red-faced cove with snowy white hair and a walking-stick said to be Admiral Seal (Retired), a Mr Fox-Beasley, Manager of a local bank, and Mrs Elphick, Chairman of the Lawnchester Bench, who looked as though she were strongly in favour of the restoration of the death penalty for cases of non-renewed dog licences. There was also a Mr Grobley, chemist and lay preacher. Finally, Marlin pointed out a tall, well-fed and handsome couple, a man and a woman in tweed suits with a certain amount of gold jewellery, tanned as though from a recent encounter with a sun-ray lamp or a fortnight in their Marbella holiday home. These, it seemed, were Mr Peter Lambert, the most successful of the Lawnchester estate agents, and his lady wife, Cynthia Lambert. By the time I had learned the names and identities of the unfriendly six, the reluctant machine, urged by Tracy's flying fingers, had coughed up a room for me. I had my bags sent up to it and we set out to visit our client.

Our way led back past the Cathedral and almost on the edge of the green grass which surrounded it there was a line of small houses and a sign which read: THIS SITE SOLD BY LAMBERT & PALFREY TO CARNATION STORES. NEW PREMISES TO OPEN HERE SHORTLY. Our accuser, Lambert, it seemed, had conned the planners into allowing him to buy a plot of land within a stone's throw of the House of God and sell it for the erection of a giant Carnation supermarket. All this had happened in spite of a pained correspondence in the *Lawnchester Herald* and a Bach evening in the Cathedral to raise funds for the Stop Carnation Society.

Canon Donkin's house turned out to be a pleasant-looking Georgian rectory just outside the Cathedral precincts. The door was opened to us by a discontented woman in her forties, whom my instructing solicitor introduced as Tim Donkin's wife, Gertrude. As she led us into the hall I could see why the Canon had had to flee, for peace and quiet, to the Saint Edithna Hotel. Up and down the stairs the two Donkin sons were practising guerrilla warfare, armed with plastic automatic rifles, uttering the realistic sounds of rapid fire and shouting orders. The dusty hall seemed to be a tip for old bicycles, supermarket baskets, broken umbrellas and cardboard boxes.

'I don't know why Tim thinks you'll save his

136

bacon,' the daunting Gertrude said. 'Just because you're his Uncle Horace.'

'Charming house,' I murmured.

'I suppose they'll chuck us out of it as soon as the case is over.' Gertrude didn't seem to give much for her husband's chances. 'I must say I can't wait. It's murder to keep clean.'

She pulled open a door to reveal Timmy trying to write letters in a living-room where every chair supported piles of mending, toy weapons and disintegrating exercise books. He looked desperate.

'It's your Uncle Horace.' Gertrude led us into the room. 'The one you're pinning your faith on.'

'My dear, perhaps our visitors would like some tea . . . ?' The Canon did his best to sound hospitable, but his wife interrupted him.

'Well, you know where the kettle is, don't you?'

Marlin and I denied any desire for tea and we stood a moment, listening to the sounds of distant gunfire.

'My dear,' Timmy made so bold as to say, 'if you could keep the children a little quiet. It seems we have things to discuss.'

'Well, you wouldn't have things to discuss, would you? Not if you'd thought for a minute about me and the children.' On which friendly note Mrs Donkin left us, slamming the door behind her.

'I'm afraid Gertrude's tired.' Our client was apologetic.

'I understand,' I told him. 'And I understand

137

why you take a hotel room to write your sermons.'

'Oh, yes. Please, Uncle Horace. Do take a seat. Frank . . .'

'May I remove the firearms?' When we were settled I asked Cousin Timmy for some further particulars of the family history.

'Odd things, families,' I started. 'We forget how many relatives we've got, knocking round the place. Let me see now, your mother Esmé Donkin was my wife's cousin. And you had just one sister?'

'Oh. Yes . . .' He sounded only vaguely interested.

'What was her name again?'

'Wendy.'

'Younger sister?'

'I suppose she'd be about forty now. We don't keep up, you know.'

'Isn't that the way with families? Not in any trouble, is she?' I remembered a bedtime conversation with She Who Must Be Obeyed.

'Trouble? Why did you ask that?' Cousin Timmy was frowning.

'No particular reason. We can't have you both in a mess, can we? Well, to business . . . I think Mr Rumpole would like to discuss the evidence. What the maid actually saw.' Frank Marlin had his brief-case open, but I wanted to establish some first principles. 'For the moment,' I said, 'I'd rather discuss theology.'

'What?' The Canon seemed shocked at the suggestion.

'You know something about faith; blind, trusting belief. Are you capable of that?'

'I like to think so.'

'Putting yourself in someone else's hands entirely. Taking the great gamble.'

'Trusting God. Yes, I can manage that.'

'How about trusting me?' I suggested. 'No criticism of the Almighty, of course, but I wonder if He's had quite as much courtroom experience?'

'I trust you, of course.' But the Canon sounded as though I had not yet engaged his interest, let alone his faith. I stood up and stretched my legs round the untidy room. 'Then tell me, who was in the bedroom with you. Someone? No one?'

My client looked up with watery blue eyes. 'I think that's a matter I'd rather leave between the two of us.'

'You and the lady concerned?'

'I really meant between me and God.' He was smiling. 'My conscience is perfectly clear. He will be my judge, Uncle Horace.'

'Maybe eventually. But tomorrow your judge is going to be Soapy Sam Ballard who just can't wait to unfrock someone. So hadn't you better tell me?'

'I don't feel called upon to answer any questions on the subject.'

'Never?'

'Never!'

I was surprised by the Canon's determination.

'Not in the witness-box when you're on your oath?'

'I shall tell them I don't consider it any of their business.'

I lit a small cigar then, and looked at him through the smoke. 'You're making my job impossible.'

'I'm sure you'll do your best for me.' He paid me a compliment but put no trust in me.

'All I can do is cross-examine the witnesses against you.' I took a bundle of witness statements from Marlin's open brief-case and gave our client a taste of the unpleasant news to come. 'Evidence of Rita O'Keefe, chambermaid. After you left the hotel she found three filter-tip cigarette ends lightly stained with lipstick in the ashtray on the dressing-table. Wear much make-up, do you, Timothy?' I chucked the script back to Marlin. 'Or is that another question you don't feel called upon to answer? Look, unless you give some sort of a reasonable explanation you're going to be out of a job and living with a wife who doesn't seem likely to forgive you. You'll be an unfrocked priest, a figure of fun for the rest of your life.'

'Perhaps that's what I've always been, to certain people.' With his schoolboy smile and the quiff of hair that wouldn't lie down Timmy seemed quite unperturbed by the idea.

'It's all very well for your God, Timothy,' I told him. 'According to you He doesn't feel called on to perform miracles. But I've got to pull off something a great deal trickier than the feeding of the five thousand, starting tomorrow morning!' That was about as far as I got with the Canon,

140

a client who seemed to think that defending himself was in some way beneath his dignity. As we left, Gertrude Donkin came out from a dark and no doubt chaotic kitchen and asked with considerable satisfaction, 'Hopeless, isn't it?'

'Is that what you'd like, Mrs Donkin?' I hadn't taken to Gertrude.

'The sooner we get out of here the better. Those stuffed shirts have always hated us; they never even asked us to their beastly dinner parties.'

Later I discovered that the disapproval of the Lawnchester upper-crust to my client didn't stop at dinner parties. A sizeable contingent had got up and left during his cathedral sermon on Miracles. I did take one further step that day in my search for a defence for Cousin Timmy. I telephoned my old friend Inspector Blackie at Criminal Records in Scotland Yard and asked him to undertake a little research on our behalf.

The wind got up that evening and there was heavy rain. The West Country Carvery was almost empty; the darkly clad figures of Rumpole, Erskine-Brown and Ballard, our judge, sat dotted about among the white tablecloths like penguins on an ice floe. I was attended to by a substantial waitress labelled 'Shirley'. I ordered the roast beef Edithna with the dewy-morning-picked mushrooms, the cottage-garden broccoli and the jumbo-sized Wessex spud with golden dairy butter. No doubt it had all been thawed from the freezer at dawn by peasants in smocks. When I

141

had placed an order for this feast, to be washed down by a bottle of the Home-from-Home Ordinaire (red), I sent out a signal to the learned friends.

'How are you, Claude? Is that you, Bollard? What time did you check in?' I was calling all tables.

'Is that you, Rumpole?' Ballard affected surprise.

'Of course not. It's the Archbishop of Canterbury travelling incognito. Perhaps we three should get together for dinner?'

'With the case coming on tomorrow? That would be hardly appropriate.'

Erskine-Brown was a stickler for legal etiquette and Ballard agreed. 'I think it more seemly, Rumpole,' he said, 'if I dine alone.'

'But you'd have the Defence *and* the Prosecution with you. I mean, neither of us could nobble you,' I reasoned.

'I suppose, Judge . . .' Erskine-Brown began but Ballard was quick to correct him. '*Chancellor*, Erskine-Brown. It *is* an ecclesiastical title.'

'Of course,' Claude apologized, '*Chancellor*. I suppose I shouldn't have any rooted objection. If both the Defence and the Prosecution were represented at your table.'

'I should make sure of that, of course. I would make it my duty to see you were both represented.' Bollard spoke with authority.

'Very right and proper, if I may say so, Chancellor.'

'Thank you, Rumpole. Of course, it wouldn't be right for us to discuss the case.'

'Oh, good heavens, no.' I did my best to re-assure him. 'For us to discuss the case would be quite improper! We can talk about anything else, though. Can't we?'

I must admit that my enthusiasm to share the Chancellor's table wasn't entirely due to the delights of Soapy Sam's company and conversation. I wanted, in my subtle way, to impress on him the serious nature of the task he was about to perform and point out the danger of stamping around in an ecclesiastical minefield where angels might well fear to tread. So, as the rain rattled against the windows and the Saint Edithna sign creaked in the wind, I took the opportunity of saying, when our dinner together drew to an end, 'A night like this makes you think of old injustices.'

'We mustn't discuss the case, Rumpole!' Ballard ruled firmly.

'Oh, no, Chancellor. Of course not. Not a word about the case. Could you unfrock the port, Erskine-Brown?'

'What's that?' Claude looked startled.

'I mean, could you pass the port, old darling?'

'Well. This is a bit of a new departure for us, isn't it?' Ballard said after the bottle had been circulated.

'Drinking port?'

'No. Ecclesiastical Law. I shall have to rely a good deal on you two fellows for the legal side.'

'I have spent the last couple of weeks boning up on the subject in Halsbury,' Claude boasted.

'It's not a question of law, is it?' I said.

'Oh, isn't it?' Claude looked disappointed, as though he'd been wasting his time.

'Like everything else in life it's a question of fact.' I ignored the Chancellor's warning 'Rumpole!' and soldiered on. 'Injustice is the same, isn't it, in a law court or a cathedral?'

'Rumpole! We really mustn't discuss . . .'

'Of course not!' I agreed, and in the following silence listened to the weather. 'Strange sound the wind's making tonight. Can you hear it?'

'It's been a dreadful summer, certainly.' Erskine-Brown has no imagination.

'Do you think you can hear,' I asked then, 'the sound of a woman . . . crying out?'

'No,' Erskine-Brown was unhelpful.

'Clearly you chaps have no belief in miracles.'

'Miracles are certainly an essential part of Christian dogma.' The faithful Ballard helped me a little. 'I'm sure we all accept that.'

'So we accept the story of the Blessed Saint Edithna?' I asked, but Erskine-Brown was still in mocking mood. 'I thought she was a hotel.'

'A Christian woman in Roman times, Erskine-Brown,' I began to tell him sadly, 'was falsely accused of adultery because her beliefs irritated the establishment. They stoned her to death. On this very spot. And where she fell dead a small stream of pure cold water came trickling from the ground.'

144

'Must have been the one that came out of my bath tap.'

'Oh, very funny. Mock on, Erskine-Brown.'

'Just a moment, Claude.' Ballard, I was pleased to see, was shocked by the fellow's levity. 'I don't think it does to take these mysteries lightly.'

'I say, I'm frightfully sorry, Chancellor.' Claude saw that there was no sense in upsetting tomorrow's judge.

'There are more things in heaven and earth, aren't there, than are dreamed of in Erskine-Brown's philosophy?' I refilled my glass and looked extra thoughtful. 'An old inn was built on Saint Edithna's well in the Middle Ages. But it's said she keeps walking . . .'

'Like Felix the cat!' Erskine-Brown couldn't resist it, but at least Ballard was impressed and slightly nervous. 'Walking, Rumpole?'

'Whenever some great injustice is done,' I assured him.

'I thought we decided we wouldn't discuss the case.' My prosecutor could see his arguments drifting away into the realms of the supernatural.

'Really, Erskine-Brown,' I rebuked him. 'Are you suggesting that Chancellor Ballard would be responsible for any sort of injustice? In *our case?*'

'Yes, really, Erskine-Brown. I must say, I take considerable exception . . .'

'Oh, terribly sorry, Chancellor. I do apologize!'

'This has got nothing whatever to do with Canon Donkin's case,' I told them clearly. 'This is a matter of history! She walks.'

'And when do they say she walked last, Rumpole?' Ballard's finger seemed anxious to loosen his collar; this was a man who took spooks seriously.

'They say, if my recollection serves me, when a Chancellor in Bloody Mary's time had a couple of extremely decent Church of England canons burnt to a cinder on the Cathedral Green' — I was inventing rapidly — 'Saint Edithna appeared on the staircase of the old inn, wringing her hands and crying out against injustice.'

'She was probably wondering what had happened to her breakfast.'

'Oh thou, Erskine-Brown' — I looked at him sadly — 'of little faith!'

'There is nothing in the teaching of our Church to suggest that miracles are no longer possible,' Ballard reminded us.

'Only too true, Chancellor. And injustice continues, from Roman times to today. We can only hope that the poor lady can rest in peace after this.'

'After this *what*, Rumpole?' Ballard seemed to think I was discussing his future judgment, but I reassured him.

'After this dinner, Chancellor. You can hear the wind, though, can't you? There seems to be a definite hint of sobbing.'

As I have said, the old central staircase had been preserved in the hotel. It was built in a well so that you could look down, let us say,

146

from a bedroom door on the third floor to the doorways on the second. Erskine-Brown was berthed on the first floor, but as Ballard and I climbed on upwards, he asked, with increasing unease, 'Was it this staircase, Rumpole? Was this where the Blessed Saint walked?'

'This very spot. Probably undergone a few repairs since those days; the muzak is new, and the abstract prints.'

'Poor woman. Poor, unfortunate woman.'

'She probably hit on a bad judge,' I told him as we parted.

Later I emerged from my room to hang a breakfast order on my door. Looking down the staircase well I could see Ballard doing the same. I moved back into the shadows and uttered a low but penetrating moan. It was the nearest I could get to the sound of a woman in distress.

From my vantage point I could see the pale face of Chancellor Ballard peering upward. It was, it seemed, the attitude of a man in terror.

The trial of Canon Timothy Donkin took place in the Chapter House of the Cathedral. For a man used to such down-market venues as Snaresbrook and the Uxbridge Magistrates, it seemed that justice, in such an environment, must be on a higher, purer level. Under the carved flowers and branches on the stone ceiling, in front of a stained-glass window depicting the expulsion from the garden of Eden surmounted by the arms of the Earls of Lawnchester, Ballard sat, robed and

147

wigged, and on a tall chair carved for a medieval bishop. Only by remembering the strict limitations of Soapy Sam's intellectual powers could I prevent a weak feeling that the Chancellor of the Diocese must be the fountain of all wisdom. Ranged around him was the Jury of four assessors, two clerics, one dark-suited elderly man, who might have been the senior partner in a firm of undertakers, and a brisk headmistress-like person, who, I thought, was regarding Cousin Timmy with particular distaste. A solicitor dressed as a barrister sat below Ballard as Clerk of the Court and another ecclesiastical hanger-on was cast as the Usher. My learned friend, Claude Erskine-Brown, was there with his cohort of official complainers, and I sat on a somewhat unyielding chair as the sole protector of the Canon. The stage was set for a trial of heresy, or at least of a little illicit love in the local Home-from-Home Hotel.

Claude opened his case at some length. It is hard for me, with advancing years, to keep fully awake during the speeches of the learned friends, and I must have dozed off, temporarily overpowered by the warmth and the smell of sunlight on stone and dusty hassocks. When I awoke the Prosecution was dealing with Timmy's reason for booking a hotel bedroom for the afternoon.

'Canon Donkin has said that he used this bedroom in the Saint Edithna Hotel to write his sermons.' Claude spoke with contempt. 'This improbable excuse becomes incredible when the Court hears that he frequently worked in the Cathedral library.'

'Did you?' I turned in my seat to whisper to my client.

'For my history of Lawnchester Cathedral,' Timmy whispered back. 'All the deeds and documents are there.'

'Then why not write your sermons in the library?' It seemed an obvious question.

'The old librarian's always chattering.'

So Cousin Tim was writing a history of Lawnchester Cathedral; the information seemed of no immediate interest so I tucked it away for possible future reference. And then Ballard, whose mind has always worked somewhat slowly, interrupted Claude's flow to say, 'Mr Erskine-Brown, what I really cannot understand is why a priest of the Church of England needs a hotel bedroom to write his sermons?'

It is never too early for a Defence Counsel to make his presence felt in a trial, so I rose slowly, but I hope impressively, to my feet. 'May I, with very great respect, your Worship, remind you of a point of legal procedure. It is customary to pass judgment at the end of a case and not at the beginning, and, sitting as your Worship does in this Cathedral, you must be particularly anxious that a great historical injustice may not be repeated!'

Ballard looked puzzled at this, but Claude kindly provided him with a clue. 'I imagine,' he said, 'my learned friend is referring to Saint Edithna.'

'Wrongly convicted of adultery,' I added.

'So far as I have read the history' — Erskine-Brown tried the approach sarcastic — 'I don't think that the Blessed Saint Edithna checked into a hotel bedroom for the purpose of writing her sermons.'

'My learned friend should not be quick to make such assumption,' I batted back.

'Mr Rumpole. Mr Erskine-Brown. Gentlemen! Shall we get on and hear the evidence?' Ballard now realized he would have done better to keep his mouth shut.

'The very course I was hoping your Worship might take!' I said, genuflecting a little. 'I'm so very much obliged.'

Claude's first witness was a Mr Thomas Campion, Manager of the Saint Edithna Hotel, a pin-striped young man with a small moustache and hair neatly combed over his ears. He produced a registration slip which showed that Canon Donkin occupied room thirty-nine on the 17th of March of that year, a double room with twin beds and a bathroom attached.

'Mr Campion, Canon Donkin had taken this room on many previous occasions?' I rose to start my cross-examination.

'He had taken similar rooms,' the witness admitted.

'You say number thirty-nine is a *double* room?'

'With twin beds, Mr Rumpole, which could be pulled *together*, no doubt, if occasion demanded it.' Ballard was clearly becoming overexcited by the evidence.

'Perhaps they could by any couple prepared to risk falling down the gap in the middle.' I was rewarded for this by a small ripple of laughter from the spectators, a call for silence from the Usher and a disapproving look from the Chancellor. I passed rapidly on to my next question. 'There is no reason, is there, why that room, number thirty-nine, shouldn't be used for occupation by a single person?'

'No reason. No.'

'And it frequently is?'

'Yes.'

'Do you, in fact, have any single rooms in your hotel?'

'No. Since our recent conversion all the rooms are either twin-bedded or have a king-sized double bed.'

'And the Canon made no particular request for a king-sized double bed?'

'Not as far as I remember,' the Manager had to admit. 'No.'

'So it doesn't look, does it, as though he came to your hotel for any sort of hanky-panky?'

'Mr Rumpole!' Chancellor Ballard was apparently outraged. 'We are within church precincts.'

'I was forgetting,' I said as innocently as possible, 'I thought we were in Court.'

'So perhaps the expression hanky . . . The

151

expression you used was not entirely appropriate!' Ballard was not appeased.

'Oh, really? What expression would you like me to use, within the Cathedral precincts?'

'The charge is conduct unbecoming.' Erskine-Brown rose, no doubt intending to ingratiate himself with the tribunal. I turned to the witness and asked quickly, to avoid further interruption from the Chancellor, 'The fact that he didn't order a bed would indicate to you that he hadn't come for any sort of conduct unbecoming a clerk in Holy Orders?'

'I didn't know why he had come.' The Manager was defensive.

'Did you not? He came to your hotel quite regularly, didn't he? Once or twice a month?'

'Yes.'

'And each time he told you he came to work on a sermon.'

'He said that. Yes.'

'Did you believe him?'

'Your Worship, I object.' Erskine-Brown rose with rare courage. 'What this witness believed is totally irrelevant!'

'Oh, do sit down, Erskine-Brown.' I got in my question while he was lost for words. 'You let him the room at a cheap rate, didn't you?'

'Yes,' the witness answered, and Erskine-Brown, having apparently lost his bottle, subsided.

'Because he was only there for the afternoon and because he was a canon of Lawnchester?'

152

'We like to do what we can to help the Cathedral authorities.' The Manager looked as pious as he could manage.

'Well, you wouldn't be helping them very much, would you, by assisting one of their clergy to commit hanky . . . to commit conduct unbecoming?'

'I suppose not.'

'I mean, are we to believe that you and Home-from-Home Hotels Limited are engaged in running some sort of church knocking-shop?'

'In *what*, Mr Rumpole?' I had lit the blue touch-paper and Ballard was about to explode again.

'I beg your Worship's pardon. I mean some sort of ecclesiastical house of ill-repute.'

'My Lord, I object. That's a perfectly monstrous suggestion!' Erskine-Brown had recovered his bottle.

'No more monstrous than the slur of gross immorality that is cast on the good name of Canon Donkin,' I answered the charge against me.

'Mr Rumpole. I rule against the admissibility of that question.' Ballard was now treating my cross-examination as though it were a rude limerick uttered during matins.

'Very well,' I told him, 'if this trial is to be conducted with all the ruthlessness of tea on the vicarage lawn, I have absolutely no more to say.'

'Mr Rumpole. Mr Erskine-Brown.' Chancellor Ballard sighed heavily. 'Perhaps this would be a convenient moment to rise for luncheon?'

It was a convenient moment indeed and I was soon back in the Carvery of the Saint Edithna Hotel toying with the Abbot's cold English platter and freshly gathered side-salad in the presence of a client who seemed unable to fancy his food. 'That judge of yours,' he said with some justice, 'doesn't seem to be able to tell the Church from Christianity.'

'I was going to ask you,' I said, more to take his mind off the present painful proceedings than for any other good reason, 'about your history of Lawnchester Cathedral.'

'Oh, yes!' Cousin Timmy suddenly returned to life and his pale eyes sparkled with excitement. 'I think I'm on the track of something interesting.'

'Orgies in the organ loft?'

'Far more interesting than that. There seems to have been a gift of land to the Cathedral from the Crown in 1672.'

'Sensational stuff! That ought to get you to the top of the best-seller list.'

'I don't want to bore you . . .'

'No, please, Timothy. Tell me about it.'

He began to tell me. I listened, at first out of politeness and then with increasing interest as he unfolded a tale which might, just possibly and if handled correctly, strengthen the Canon's precarious hold on his frock.

The afternoon witness was the chambermaid, Rita O'Keefe. She stood in the witness-box, a woman with untidy hair and bitten fingernails, who must once have been beautiful but who now looked overworked and anxious. Claude Erskine-Brown established that she had worked at the hotel for the past four years and that she was unmarried and lived on the premises. He then brought her gently to the afternoon of March the 17th and asked her to tell the Court exactly what she saw.

'I was standing at the end of the corridor,' Miss O'Keefe told us.

'That is, the third-floor corridor?'

'Yes. Well, I was standing there and the door from the emergency staircase opened and I saw a woman.'

'Can you describe her?' Claude asked.

'Not too well. The light was behind her. She was thin. I think she was dressed in a sort of grey suit. Reddish hair, from what I remember.'

'Was she an elderly lady?'

'No, I'd say, sir, about my age.'

'Then certainly not elderly.' Soapy Sam was indulging the well-known judicial habit of buttering up a prosecution witness.

'What happened then?' Claude got us back to business.

'She walked quickly, like, to the door of number thirty-nine.'

'We know that was Canon Donkin's room,' the Chancellor reminded us, unnecessarily I thought.

'She knocked at the door and I saw him open it to her.'

'By him, you mean Canon Donkin?' Claude was dotting all the 'i's.

'Yes, sir.'

'And then?'

'He let her into the room and shut the door on the both of them, sir.' At this the accusers indulged in a few sad sighs and the assessors looked more beadily than ever at the accused.

'And after that?' Claude spoke very solemnly, as though a service were in progress.

'I stayed watching for some time, but they didn't come out.'

'How long did you stand in the corridor?'

'About three quarters of an hour.' I found that answer somewhat astonishing and made a note of it.

'And then what did you do?'

'I went downstairs to the reception area. At about six o'clock I saw that gentleman.' She turned her still beautiful eyes sadly on the Canon. 'I saw him leave the hotel. Then I went up to number thirty-nine.'

'Did you notice anything about the room?'

'The beds were made up, like. But there were cigarettes with lipstick on them, in the ashtray beside the bed.'

As you can see, there seemed little enough to be said on Canon Timmy's behalf by the time Miss O'Keefe had finished her account. I began with a smile, calculated to lure the witness into a sense of false security, and asked very gently, 'Miss O'Keefe. What did you do with the lip-

156

stick-stained cigarette ends. Did you keep them?'

'I chucked them away.' The chambermaid gave a slight toss of her head, remembered from her more flirtatious years. 'In the rubbish bin.'

'And I suggest you might have done the same with the rest of your worthless evidence.' I was still being charming but Ballard gave me a warning 'Mr Rumpole!'

'Oh, very well, let's try to take it seriously. You say that after the Canon had left the beds were still made?'

'They could have been made *after* use, Mr Rumpole.' Ballard had clearly cast himself as leading Counsel for the Prosecution.

'If they were singularly domesticated lovers, yes,' I agreed with the Chancellor and then gave my full attention to the witness. 'Miss O'Keefe. You told us you stood watching in the corridor for about three quarters of an hour after you saw a woman was admitted.'

'Yes, sir.'

'You stood there, neglecting your other duties?'

'I didn't have any other duties.'

'It was three o'clock in the afternoon, Mr Rumpole,' Erskine-Brown reminded us all unnecessarily. I told him I was perfectly capable of cross-examining a witness without his assistance and then gave my full attention to Rita. 'Am I to understand that you had no duties on the third floor that afternoon?'

'That's right. It was my afternoon off.'

'Your afternoon off?' I looked round the Court

as though astonished. 'So what on earth were you doing spying on Canon Donkin?'

'Mr Rumpole. She has told us she happened to be watching . . .' Ballard began another protest, but I cut him short now with '*Spying,* my Lord. There is no other word for it, even though we are in a cathedral.'

'The gentleman had asked me to keep an eye on the Reverend. When he came to the hotel, like,' Rita told us.

'So you did that, on your afternoon off?'

'Well, yes. To oblige the gentleman.'

'How much did the gentleman pay you? Thirty pieces of silver?'

'I do object!' Claude objected.

'Yes, Mr Rumpole!' Ballard sounded, as ever, pained. 'I think we should try to keep the Bible out of it.'

'Am I to understand,' I asked as innocently as I could manage, 'that the Gospels do not apply in the Ecclesiastical Court?'

'No, no. Of course not. Certainly not!' Ballard escaped my question by turning to the witness. 'Miss O'Keefe. I want to understand your evidence. Did some gentleman pay you to keep some sort of watch on the Reverend Timothy Donkin?'

'Ten pounds he gave me. For the afternoon.'

'And who was this generous gentleman?' I asked. 'This open-minded spy-master?'

'I assume it was the Manager.' Claude rose to make the uncalled-for assumption.

'Sit down, Mr Erskine-Brown! It wasn't Mr Campion, the hotel manager, was it?'

'No.'

There was a long silence and Miss Rita O'Keefe looked round the Court, seeming to be asking permission to answer the question. 'Who was it, Miss O'Keefe?' I repeated.

'It was . . . that gentleman.' She was pointing past Claude at one of our six accusers, straight at the suntanned face of the leading estate agent and property developer of Lawnchester and the man responsible for selling to Carnation super-markets a prime site within a prayer's whisper of the Cathedral.

'You're pointing to Mr Peter Lambert?'

'Yes, sir.'

The evidence of Miss Rita O'Keefe threw the Prosecution ranks into some considerable confusion. Claude Erskine-Brown asked for a brief adjournment in order that he could consider 'an unexpected development'. Chancellor Ballard immediately retired, I suppose to some hallowed spot in which he might pray for guidance. I took a turn around the Cathedral close, smoked a small cigar, and wondered if my old friend Inspector Blackie at Criminal Records had managed to turn up the information I wanted. It had not been an unsuccessful afternoon in Court and I had the encouraging feeling that the Almighty, unlike his representative Ballard, had accepted a watching brief on behalf of the Defence.

Back in Court I had five minutes with my client to check the details of a subject he had broached at lunchtime, his research into the grant of certain Crown lands to the Cathedral by Charles II. Then Soapy Sam returned to the Seat of Judgment and Claude called Mr Peter Lambert to explain his employment of a hotel chambermaid to spy on a clerk in Holy Orders. 'I certainly paid Miss O'Keefe to keep watch on Canon Donkin,' Peter Lambert smiled, showing a lot of white teeth and the appearance of candour which must have helped him through a thousand dubious property deals. 'I had every reason to suspect that he was indulging in immoral behaviour and I thought he should be exposed. Miss O'Keefe's observation proved me absolutely right.' After this, Claude sat down as though the whole matter had now been settled quite satisfactorily, an illusion which I did my best to dispel when I rose to cross-examine.

'Mr Lambert.' Again I started politely. 'I think you're anxious to develop a site very near to the Cathedral Green as a new Carnation shopping market?'

'My Lord. I really don't know what this can have to do with this case.' Claude tried to give the witness time to think by his interruption, and I had to speak sharply to my learned friend. 'Sit still and listen, and you may find out. What's the answer?'

'Yes,' Lambert agreed, as he had to.

'In order that the view of the Cathedral may

be spoiled and the citizens of Lawnchester may wander round a concrete super-store filling little wire wheelbarrows with things they never wanted in the first place.' I felt the assessors were warming to me for the first time, but Lambert flashed his teeth at them and said, 'We do hope to develop the site, yes.'

'And you knew that my client, Canon Donkin, has been delving into the history of the Cathedral?'

'When he was not otherwise engaged in his amorous affairs, yes.' Lambert couldn't resist the gibe, which I ignored.

'Did you not get wind of the fact, no doubt from the talkative librarian, that he was hoping to be in a position to prove that the very piece of land you want to develop as a supermarket was granted to the Cathedral by King Charles II in the year 1672 and has been Cathedral property ever since?'

There was a silence which lasted a little too long for Mr Lambert's credibility, and then he tried to sound unconcerned. 'I heard he had some wild idea about that. Yes.'

'If you have no title to that site whatsoever, bang goes your idea of making a packet out of a new, unwanted supermarket?'

'It seems that's what he was trying to prove. Yes.'

'So that's why you and your cronies, the Bank Manager and the Admiral and the Chairman of the Bench' — I looked round at our six accusers — 'that motley crew of self-interested guardians of public morality who have invested in the Carnation stores site, all want to get rid of the Reverend Timothy Donkin?' Now the silence produced no answer. 'Is that the truth and the whole truth about this case, Mr Lambert?'

'We honestly believe he's guilty of immorality, sir.' Lambert avoided the question as blatantly as any politician on television, and supplied a smile of sickening sincerity for good measure.

'Oh, really! How very convenient for you!'

'Mr Rumpole.' Ballard looked worried and as though he had completely underestimated the worldliness of the Ecclesiastical Court. 'Even if Mr Lambert and his friends have some financial interest in this case . . .'

'*Even* if, my Lord?' I raised the Rumpole eyebrows.

'I still have to consider Miss O'Keefe's evidence about the woman who came to the Canon's room.' He looked around anxiously as though eager for a sign; when none was forthcoming he decided to knock off. 'Very well, gentlemen. Shall we say ten thirty tomorrow morning?'

When I got back to the Saint Edithna Hotel I shut myself in the telephone booth in the hall and got through to Inspector Blackie at the Yard who gave me some information which I knew might be to the considerable advantage of Canon Donkin if only he had the wit to make use of it. Then I walked into the lounge area and saw a sight which proved, if proof were ever needed, that God moves in a mysterious way his wonders to perform. For there sat She Who Must Be Obeyed, wearing a hat and consuming tea and scones with the air of a woman on a mission.

'Do I come as a bit of a shock to you, Rumpole?' Hilda asked as I sat down to await her explanation. I answered her as cheerfully as I could. 'Of course not. Come to see all the fun of the Ecclesiastical Court, have you?'

'I would hardly call adultery by a priest in Holy Orders fun, Rumpole.'

'No. I suppose you wouldn't. All the same, they may have quite enjoyed it at the time . . .'

'That seems to me a remark in extremely poor taste!'

Shirley, the waitress, flitted heavily by and I ordered a large claret. 'What's yours to be?' I tried to include Hilda in any little conviviality going, but She was clearly not in a party mood. 'I didn't come all this way to drink with you, Rumpole.'

'Then why did you come? Sightseeing? A tour of English cathedral cities? Salisbury next?'

'The sight I have come to see is you, Rumpole.'

'I might be known as an ancient monument in some quarters, but . . .'

'Far too ancient to stay in hotels with girls about you.'

I began to understand the reason for Hilda's visit. Delinquent clerics, hotel bedrooms and Mizz Liz Probert had weighed on her mind to produce

163

a green-eyed monster which had driven her to take British Rail to the West Country. It was, I supposed, a sign of affection not often apparent in her day-to-day treatment of a husband with little time and almost no inclination for philandering. After a hard day in Court and a bottle or two of the ordinary red, my favoured pastime is sleep; I should hate to be kept awake by the pillow talk of such as Mizz Liz Probert.

I reassured her. 'Girls? Not one girl, Hilda. Until you arrived, of course.'

'Well. Where is she?'

'Where's who?'

'You know perfectly well who I mean. Upstairs, I suppose. Helping you with your work. You men are all exactly the same. Birds of a feather, you and Cousin Timmy. Miss Probert. That's who I'm talking about. And don't try to look innocent.'

'Mizz Liz! You came all this way to see *her?*' I asked and Hilda gave me the full explanation: ' "Will she be coming with you?" I asked. "Oh yes," you said, "if she's got nothing better to do." I'm sure she had nothing better to do! I expect she's been looking forward to the away-days. Bought a new outfit, quite likely. And now she's getting ready for a little bit of dinner. Well, all I can say is, you'd better make it a table for three.'

'Two,' I told her firmly.

'You and that Probert person?'

'You and I. We shall be having dinner *à deux*, Hilda. Mizz Liz Probert's doing a spot of indecency at Snaresbrook. She's getting work of her own nowadays.'

There was a silence between us then, while Hilda tried not to look like someone who's come bravely downstairs to catch a burglar and found nothing but the cat knocking over the milk bottles.

'She's not here?'

'I'm so sorry, Hilda. Are you very disappointed?'

'Oh. Well. She's not here, then. I wanted to take another look at Lawnchester, anyway.' Say what you like about She Who Must Be Obeyed, She manages never to feel foolish for long. Hilda looked at her watch and announced, 'It's too late for me to go back home tonight.'

'I'm afraid it is. We'll find a restaurant. The food here is rather like my jokes.'

'Whatever do you mean?'

'Not always, old girl, in the very best of taste.'

The events that followed may be cited as proof that the Almighty has revised his thoughts on miracles and no longer feels them to be beneath his dignity. Mind you the miraculous events which took place that night in the Saint Edithna Hotel would not have had their effect on the trial of Canon Donkin without a little worldly assistance from Rumpole. Miraculous fish may be provided, but some human hand still has to cook them and add the lemon wedge and the sprig of parsley. But enough of this theological discussion, let me briefly describe the events which occurred after

Hilda and I returned to my room, filled with a rapidly evaporating dinner taken in the Swinging Bamboo, Lawnchester.

The miraculous events of that night had begun with a cloud no bigger than a man's hand. The loo wasn't working. The plumbing in the Saint Edithna appeared temperamental and I had to complain of the flushing system in my *en suite* facility. Accordingly we returned to find a note taped to the seat of the lavatory informing us that it was temporarily out of order and would we please use the toilet situated at the end of the corridor. Hilda, who had already put on her nightdress and covered it with a long white dressing-gown, was considerably irked by the situation. 'These things happen, Hilda,' I told her. 'Even in the best regulated hotels.' A plan was already stirring in my mind, whether by divine inspiration or not I leave my reader to decide. Suffice it to say that our broken loo changed the course of history, at least the history of Canon Donkin.

When Hilda was safely installed along the corridor I emerged from our room. The lights were already dimmed sufficiently for my purpose. It was the work of a few moments to run, as lightly and as swiftly as I could manage, which was not all that lightly and swiftly to be honest, to Ballard's bedroom. As soon as I heard the sound of rushing water from above I knocked on the Chancellor's door and then stood back against the wall so I should be hidden from his view when he opened it.

Fate, if that is what you wish to call it, was on our side that night. Ballard in pyjamas opened the door and peered out into the gloaming. What he saw, on the landing above, must have filled him with terror and foreboding. A tallish woman, clothed all in white, was passing in a terrible and unearthly silence, her hands clasped together. Struck, I have no doubt, by the awful significance of this miracle, Soapy Sam uttered a strangled cry and bolted back into his room, there to contemplate the dreadful results of human error in the Courts of Law.

Hilda rose early the next day and, declaring that She could stay no longer in a hotel with such primitive sanitary arrangements, took a taxi back to the station. Her mission, although She didn't know it, had been a triumphant success. Before the Court sat, I walked my client round the Cathedral Close and gave him the information I had got from Criminal Records, facts which I knew would come as no surprise to him.

'Miss Wendy Donkin,' I reminded him. 'Convicted two years ago for fraud and false pretences. Released on licence. Wanted for twenty other offences concerning cheques and stolen credit cards. So far she's avoided re-arrest. If they catch her, your sister'll be sent back to do the rest of her sentence, as well as any further bird she gets.'

'Poor Wendy.' The Canon shook his head sadly.

'Exactly.' I told my client what he already

knew, what had happened on the afternoon of March the 17th. 'She telephoned you and you arranged to meet her in the hotel bedroom where you are eccentric enough to compose your sermons. Neither of you bargained for Mr Lambert or his spy. No doubt you gave your sister money.'

'I gave her a promise.'

'What?'

'Not to tell anyone that I'd seen her.'

'Well, it's a promise you'll have to break. I'm going to put you in the witness-box and you can tell Soapy Sam all about it.'

'No.'

'What?' We had reached the door of the Chapter House. The Canon faced me with a look of gentle obstinacy. 'No, Uncle Horace, I gave my word. I'm not bringing Wendy into it.'

'Look. Tim. Reverend Tim. Are you totally insane?'

'I don't think so, but I'm quite determined.'

'For God's sake, resist the temptation to be a martyr.'

'It's not that. I'm not going to go back on my word because of Peter Lambert.' He gave me, then, a look of infuriating sympathy. 'I'm sorry to disappoint you, Uncle Horace.'

'I must say, it adds a new terror to my job,' I told him, with ill-concealed irritation, 'having some sort of saint for a client.'

Further argument between us was avoided by the temporary, part-time Ecclesiastical Usher emerging from the shadows to tell us that Mr

Chancellor Ballard would like to see both Counsel in private before the Court sat that morning.

The Chancellor, when Claude and I joined him in some sanctum behind the Chapter House, looked pale and weary as a man who had spent a rough night on the road to Damascus. However, he spoke like a man who had wrestled with his soul and reached some inner certainty.

'Come along in, Claude. Sit you down, Rumpole. Make yourselves comfortable, both you chaps.' His welcome was almost embarrassing. 'I must tell you both, I have given this case most anxious consideration.'

'I shouldn't have thought there was much doubt about it' — Claude Erskine-Brown tried to sound confident — 'on the facts.'

'Facts?' Ballard looked at him somewhat sadly. 'Facts are not everything. This isn't an ordinary Court and we are here exercising a very special jurisdiction. We must be particularly careful that we don't commit an injustice against a person who may very well be entirely innocent. We have, of course, the memory of a certain martyr very much in our minds.'

'Oh, very much, Chancellor. It's in my mind constantly,' I assured him.

'We must also be grateful for any sort of guidance this holy city of Lawnchester can give us.'

'Guidance, Chancellor?' Claude was puzzled.

'Guidance comes to us, Erskine-Brown, from many unexpected sources.'

'I think what his Worship means, Claude,' I translated for the benefit of the heathen, 'is that there are more things in heaven and earth than are dreamt of in your philosophy.'

'Exactly, Rumpole! Very well put, if I may say so.' The Chancellor moved me up to the top of the class. 'I have thought anxiously about this case, and I am not ashamed to say that I have prayed.'

'Haven't we all? You've prayed too, haven't you, Claude?' I put on my most pious expression.

'Well. Well, yes, but . . .'

'And I've come to a clear decision,' Ballard pronounced. 'Having regard to the evidence about the financial interests involved, and the possibility that Miss O'Keefe might have been tempted to, shall we say, invent for money . . .'

'All too possible, I'm afraid, Chancellor,' I agreed. 'Such a lot of original sin about nowadays.'

'. . . I have come to the conclusion that it would not be safe to proceed any further against Canon Donkin on this evidence. I propose to direct the Assessors to acquit. Of course, I'll hear argument if you want to address me.'

This last remark was directed at Claude Erskine-Brown who did seem about to open his mouth. In a penetrating aside, I gave him my best legal advice. 'Give up gracefully, Claude,' I warned the fellow, 'God's against you.'

When the Canon and his frock were both safe and clear of the Courtroom, I received the some-

170

what distracted thanks of Cousin Timmy and he went off, with well-justified apprehension, to break the good news to Gertrude. I lunched at leisure and took the train back to London, returning to the matrimonial home in Froxbury Mansions on the Gloucester Road in the early evening. I opened the front door to be greeted by Hilda's usual cry of 'Who's that?' from the kitchen. 'Fear not,' I told her. 'It is I Saint Rumpole and all angels.'

'I'm sorry your little holiday to the West Country was so short,' I told her later as we were sitting over our chops and two veg in the kitchen.

'I don't know why I came down in the first place.'

'Oh, it was enormously kind of you, Hilda. You were a power for good.'

'It's not because I'm jealous, Rumpole,' she hastened to assure me. 'Don't flatter yourself about that.' I was smiling, I must confess, as I poured myself another glass of Pommeroy's Very Ordinary, and this led Hilda to add, 'And don't look so pleased with yourself, just because you won a case.'

'A total victory,' I agreed. 'The Age of Miracles is not past.' And I said, as I raised my glass, 'Let us drink to the Blessed Saint Edithna. Also known,' I added, but not aloud, 'as She Who Must Be Obeyed.'

# Rumpole and the Tap End

There are many reasons why I could never become one of Her Majesty's judges. I am unable to look at my customer in the dock without feeling 'There but for the Grace of God goes Horace Rumpole.' I should find it almost impossible to order any fellow citizen to be locked up in a Victorian slum with a couple of psychopaths and three chamber-pots, and I cannot imagine a worse way of passing your life than having to actually listen to the speeches of the learned friends. It also has to be admitted that no sane Lord Chancellor would ever dream of the appointment of Justice Rumpole. There is another danger inherent in the judicial office: a judge, any judge, is always liable to say, in a moment of boredom or impatience, something downright silly. He is then denounced in the public prints, his resignation is called for, he is stigmatized as malicious or at least mad and his Bench becomes a bed of nails and his ermine a hair-shirt. There is, perhaps, no judge more likely to open his mouth and put his foot in it than that, on the whole well meaning, old darling, Mr Justice Featherstone, once Guthrie Featherstone, Q.C., M.P., a Member of Parliament so uninterested in politics that he joined the Social Democrats and who, during many eventful years of my life, was Head of our Chambers in Equity Court. Now, as a judge, Guthrie Featherstone had swum somewhat out of our ken; but he hadn't lost his old talent for giving voice to the odd uncalled-for and disastrous phrase. He, I'm sure, will never forget the furore that arose when, in passing sentence in a case of attempted murder in which I was engaged for the Defence, his Lordship made an unwise reference to the 'tap end' of a matrimonial bath-tub. At least the account which follows may serve a terrible warning to anyone contemplating a career as a judge.

I have spoken elsewhere, and on frequent occasions, of my patrons the Timsons, that extended family of South London villains for whom, over the years, I have acted as Attorney-General. Some of you may remember Tony Timson, a fairly mild-mannered receiver of stolen video-recorders, hi-fi sets and microwave ovens, married to that April Timson who once so offended her husband's male chauvinist prejudices by driving a getaway car at a somewhat unsuccessful bank robbery.* Tony and April lived in a semi on a large housing estate with their offspring, Vincent Timson, now aged eight, who I hoped would grow up in the family business and thus ensure a steady flow of briefs for Rumpole's future. Their house was brightly, not to say garishly, furnished with mock tiger-skin rugs, Italian-tile-style linoleum and

* See 'Rumpole and the Female of the Species' in *Rumpole and the Golden Thread*, Penguin Books, 1983.

wallpaper which simulated oak panelling. (I knew this from a large number of police photographs in various cases.) It was also equipped with almost every labour-saving device which ever dropped off the back of a lorry. On the day when my story starts this desirable home was rent with screams from the bathroom and a stream of soapy water flowing out from under the door. In the screaming, the word 'murderer' was often repeated at a volume which was not only audible to young Vincent, busy pushing a blue-flashing toy police car round the hallway, but to the oc-cupants of the adjoining house and those of the neighbours who were hanging out their wash-ing. Someone, it was not clear who it was at the time, telephoned the local cop shop for as-sistance.

In a surprisingly short while a real, flashing police car arrived and the front door was flung open by a wet and desperate April Timson, her leopard-skin-style towelling bath-robe clutched about her. As Detective Inspector Brush, an of-ficer who had fought a running battle with the Timson family for years, came up the path to meet her she sobbed out, at the top of her voice, a considerable voice for so petite a redhead, 'Thank God, you've come! He was only trying to bloody murder me.' Tony Timson emerged from the bathroom a few seconds later, water dripping from his ear-lobe-length hair and his gaucho moustache. In spite of the word RAMBO emblazoned across his bath-robe, he was by no means a man of formidable physique. Looking down the stairs, he saw his wife in hysterics and his domestic hearth invaded by the Old Bill. No sooner had he reached the hallway than he was arrested and charged with attempted murder of his wife, the particulars being, that, while sharing a bath with her preparatory to going to a neighbour's party, he had tried to cause her death by drowning.

In course of time I was happy to accept a brief for the defence of Tony Timson and we had a conference in Brixton prison where the alleged wife-drowner was being held in custody. I was attended, on that occasion, by Mr Bernard, the Timsons' regular solicitor, and that up-and-coming young radical barrister, Mizz Liz Probert, who had been briefed to take a note and generally assist me in the *cause célèbre*.

'Attempted murderer, Tony Timson?' I opened the proceedings on a somewhat incredulous note. 'Isn't that rather out of your league?'

'April told me,' he began his explanation, 'she was planning on wearing her skin-tight leatherette trousers with the revealing halter-neck satin top. That's what she was planning on wearing, Mr Rumpole!'

'A somewhat tasteless outfit, and not entirely *haute couture*,' I admitted. 'But it hardly entitles you to drown your wife, Tony.'

'We was both invited to a party round her friend Chrissie's. And that was the outfit she was keen on wearing . . .'

'She says you pulled her legs and so she became submerged.' Bernard, like a good solicitor, was reading the evidence.

' "The Brides in the Bath"!' My mind went at once to one of the classic murders of all times. 'The very method! And you hit on it with no legal training. How did you come to be in the same bath, anyway?'

'We always shared, since we was courting.' Tony looked surprised that I had asked. 'Don't all married couples?'

'Speaking for myself and She Who Must Be Obeyed the answer is, thankfully, no. I can't speak for Mr Bernard.'

'Out of the question.' Bernard shook his head sadly. 'My wife has a hip.'

'Sorry, Mr Bernard. I'm really sorry.' Tony Timson was clearly an attempted murderer with a soft heart.

'Quite all right, Mr Timson,' Bernard assured him. 'We're down for a replacement.'

'April likes me to sit up by the taps.' Tony gave us further particulars of the Timson bathing habits. 'So I can rinse off her hair after a shampoo. Anyway, she finds her end that much more comfortable.'

'She makes you sit at the tap end, Tony?' I began to feel for the fellow.

'Oh, I never made no objection,' my client assured me. 'Although you can get your back a bit scalded. And those old taps does dig into you sometimes.'

'So were you on friendly terms when you both entered the water?' My instructing solicitor was quick on the deductions. 'She was all right then. We was both, well, affectionate. Looking forward to the party, like.'

'She didn't object to what you planned on wearing?' I wanted to cover all the possibilities.

'My non-structured silk-style suiting from Toy Boy Limited!' Tony protested. 'How could she object to that, Mr Rumpole? No. She washed her hair as per usual. And I rinsed it off for her. Then she told me who was going to be at the party, like.'

'Mr Peter Molloy,' Bernard reminded me. 'It's in the brief, Mr Rumpole.' Now I make it a rule to postpone reading my brief until the last possible moment so that it's fresh in my mind when I go into Court, so I said, somewhat testily, 'Of course I know that, but I thought I'd like to get the story from the client. Peanuts Molloy! Mizz Probert, we have a defence. Tony Timson's wife was taking him to a party attended by Peanuts Molloy.'

The full implications of this piece of evidence won't be apparent to those who haven't made a close study of my previous handling of the Timson affairs. Suffice it to say the Molloys are to the Timsons as the Montagues were to the Capulets or the Guelphs to the Ghibellines, and their feud goes back to the days when the whole of South London was laid down to pasture, and they were quarrelling about stolen sheep. The latest outbreak of hostilities occurred when certain Molloys, robbing a couple of elderly Timsons as *they* were robbing a bank, almost succeeded in getting Tony's relatives convicted for an offence they had not committed.[*] Peter, better known as 'Peanuts', Molloy was the young hopeful of the clan Molloy and it was small wonder that Tony Timson took great exception to his wife putting on her leatherette trousers for the purpose of meeting the family enemy.

Liz Probert, however, a white-wig at the Bar who knew nothing of such old legal traditions as the Molloy–Timson hostility, said, 'Why should Mrs Timson's meeting Molloy make it all right to drown her?' I have to remind you that Mizz Liz was a pillar of the North Islington women's movement.

'It wasn't just that she was meeting him, Mr Rumpole,' Tony explained. 'It was the words she used.'

'What did she say?'

'I'd rather not tell you if you don't mind. It was humiliating to my pride.'

'Oh, for heaven's sake, Tony. Let's hear the worst.' I had never known a Timson behave so coyly.

'She made a comparison like, between me and Peanuts.'

[*] See 'Rumpole's Last Case' in *Rumpole's Last Case*, Penguin Books, 1987.

'What comparison?'

Tony looked at Liz and his voice sank to a whisper. 'Ladies present,' he said.

'Tony,' I had to tell him, 'Mizz Liz Probert has not only practised in the criminal courts, but in the family division. She is active on behalf of gay and lesbian rights in her native Islington. She marches, quite often, in aid of abortion on demand. She is a regular reader of the woman's page of the *Guardian*. You and I, Tony, need have no secrets from Mizz Probert. Now, what was this comparison your wife made between you and Peanuts Molloy?'

'On the topic of virility. I'm sorry, Miss.'

'That's quite all right.' Liz Probert was unshocked and unamused.

'What we need, I don't know if you would agree, Mr Rumpole,' Mr Bernard suggested, 'is a predominance of *men* on the Jury.'

'Underendowed males would condone the attempted murder of a woman, you mean?' The Probert hackles were up.

'Please. Mizz Probert.' I tried to call the meeting to order. 'Let us face this problem in a spirit of detachment. What we need is a sympathetic judge who doesn't want to waste his time on a long case. Have we got a fixed date for this, Mr Bernard?'

'We have, sir. Before the Red Judge.' Mr Bernard meant that Tony Timson was to be tried before the High Court judge visiting the Old Bailey.

'They're pulling out all the stops.' I was impressed.

'It *is* attempted murder, Mr Rumpole. So we're fixed before Mr Justice Featherstone.'

'Guthrie Featherstone.' I thought about it. 'Our one-time Head of Chambers. Now, I just wonder . . .'

We were in luck. Sir Guthrie Featherstone was in no mood to try a long case, so he summoned me and Counsel for the Prosecution to his room before the start of the proceedings. He sat robed but with his wig on the desk in front of him, a tall, elegant figure who almost always wore the slightly hunted expression of a man who's not entirely sure what he's up to — an unfortunate state of mind for a fellow who has to spend his waking hours coming to firm and just decisions. For all his indecision, however, he knew for certain that he didn't want to spend the whole day trying a ticklish attempted murder.

'Is this a long case?' the Judge asked. 'I am bidden to take tea in the neighbourhood of Victoria. Can you fellows guess where?'

'Sorry, Judge. I give up.' Charles Hearthstoke, our serious-minded young prosecutor, seemed in no mood for party games.

'The station buffet?' I hazarded a guess.

'The station buffet!' Guthrie enjoyed the joke. 'Isn't that you all over, Horace? You will have your joke. Not far off, though.' The joke was over and he went on impressively. 'Buck House.

Her Majesty has invited me — no, correction — "commanded" me to a Royal Garden Party.'

'God Save The Queen!' I murmured loyally.

'Not only Her Majesty,' Guthrie told us, 'more seriously one's lady wife, would be extremely put out if one didn't parade in grey top-hat order!'

'He's blaming it on his wife!' Liz Probert, who had followed me into the presence, said in a penetrating aside.

'So naturally one would have to be free by lunch-time. Hearthstoke, is this a long case from the prosecution point of view?' the Judge asked.

'It is an extremely serious case, Judge.' Our prosecutor spoke like a man of twice his years. 'Attempted murder. We've put it down for a week.' I have always thought young Charlie Hearthstoke a mega-sized pill ever since he joined our Chambers for a blessedly brief period and tried to get everything run by a computer.*

'I'm astonished,' I gave Guthrie a little comfort, 'that my learned friend Mr Hearthrug should think it could possibly last so long.'

'Hearthstoke,' young Charlie corrected me.

'Have it your own way. With a bit of common sense we could finish this in half an hour.'

'Thereby saving public time and money.' Hope sprang eternal in the Judge's breast.

'Exactly!' I cheered him up. 'As you know, it is an article of my religion never to plead guilty.

* See 'Rumpole and the Judge's Elbow' in *Rumpole's Last Case*, Penguin Books, 1987.

181

But, bearing in mind all the facts in this case, I'm prepared to advise Timson to put his hands up to common assault. He'll agree to be bound over to keep the peace.'

'Common assault?' Hearthstoke was furious. 'Binding over? Hold on a minute. He tried to drown her!'

'Judge.' I put the record straight. 'He was seated at the tap end of the bath. His wife, lying back comfortably in the depths, passed an extremely wounding remark about my client's virility.'

It was then I saw Mr Justice Featherstone looking at me, apparently shaken to the core. 'The *tap end*,' he gasped. 'Did you say he was seated at the *tap end*, Horace?'

'I'm afraid so, Judge.' I confirmed the information sorrowfully.

'This troubles me.' Indeed the Judge looked extremely troubled. 'How does it come about that he was seated at the tap end?'

'His wife insisted on it.' I had to tell him the full horror of the situation.

'This woman insisted that her husband sat with his back squashed up against the taps?' The Judge's voice rose in incredulous outrage.

'She made him sit in that position so he could rinse off her hair.'

'At the *tap end?*' Guthrie still couldn't quite believe it.

'Exactly so.'

'You're sure?'

'There can be no doubt about it.'

'Hearthrug . . . I mean, *stoke*. Is this one of the facts agreed by the Prosecution?'

'I can't see that it makes the slightest difference.' The Prosecution was not pleased with the course its case was taking.

'You can't see! Horace, was this conduct in any way typical of this woman's attitude to her husband?'

'I regret to say, entirely typical.'

'Rumpole . . .' Liz Probert, appalled by the chauvinist chatter around her, seemed about to burst, and I calmed her with a quiet 'Shut up, Mizz.'

'So you are telling me that this husband deeply resented the position in which he found himself.' Guthrie was spelling out the implications exactly as I had hoped he would.

'What married man wouldn't, Judge?' I asked mournfully.

'And his natural resentment led to a purely domestic dispute?'

'Such as might occur, Judge, in the best bathrooms.'

'And you are content to be bound over to keep the peace?' His Lordship looked at me with awful solemnity.

'Reluctantly, Judge,' I said after a suitable pause for contemplation, 'I would agree to that restriction on my client's liberty.'

'Liberty to drown his wife!' Mizz Probert had to be 'shushed' again.

'Hearth*stoke*.' The Judge spoke with great authority. 'My compliments to those instructing you and in my opinion it would be a gross waste of public funds to continue with this charge of attempted murder. We should be finished by half past eleven.' He looked at his watch with the deep satisfaction of a man who was sure that he would be among those present at the Royal Garden Party, after the ritual visit to Moss Bros to hire the grey topper and all the trimmings. As we left the sanctum, I stood aside to let Mizz Probert out of the door. 'Oh, no, Rumpole, you're a man,' she whispered with her fury barely contained. 'Men always go first, don't they?'

So we all went into Court to polish off *R.* v. *Timson* and to make sure that Her Majesty had the pleasure of Guthrie's presence over the tea and strawberries. I made a token speech in mitigation, something of a formality as I knew that I was pushing at an open door. Whilst I was speaking, I was aware of the fact that the Judge wasn't giving me his full attention. That was reserved for a new young shorthand writer, later to become known to me as a Miss (not, I'm sure in her case, a Mizz) Lorraine Frinton. Lorraine was what I believe used to be known as a 'bit of an eyeful', being young, doe-eyed and clearly surrounded by her own special fragrance. When I sat down, Guthrie thanked me absent-mindedly and reluctantly gave up the careful perusal of Miss Frinton's beauty. He then proceeded to pass sentence on Tony Timson in a number of peculiarly ill-chosen words.

'Timson,' his Lordship began harmlessly enough. 'I have heard about you and your wife's habit of taking a bath together. It is not for this Court to say that communal bathing, in time of peace when it is not in the national interest to save water, is appropriate conduct in married life. *Chacun à son goût*, as a wise Frenchman once said.' Miss Frinton, the shorthand writer, looked hopelessly confused by the words of the wise Frenchman. 'What throws a flood of light on this case,' the Judge went on, 'is that you, Timson, habitually sat at the tap end of the bath. It seems you had a great deal to put up with. And your wife, she, it appears from the evidence, washed her hair in the more placid waters of the other end. I accept that this was a purely domestic dispute. For the common assault to which you have pleaded guilty you will be bound over to keep the peace . . .' And the Judge added the terrible words, '. . . in the sum of fifty pounds.'

So Tony Timson was at liberty, the case was over and a furious Mizz Liz Probert banged out of Court before Guthrie was half way out of the door. Catching up with her, I rebuked my learned Junior. 'It's not in the best traditions of the Bar to slam out before the Judge in any circumstances. When we've just had a famous victory it's quite ridiculous.'

'A famous victory.' She laughed in a cynical fashion. 'For men!'

'Man, woman or child, it doesn't matter who the client is. We did our best and won.'

'Because he was a man! Why shouldn't he sit at the tap end? I've got to do something about it!' She moved away purposefully. I called after her. 'Mizz Probert! Where're you going?'

'To my branch of the women's movement. The protest's got to be organized on a national level. I'm sorry, Rumpole. The time for talking's over.'

And she was gone. I had no idea, then, of the full extent of the tide which was about to overwhelm poor old Guthrie Featherstone, but I had a shrewd suspicion that his Lordship was in serious trouble.

The Featherstones' two children were away at university, and Guthrie and Marigold occupied a flat which Lady Featherstone found handy for Harrods, her favourite shopping centre, and a country cottage near Newbury. Marigold Featherstone was a handsome woman who greatly enjoyed life as a judge's wife and was full of that strength of character and quickness of decision his Lordship so conspicuously lacked. They went to the Garden Party together with three or four hundred other pillars of the establishment: admirals, captains of industry, hospital matrons and drivers of the Royal Train. Picture them, if you will, safely back home with Marigold kicking off her shoes on the sofa and Guthrie going out to the hall to fetch that afternoon's copy of the *Evening Sentinel*, which had just been delivered. You must, of course, understand that I was not present at the scene or other similar scenes which are necessary to this narrative. I can only do my best to reconstruct it from what I know of subsequent events and what the participants told me afterwards. Any gaps I have been able to fill in are thanks to the talent for fiction which I have acquired during a long career acting for the Defence in criminal cases.

'There might just be a picture of us arriving at the Palace.' Guthrie brought back the *Sentinel* and then stood in horror, rooted to the spot by what he saw on the front page.

'Well, then. Bring it in here.' Marigold, no doubt, called from her reclining position.

'Oh, there's absolutely nothing to read in it. The usual nonsense. Nothing of the slightest interest. Well, I think I'll go and have a bath and get changed.' And he attempted to sidle out of the room, holding the newspaper close to his body in a manner which made the contents invisible to his wife.

'Why're you trying to hide that *Evening Sentinel*, Guthrie?'

'Hide it? Of course I'm not trying to hide it. I just thought I'd take it to read in the bath.'

'And make it all soggy? Let me have it, Guthrie.'

'I told you . . .'

'Guthrie. I want to see what's in the paper.' Marigold spoke in an authoritative manner and her husband had no alternative but to hand it over, murmuring the while, 'It's completely

187

inaccurate, of course.'

And so Lady Featherstone came to read, under a large photograph of his Lordship in a full-bottomed wig, the story which was being enjoyed by every member of the legal profession in the Greater London area. CARRY ON DROWNING screamed the banner headline. TAP END JUDGE'S AMAZING DECISION. And then came the full denunciation:

*Wives who share baths with their husbands will have to be careful where they sit in the future. Because 29-year-old April Timson of Bexley Heath made her husband Tony sit at the tap end the Judge dismissed a charge of attempted murder against him. 'It seems you had a good deal to put up with,' 55-year-old Mr Justice Featherstone told Timson, a 36-year-old window cleaner. 'This is male chauvinism gone mad,' said a spokesperson of the Islington Women's Organization. 'There will be protests up and down the country and questions asked in Parliament. No woman can sit safely in her bath while this Judge continues on the bench.'*

'It's a travesty of what I said, Marigold. You know exactly what these Court reporters are. Head over heels in Guinness after lunch.' Guthrie no doubt told his wife.

'This must have been in the morning. We went to the Palace after lunch.'

'Well, anyway. It's a travesty.'

'What do you mean, Guthrie? Didn't you say

all that about the tap end?'

'Well, I may just have mentioned the tap end. Casually. In passing. Horace told me it was part of the evidence.'

'Horace?'

'Rumpole.'

'I suppose he was defending.'

'Well, yes . . .'

'You're clay in the hands of that little fellow, Guthrie. You're a Red Judge and he's only a Junior, but he can twist you round his little finger,' I rather hope she told him.

'You think Horace Rumpole led me up the garden?'

'Of course he did! He got his chap off and he encouraged you to say something monumentally stupid about tap ends. Not, I suppose, that you needed much encouragement.'

'This gives an entirely false impression. I'll put it right, Marigold. I promise you. I'll see it's put right.'

'I think you'd better, Guthrie.' The Judge's wife, I knew, was not a woman to mince her words. 'And for heaven's sake try not to put your foot in it again.'

So Guthrie went off to soothe his troubles up to the neck in bath water and Marigold lay brooding on the sofa until, so she told Hilda later, she was telephoned by the Tom Creevey Diary Column on the *Sentinel* with an inquiry as to which end of the bath she occupied when she and her husband were at their ablutions. Famous couples all over London, she was assured, were being asked the same question. Marigold put down the instrument without supplying any information, merely murmuring to herself, 'Guthrie! what have you done to us now?'

Marigold Featherstone wasn't the only wife appalled by the Judge's indiscretions. As I let myself in to our mansion flat in the Gloucester Road, Hilda, as was her wont, called to me from the living-room, 'Who's that?'

'I am thy father's spirit,' I told her in sepulchral tones.

> 'Doomed for a certain term to
>  walk the night,
> And for the day confined to fast
>  in fires,
> Till the foul crimes done in my
>  days of nature
> Are burnt and purged away.'

'I suppose you think it's perfectly all right.' She was, I noticed, reading the *Evening Sentinel.*

'What's perfectly all right?'

'Drowning wives!' She said in the unfriendliest of tones. 'Like puppies. I suppose you think that's all perfectly understandable. Well, Rumpole, all I can say is, you'd better not try anything like that with me!'

'Hilda! It's never crossed my mind. Anyway, Tony Timson didn't drown her. He didn't come anywhere near drowning her. It was just a matrimonial tiff in the bathroom.'

'Why should *she* have to sit at the tap end?'

'Why indeed?' I made for the sideboard and a new bottle of Pommeroy's plonk. 'If she had, and if she'd tried to drown him because of it, I'd have defended her with equal skill and success. There you are, you see. Absolutely no prejudice when it comes to accepting a brief.'

'You think men and women are entirely equal?'

'Everyone is equal in the dock.'

'And in the home?'

'Well, yes, Hilda. Of course. Naturally. Although I suppose some are born to command.' I smiled at her in what I hoped was a soothing manner, well designed to unruffle her feathers, and took my glass of claret to my habitual seat by the gas fire. 'Trust me, Hilda,' I told her. 'I shall always be a staunch defender of Women's Rights.'

'I'm glad to hear that.'

'I'm glad you're glad.'

'That means you can do the weekly shop for us at Safeways.'

'Well, I'd really love that, Hilda,' I said eagerly. 'I should regard that as the most tremendous fun. Unfortunately I have to earn the boring stuff that pays for our weekly shop. I have to be at the service of my masters.'

'Husbands who try to drown their wives?' she asked unpleasantly.

'And vice versa.'

191

'They have late-night shopping on Thursdays, Rumpole. It won't cut into your work-time at all. Only into your drinking time in Pommeroy's Wine Bar. Besides which I shall be far too busy for shopping from now on.'

'Why, Hilda? What on earth are you planning to do?' I asked innocently. And when the answer came I knew the sexual revolution had hit Froxbury Mansions at last.

'Someone has to stand up for Women's Rights,' Hilda told me, 'against the likes of you and Guthrie Featherstone. I shall read for the Bar.'

Such was the impact of the decision in *R. v. Timson* on life in the Rumpole home. When Tony Timson was sprung from custody he was not taken lovingly back into the bosom of his family. April took her baths alone and frequently left the house tricked out in her skin-tight, wet-look trousers and the exotic halter-neck. When Tony made so bold as to ask where she was going, she told him to mind his own business. Vincent, the young hopeful, also treated his father with scant respect and, when asked where he was off to on his frequent departures from the front door, also told his father to mind his own business.

When she was off on the spree, April Timson, it later transpired, called round to an off licence in neighbouring Morrison Avenue. There she met the notorious Peanuts Molloy, also dressed in alluring leather, who was stocking up from Ruby, the large black lady who ran the 'offey', with raspberry crush, Champanella, crème de cacao and three-star cognac as his contribution to some party or other. He and April would embrace openly and then go off partying together. On occasion Peanuts would ask her how 'that wally of a husband' was getting on, and express his outrage at the lightness of the sentence inflicted on him. 'Someone ought to give that Tony of yours a bit of justice,' was what he was heard to say.

Peanuts Molloy wasn't alone in feeling that being bound over in the sum of fifty pounds wasn't an adequate punishment for the attempted drowning of a wife. This view was held by most of the newspapers, a large section of the public, and all the members of the North Islington Women's Movement (Chair, Mizz Liz Probert). When Guthrie arrived for business at the Judge's entrance of the Old Bailey, he was met by a vociferous posse of women, bearing banners with the following legend: WOMEN OF ENGLAND, KEEP YOUR HEADS ABOVE WATER. GET JUSTICE FEATHERSTONE SACKED. As the friendly police officers kept these angry ladies at bay, Guthrie took what comfort he might from the thought that a High Court judge can only be dismissed by a Bill passed through both Houses of Parliament.

Something, he decided, would have to be done to answer his many critics. So Guthrie called Miss Lorraine Frinton, the doe-eyed shorthand writer, into his room and did his best to correct the record of his ill-considered judgment. Miss Frinton, breathtakingly decorative as ever, sat with her long legs neatly crossed in the Judge's armchair and tried to grasp his intentions with regard to her shorthand note. I reconstruct this conversation thanks to Miss Frinton's later recollection. She was, she admits, very nervous at the time because she thought that the Judge had sent for her because she had, in some way, failed in her duties. 'I've been living in dread of someone pulling me up about my shorthand,' she confessed. 'It's not my strongest suit, quite honestly.'

'Don't worry, Miss Frinton,' Guthrie did his best to reassure her. 'You're in no sort of trouble at all. But you are a shorthand writer, of course you are, and if we could just get to the point when I passed sentence. Could you read it out?'

The beautiful Lorraine looked despairingly at her notebook and spelled out, with great difficulty, 'Mr Hearthstoke has quite wisely . . .'

'A bit further on.'

'Jackie a saw goo . . . a wise Frenchman . . .' Miss Frinton was decoding.

'*Chacun à son goût!*'

'I'm sorry, my Lord. I didn't quite get the name.'

'*Ça ne fait rien.*'

'How are you spelling that?' She was now lost.

'Never mind.' The Judge was at his most patient. 'A little further on, Miss Frinton. Lorraine. I'm sure you and I can come to an agreement. About a full stop.'

After much hard work, his Lordship had his way with Miss Frinton's shorthand note, and Counsel and solicitors engaged in the case were assembled in Court to hear, in the presence of the gentlemen of the Press, his latest version of his unfortunate judgment.

'I have had my attention drawn to the report of the case in *The Times*,' he started with some confidence, 'in which I am quoted as saying to Timson, "It seems you had a great deal to put up with. And your wife, she, it appears from the evidence, washed her hair in the more placid waters" etc. It's the full stop that has been misplaced. I have checked this carefully with the learned shorthand writer and she agrees with me. I see her nodding her head.' He looked down at Lorraine who nodded energetically, and the Judge smiled at her. 'Very well, yes. The sentence in my judgment in fact read "It seems you had a great deal to put up with, and your wife." Full stop! What I intended to convey, and I should like the Press to take note of this, was that both Mr and Mrs Timson had a good deal to put up with. At different ends of the bath, of course. Six of one and half a dozen of the other. I hope that's clear?' It was, as I whispered to Mizz Probert sitting beside me, as clear as mud.

The Judge continued. 'I certainly never said that I regarded being seated at the tap end as legal provocation to attempted murder. I would have said it was one of the facts that the Jury

195

might have taken into consideration. It might have thrown some light on this wife's attitude to her husband.'

'What's he trying to do?' *sotto voce* Hearthstoke asked me.

'Trying to get himself out of hot water,' I suggested.

'But the attempted murder charge was dropped,' Guthrie went on.

'He twisted my arm to drop it,' Hearthstoke was muttering.

'And the entire tap end question was really academic,' Guthrie told us, 'as Timson pleaded guilty to common assault. Do you agree, Mr Rumpole?'

'Certainly, my Lord.' I rose in my most servile manner. 'You gave him a very stiff binding over.'

'Have you anything to add, Mr Hearthstoke?'

'No, my Lord.' Hearthstoke couldn't very well say anything else, but when the Judge had left us he warned me that Tony Timson had better watch his step in future as Detective Inspector Brush was quite ready to throw the book at him.

Guthrie Featherstone left Court well pleased with himself and instructed his aged and extremely disloyal clerk, Wilfred, to send a bunch of flowers, or, even better, a handsome pot plant to Miss Lorraine Frinton in recognition of her loyal services. So Wilfred told me he went off to telephone Interflora and Guthrie passed his day happily trying a perfectly straightforward robbery. On rising he retired to his room for a cup of weak Lapsang and a glance at the *Evening Sentinel*. This glance was enough to show him that he had achieved very little more, by his statement in open Court, than inserting his foot into the mud to an even greater depth.

BATHTUB JUDGE SAYS IT AGAIN screamed the headline. *Putting her husband at the tap end may be a factor to excuse the attempted murder of a wife.* 'Did I say that?' the appalled Guthrie asked old Wilfred who was busy pouring out the tea.

'To the best of my recollection, my Lord. Yes.'

There was no comfort for Guthrie when the telephone rang. It was old Keith from the Chancellor's office saying that the Lord Chancellor, as Head of the Judiciary, would like to see Mr Justice Featherstone at the earliest available opportunity.

'A Bill through the Houses of Parliament.' A stricken Guthrie put down the telephone. 'Would they do it to me, Wilfred?' he asked, but answer came there none.

'You do look, my clerk, in a moved sort, as if you were dismayed.' In fact, Henry, when I encountered him in the clerk's room, seemed distinctly rattled. 'Too right, sir. I am dismayed. I've just had Mrs Rumpole on the telephone.'

'Ah. She Who Must wanted to speak to me?'

'No, Mr Rumpole. She wanted to speak to me. She said I'd be clerking for her in the fullness of time.'

'Henry,' I tried to reassure the man, 'there's

no immediate cause for concern.'

'She said as she was reading for the Bar, Mr Rumpole, to make sure women get a bit of justice in the future.'

'Your missus coming into Chambers, Rumpole?' Uncle Tom, our oldest and quite briefless inhabitant, was pursuing his usual hobby of making approach shots to the waste-paper basket with an old putter.

'Don't worry, Uncle Tom.' I sounded as confident as I could. 'Not in the foreseeable future.'

'My motto as a barrister's clerk, sir, is anything for a quiet life,' Henry outlined his philosophy. 'I have to say that my definition of a quiet life does not include clerking for Mrs Hilda Rumpole.'

'Old Sneaky MacFarlane in Crown Office Row had a missus who came into his Chambers.' Uncle Tom was off down Memory Lane. 'She didn't come in to practice, you understand. She came in to watch Sneaky. She used to sit in the corner of his room and knit during all his conferences. It seems she was dead scared he was going to get off with one of his female divorce petitioners.'

'Mrs Rumpole, Henry, has only just written off for a legal course in the Open University. She can't yet tell provocation from self defence or define manslaughter.' I went off to collect things from my tray and Uncle Tom missed a putt and went on with his story. 'And you know what? In the end Mrs MacFarlane went off with a co-respondent she'd met at one of these conferences. Some awful fellow, apparently, in black and white shoes! Left poor old Sneaky high and dry. So, you see, it doesn't do to have wives in Chambers.'

'Oh, I meant to ask you, Henry. Have you seen my Ackerman on *The Causes of Death*?' One of my best-loved books had gone missing.

'I think Mr Ballard's borrowed it, sir.' And then Henry asked, still anxious, 'How long do they take then, those courses at the Open University?'

'Years, Henry,' I told him. 'It's unlikely to finish during our lifetime.'

When I went up to Ballard's room to look for my beloved Ackerman, the door had been left a little open. Standing in the corridor I could hear the voices of those arch-conspirators, Claude Erskine-Brown and Soapy Sam Ballard, Q.C. I have to confess that I lingered to catch a little of the dialogue.

'Keith from the Lord Chancellor's office sounded *you* out about Guthrie Featherstone?' Erskine-Brown was asking.

'As the fellow who took over his Chambers. He thought I might have a view.'

'And have you? A view, I mean.'

'I told Keith that Guthrie was a perfectly charming chap, of course.' Soapy Sam was about to damn Guthrie with the faintest of praise.

'Oh, perfectly charming. No doubt about that,' Claude agreed.

'But as a judge, perhaps, he lacks judgment.'

'Which is a pretty important quality in a judge,' Claude thought.

'Exactly. And perhaps there is some lack of . . .'

'Gravitas?'

'The very word I used, Claude.'

'There was a bit of lack of gravitas in Chambers, too,' Claude remembered, 'when Guthrie took a shine to a temporary typist . . .'

'So the upshot of my talk with Keith was . . .'

'What was the upshot?'

'I think we may be seeing a vacancy on the High Court Bench.' Ballard passed on the sad news with great satisfaction. 'And old Keith was kind enough to drop a rather interesting hint.'

'Tell me, Sam?'

'He said they might be looking for a replacement from the same stable.'

'Meaning these Chambers in Equity Court?'

'How could it mean anything else?'

'Sam, if you go on the Bench, we should need another silk in Chambers!' Claude was no doubt licking his lips as he considered the possibilities.

'I don't see how they could refuse you.' These two were clearly hand in glove.

'There's no doubt Guthrie'll have to go.' Claude pronounced the death sentence on our absent friend.

'He comes out with such injudicious remarks.' Soapy Sam put in another drop of poison. 'He was just like that at Marlborough.'

'Did you tell old Keith that?' Claude asked and then sat open-mouthed as I burst from my hiding-place with 'I bet you did!'

'Rumpole!' Ballard also looked put out. 'What on earth have you been doing?'

'I've been listening to the Grand Conspiracy.'

'You must admit, Featherstone J. has made the most tremendous boo-boo.' Claude smiled as though he had never made a boo-boo in his life.

'In the official view,' Soapy Sam told me, 'he's been remarkably stupid.'

'He wasn't stupid.' I briefed myself for Guthrie's defence. 'As a matter of fact he understood the case extremely well. He came to a wise decision. He might have phrased his judgment more elegantly, if he hadn't been to Marlborough. And let me tell you something, Ballard. My wife, Hilda, is about to start a law course at the Open University. She is a woman, as I know to my cost, of grit and determination. I expect to see her Lord Chief Justice of England before you get your bottom within a mile of the High Court Bench!'

'Of course you're entitled to your opinion.' Ballard looked tolerant. 'And you got your fellow off. All I know for certain is that the Lord Chancellor has summoned Guthrie Featherstone to appear before him.'

The Lord Chancellor of England was a small, fat, untidy man with steel-rimmed spectacles which gave him the schoolboy look which led to his nickname 'The Owl of the Remove'. He

201

was given to fits of teasing when he would laugh aloud at his own jokes and unpredictable bouts of biting sarcasm during which he would stare at his victims with cold hostility. He had been, for many years, the Captain of the House of Lords croquet team, a game in which his ruthless cunning found full scope. He received Guthrie in his large, comfortably furnished room overlooking the Thames at Westminster, where his long wig was waiting on its stand and his gold-embroidered purse and gown were ready for his procession to the woolsack. Two years after this confrontation, I found myself standing with Guthrie at a Christmas party given in our Chambers to members past and present, and he was so far gone in *Brut* (not to say Brutal) Pommeroy's *Méthode Champenoise* as to give me the bare bones of this historic encounter. I have fleshed them out from my knowledge of both characters and their peculiar habits of speech.

'Judgeitis, Featherstone,' I hear the Lord Chancellor saying. 'It goes with piles as one of the occupational hazards of the judicial profession. Its symptoms are pomposity and self-regard. It shows itself by unnecessary interruptions during the proceedings or giving utterance to private thoughts far, far better left unspoken.'

'I did correct the press report, Lord Chancellor, with reference to the shorthand writer.' Guthrie tried to sound convincing.

'Oh, I read that.' The Chancellor was unimpressed. 'Far better to have left the thing alone.

Never give the newspapers a second chance. That's my advice to you.'

'What's the cure for judgeitis?' Guthrie asked anxiously.

'Banishment to a golf club where the sufferer may bore the other members to death with recollections of his old triumphs on the Western Circuit.'

'You mean, a Bill through two Houses of Parliament?' The Judge stared into the future, dismayed.

'Oh, that's quite unnecessary!' The Chancellor laughed mirthlessly. 'I just get a Judge in this room and say, "Look here, old fellow. You've got it badly. Judgeitis. The Press is after your blood and quite frankly you're a profound embarrassment to us all. Go out to Esher, old boy," I say, "and improve your handicap. I'll give it out that you're retiring early for reasons of health." And then I'll make a speech defending the independence of the Judiciary against scurrilous and unjustified attacks by the Press.'

Guthrie thought about this for what seemed a silent eternity and then said, 'I'm not awfully keen on golf.'

'Why not take up croquet?' The Chancellor seemed anxious to be helpful. 'It's a top-hole retirement game. The women of England are against you. I hear they've been demonstrating outside the Old Bailey.'

'They were only a few extremists.'

'Featherstone, all women are extremists. You

must know that, as a married man.'

'I suppose you're right, Lord Chancellor.' Guthrie now felt his position to be hopeless. 'Retirement! I don't know how Marigold's going to take it.'

The Lord Chancellor still looked like a hanging judge, but he stood up and said in businesslike tones, 'Perhaps it can be postponed in your case. I've talked it over with old Keith.'

'Your right-hand man?' Guthrie felt a faint hope rising.

'Exactly.' The Lord Chancellor seemed to be smiling at some private joke. 'You may have an opportunity some time in the future, in the not-too-distant future, let us hope, to make your peace with the women of England. You may be able to put right what they regard as an injustice to one of their number.'

'You mean, Lord Chancellor, my retirement is off?' Guthrie could scarcely believe it.

'Perhaps adjourned. *Sine die.*'

'Indefinitely?'

'Oh, I'm so glad you keep up with your Latin.' The Chancellor patted Guthrie on the shoulder. It was an order to dismiss. 'So many fellows don't.'

So Guthrie had a reprieve and, in the life of Tony Timson also, dramatic events were taking place. April's friend Chrissie was once married to Shaun Molloy, a well-known safe breaker, but their divorce seemed to have severed her con-

204

nections with the Molloy clan and Tony Timson had agreed to receive and visit her. It was Chrissie who lived on their estate and had given the party before which April and Tony had struggled in the bath together; but it was at Chrissie's house, it seemed, that Peanuts Molloy was to be a visitor. So Tony's friendly feelings had somewhat abated, and when Chrissie rang the chimes on his front door one afternoon when April was out, he received her with a brusque 'What you want?'

'I thought you ought to know, Tony. It's not right.'

'What's not right?'

'Your April and Peanuts. It's not right.'

'You're one to talk, aren't you, Chrissie? April was going round yours to meet Peanuts at a party.'

'He just keeps on coming to mine. I don't invite him. Got no time for Peanuts, quite honestly. But him and your April. They're going out on dates. It's not right. I thought you ought to know.'

'What you mean, dates?' As I have said, Tony's life had not been a bed of roses since his return home, but now he was more than usually troubled.

'He takes her out partying. They're meeting tonight round the offey in Morrison Avenue. Nine thirty time, she told me. Just thought you might like to know, that's all,' the kindly Chrissie added.

So it happened that at nine thirty that night, when Ruby was presiding over an empty off licence in Morrison Avenue, Tony Timson entered it and stood apparently surveying the tempting bottles on display but really waiting to confront

205

the errant April and Peanuts Molloy. He heard a door bang in some private area behind Ruby's counter and then the strip lights stopped humming and the off licence was plunged into darkness. It was not a silent darkness, however; it was filled with the sound of footsteps, scuffling and heavy blows.

Not long afterwards a police car with a wailing siren was screaming towards Morrison Avenue; it was wonderful with what rapidity the Old Bill was summoned whenever Tony Timson was in trouble. When Detective Inspector Brush and his sergeant got into the off licence, their torches illuminated a scene of violence. Two bodies were on the floor. Ruby was lying by the counter, unconscious, and Tony was lying beside some shelves, nearer to the door, with a wound in his forehead. The Sergeant's torch beam showed a heavy cosh lying by his right hand and pound notes scattered around him. 'Can't you leave the women alone, boy?' the Detective Inspector said as Tony Timson slowly opened his eyes.

So another Timson brief came to Rumpole, and Mr Justice Featherstone got a chance to redeem himself in the eyes of the Lord Chancellor and the women of Islington.

Like two knights of old approaching each other for combat, briefs at the ready, helmeted with wigs and armoured with gowns, the young black-haired Sir Hearthrug and the cunning old Sir Horace, with his faithful page Mizz Liz in attendance, met outside Number One Court at the Old Bailey and threw down their challenges.

'Nemesis,' said Hearthrug.

'What's that meant to mean?' I asked him.

'Timson's for it now.'

'Let's hope justice will be done,' I said piously.

'Guthrie's not going to make the same mistake twice.'

'Mr Justice Featherstone's a wise and upright judge,' I told him, 'even if his foot does get into his mouth occasionally.'

'He's a judge with the Lord Chancellor's beady eye upon him, Rumpole.'

'I wasn't aware that this case was going to be decided by the Lord Chancellor.'

'By him and the women of England.' Hearthstoke smiled at Mizz Probert in what I hoped she found a revolting manner. 'Ask your learned Junior.'

'Save your breath for Court, Hearthrug. You may need it.' So we moved on, but as we went my learned Junior disappointed me by saying, 'I don't think Tony Timson should get away with it again.' 'Happily, that's not for you to decide,' I told her. 'We can leave that to the good sense of the Jury.'

However, the Jury, when we saw them assembled, were not a particularly cheering lot. For a start, the women outnumbered the men by eight to four and the women in question looked large and severe. I was at once reminded of the mothers' meetings that once gathered round the guillotine and I seemed to hear, as Hearthstoke opened the prosecution case, the ghostly click of knitting needles.

His opening speech was delivered with a good deal of ferocity and he paused now and again to flash a white-toothed smile at Miss Lorraine Frinton, who sat once more, looking puzzled, in front of her shorthand notebook.

'Members of the Jury,' Hearthrug intoned with great solemnity. 'Even in these days, when we are constantly sickened by crimes of violence, this is a particularly horrible and distressing event. An attack with this dangerous weapon' — here he picked up the cosh, Exhibit One, and waved it at the Jury — 'upon a weak and defenceless woman.'

'Did you say a *woman*, Mr Hearthstoke?' Up spoke the anxious figure of the Red Judge upon the Bench. I cannot believe that pure chance had selected Guthrie Featherstone to preside over Tony Timson's second trial.

Our Judge clearly meant to redeem himself and appear, from the outset, as the dedicated protector of that sex which is sometimes called the weaker by those who have not the good fortune to be married to She Who Must Be Obeyed.

'I'm afraid so, my Lord,' Hearthstoke said, more in anger than in sorrow.

'This man Timson attacked a *woman!*' Guthrie gave the Jury the benefit of his full outrage. I had to put some sort of a stop to this so I rose to say, 'That, my Lord, is something the Jury has to decide.'

'Mr Rumpole,' Guthrie told me, 'I am fully aware of that. All I can say about this case is that should the Jury convict, I take an extremely serious view of any sort of attack on a woman.'

'If they were bathing it wouldn't matter,' I muttered to Liz as I subsided.

'I didn't hear that, Mr Rumpole.'

'Not a laughing matter, my Lord,' I corrected myself rapidly.

'Certainly not. Please proceed, Mr Hearth-stoke.' And here his Lordship whispered to his clerk, Wilfred, 'I'm not having old Rumpole twist me round his little finger in *this* case.'

'Very wise, if I may say so, my Lord,' Wilfred whispered back as he sat beside the Judge, sharpening his pencils.

'Members of the Jury,' an encouraged Hearthstoke proceeded. 'Mrs Ruby Churchill, the innocent victim, works in an off licence near the man Timson's home. Later we shall look at a plan of the premises. The Prosecution does not allege that Timson carried out this robbery alone. He no doubt had an accomplice who entered by an open window at the back of the shop and turned out the lights. Then, we say, under cover of darkness, Timson coshed the unfortunate Mrs Churchill, whose evidence you will hear. The accomplice escaped with most of the money from the till. Timson, happily for justice, slipped and struck his head on the corner of the shelves. He was found in a half-stunned condition, with the cosh and some of the money. When arrested by Detective Inspector Brush he said, "You got me this time, then". You may think that a clear admission of guilt.' And now Hearthstoke was into his peroration. 'Too long, Members of the Jury,' he said, 'have women suffered in our Courts. Too long have men seemed licensed to attack them. Your verdict in this case will be awaited eagerly and hopefully by the women of England.'

I looked at Mizz Liz Probert and I was grieved to note that she was receiving this hypocritical balderdash with starry-eyed attention. During the mercifully short period when the egregious Hearthrug had been a member of our Chambers in Equity Court, I remembered, Mizz Liz had developed an inexplicably soft spot for the fellow. I was pained to see that the spot remained as soft as ever.

Even as we sat in Number One Court, the Islington women were on duty in the street outside bearing placards with the legend JUSTICE FOR WOMEN. Claude Erskine-Brown and Soapy Sam Ballard passed these demonstrators and smiled with some satisfaction. 'Guthrie's in the soup again, Ballard,' Claude told his new friend. 'They're taking to the streets!'

Ruby Churchill, large, motherly, and clearly anxious to tell the truth, was the sort of witness it's almost impossible to cross-examine effectively. When she had told her story to Hearthstoke, I

210

rose and felt the silent hostility of both Judge and Jury.

'Before you saw him in your shop on the night of this attack,' I asked her, 'did you know my client, Mr Timson?'

'I knew him. He lives round the corner.'

'And you knew his wife, April Timson?'

'I know her. Yes.'

'She's been in your shop?'

'Oh, yes, sir.'

'With her husband?'

'Sometimes with him. Sometimes without.'

'Sometimes without? How interesting.'

'Mr Rumpole. Have you many more questions for this unfortunate lady?' Guthrie seemed to have been converted to the view that female witnesses shouldn't be subjected to cross-examination.

'Just a few, my Lord.'

'Please. Mrs Churchill,' his Lordship gushed at Ruby. 'Do take a seat. Make yourself comfortable. I'm sure we all admire the plucky way in which you are giving your evidence. *As a woman.*'

'And as a woman,' I made bold to ask, after Ruby had been offered all the comforts of the witness-box, 'did you know that Tony Timson had been accused of trying to drown his wife in the bath? And that he was tried and bound over?'

'My Lord. How can that possibly be relevant?' Hearthrug arose, considerably narked.

'I was about to ask the same question.' Guthrie

sided with the Prosecution. 'I have no idea what Mr Rumpole is driving at!'

'Oh, I thought your Lordship might remember the case,' I said casually. 'There was some newspaper comment about it at the time.'

'Was there really?' Guthrie affected ignorance. 'Of course, in a busy life one can't hope to read every little paragraph about one's cases that finds its way into the newspapers.'

'This found its way slap across the front page, my Lord.'

'Did it really? Do you remember that, Mr Hearthstoke?'

'I think I remember some rather ill-informed comment, my Lord.' Hearthstoke was not above buttering up the Bench.

'Ill-informed. Yes. No doubt it was. One has so many cases before one . . .' As Guthrie tried to forget the past, I hastily drew the witness back into the proceedings. 'Perhaps your memory is better than his Lordship's?' I suggested to Ruby. 'You remember the case, don't you, Mrs Churchill?'

'Oh, yes. I remember it.' Ruby had no doubt.

'Mr Hearthstoke. Are you objecting to this?' Guthrie was looking puzzled.

'If Mr Rumpole wishes to place his client's previous convictions before the Jury, my Lord, why should I object?' Hearthstoke looked at me complacently, as though I were playing into his hands, and Guthrie whispered to Wilfred, 'Bright chap, this prosecutor.'

212

'And can you remember what you thought about it at the time?' I went on plugging away at Ruby.

'I thought Mr Timson had got away with murder!'

The Jury looked severely at Tony, and Guthrie appeared to think I had kicked a sensational own goal. 'I suppose that was hardly the answer you wanted, Mr Rumpole,' he said.

'On the contrary, my Lord. It was exactly the answer I wanted! And having got away with it then, did it occur to you that someone . . . some avenging angel, perhaps, might wish to frame Tony Timson on this occasion?'

'My lord. That is pure speculation!' Hearthstoke arose, furious, and I agreed with him. 'Of course it is. But it's a speculation I wish to put in the mind of the Jury at the earliest possible opportunity.' So I sat down, conscious that I had at least chipped away at the Jury's certainty. They knew that I should return to the possibility of Tony having been framed and were prepared to look at the evidence with more caution.

That morning two events of great pith and moment occurred in the case of the Queen against Tony Timson. April went shopping in Morrison Avenue and saw something which considerably changed her attitude. Peanuts Molloy and her friend Chrissie were coming out of the off licence with a plastic bag full of assorted bottles. As Peanuts held his car door open for Chrissie they engaged in a passionate and public embrace, unaware that they were doing so in the full view of Mrs April Timson, who uttered the single word 'Bastard!' in the hearing of the young hopeful Vincent who, being on his school holidays, was accompanying his mother. The other important matter was that Guthrie, apparently in a generous mood as he saw a chance of reestablishing his judicial reputation, sent a note to me and Hearthstoke asking if we would be so kind as to join him, and the other judges sitting at the Old Bailey, for luncheon.

Guthrie's invitation came as Hearthstoke was examining Miss Sweating, the schoolmistresslike scientific officer, who was giving evidence as to the bloodstains found about the off licence on the night of the crime. As this evidence was of some importance I should record that blood of Tony Timson's group was traced on the floor and on the corner of the shelf by which he had fallen. Blood of the same group as that which flowed in Mrs Ruby Churchill's veins was to be found on the floor where she lay and on the cosh by Tony's hand. Talk of blood groups, as you will know, acts on me like the smell of greasepaint to an old actor, or the cry of hounds to John Peel. I was pawing the ground and snuffing a little at the nostrils as I rose to cross-examine.

'Miss Sweating,' I began. 'You say there was blood of Timson's group on the corner of the shelf?'

'There was. Yes.'

'And from that you assumed that he had hit his head against the shelf?'

'That seemed the natural assumption. He had been stunned by hitting his head.'

'Or by someone else hitting his head?'

'But the Detective Inspector told me . . .' the witness began, but I interrupted her with 'Listen to me and don't bother about what the Detective Inspector told you!'

'Mr Rumpole!' That grave protector of the female sex on the Bench looked pained. 'Is that the tone to adopt? The witness is a woman!'

'The witness is a scientific officer, my Lord,' I pointed out, 'who pretends to know something about bloodstains. Looking at the photograph of the stains on the corner of the shelf, Miss Sweating, might not they be splashes of blood which fell when the accused was struck in that part of the room?'

Miss Sweating examined the photograph in question through her formidable horn-rims and we were granted two minutes' silence which I broke into at last with 'Would you favour us with an answer, Miss Sweating? Or do you want to exercise a woman's privilege and not make up your mind?'

'Mr Rumpole!' The newly converted feminist judge was outraged. But the witness admitted, 'I suppose they might have got there like that. Yes.'

'They are consistent with his having been struck by an assailant. Perhaps with another weapon sim-

215

ilar to this cosh?'

'Yes,' Miss Sweating agreed, reluctantly.

'Thank you. "Trip no further, pretty sweeting" . . .' I whispered as I sat down, thereby shocking the shockable Mizz Probert.

'Miss Sweating' — Guthrie tried to undo my good work — 'you have also said that the bloodstains on the shelf are consistent with Timson having slipped when he was running out of the shop and striking his head against it?'

'Oh, yes,' Miss Sweating agreed eagerly. 'They are consistent with that, my Lord.'

'Very well.' His Lordship smiled ingratiatingly at the women of the Jury. 'Perhaps the ladies of the Jury would like to take a little light luncheon now?' And he added, more brusquely, 'The gentlemen too, of course. Back at five past two, Members of the Jury.'

When we got out of Court, I saw my learned friend Charles Hearthstoke standing in the corridor in close conversation with the beautiful shorthand writer. He was, I noticed, holding her lightly and unobtrusively by the hand. Mizz Probert, who also noticed this, walked away in considerable disgust.

A large variety of judges sit at the Old Bailey. These include the Old Bailey regulars, permanent fixtures such as the Mad Bull Bullingham and the sepulchral Graves, judges of the lower echelon who wear black gowns. They also include a judge called the Common Sergeant, who is neither common nor a sergeant, and the Recorder who wears red and is the senior Old Bailey judge — a man who has to face, apart from the usual diet of murder, robbery and rape, a daunting number of City dinners. These are joined by the two visiting High Court judges, the Red Judges of the Queen's Bench, of whom Guthrie was one, unless and until the Lord Chancellor decided to put him permanently out to grass. All these judicial figures trough together at a single long table in a back room of the Bailey. They do it, and the sight comes as something of a shock to the occasional visitor, wearing their wigs. The sight of Judge Bullingham's angry and purple face ingesting stew and surmounted with horse-hair is only for the strongest stomachs. They are joined by various City aldermen and officials wearing lace jabots and tailed coats and other guests from the Bar or from the world of business.

Before the serious business of luncheon begins, the company is served sherry, also taken whilst wearing wigs, and I was ensconced in a corner where I could overhear a somewhat strange preliminary conversation between our judge and Counsel for the Prosecution.

'Ah, Hearth*stoke*,' Guthrie greeted him. 'I thought I'd invite both Counsel to break bread with me. Just want to make sure neither of you had anything to object to about the trial.'

'Of course not, Judge!' Hearthstoke was smiling. 'It's been a very pleasant morning. Made even more pleasant by the appearance of the shorthand writer.'

'The . . . ? Oh, yes! Pretty girl, is she? I hadn't noticed,' Guthrie fibbed.

'Hadn't you? Lorraine said you'd been extraordinarily kind to her. She so much appreciated the beautiful pot plant you sent her.'

'Pot plant?' Guthrie looked distinctly guilty, but Hearthstoke pressed on with 'Something rather gorgeous she told me. With pink blooms. Didn't she help you straighten out the shorthand note in the last Timson case?'

'She corrected her mistake,' Guthrie said carefully.

'*Her* mistake, was it?' Hearthstoke was looking at the Judge. 'She said it'd been yours.'

'Perhaps we should all sit down now.' Guthrie was keen to end this embarrassing scene. 'Oh and, Hearthstoke, no need to mention that business of the pot plant around the Bailey. Otherwise they'll all be wanting one.' He gave a singularly unconvincing laugh. 'I can't give pink blooms to everyone, including Rumpole!'

'Of course, Judge.' Hearthstoke was understanding. 'No need to mention it at all *now*.'

'*Now?*'

'Now,' the Prosecutor said firmly, 'justice is going to be done to Timson. At last.'

Guthrie seemed thankful to move away and find his place at the table, until he discovered that I had been put next to him. He made the best of it, pushed one of the decanters in my direction and hoped I was quite satisfied with the fairness of the proceedings.

'Are *you* content with the fairness of the proceedings?' I asked him.

'Yes, of course. I'm the Judge, aren't I?'

'Are you sure?'

'What on earth's that meant to mean?'

'Haven't you asked yourself why you, a High Court judge, a Red Judge, have been given a paltry little robbery with violence?' I refreshed myself with a generous gulp of the City of London's claret.

'I suppose it's the luck of the draw.'

'Luck of the draw, my eye! I detect the subtle hand of old Keith from the Lord Chancellor's office.'

'Keith?' His Lordship looked around him nervously.

'Oh, yes. "Give Guthrie *Timson*," he said. "Give him a chance to redeem himself by potting the fellow and sending him down for ten years. The women of England will give three hearty cheers and Featherstone will be the Lord Chancellor's blue-eyed boy again." Don't fall for it! You can be better than that, if you put your mind to it. Sum up according to the evidence and the hell with the Lord Chancellor's office!'

'Horace! I don't think I've heard anything you've been saying.'

'It's up to you, old darling. Are you a man or a rubber stamp for the Civil Service?'

Guthrie looked round desperately for a new subject of conversation and his eye fell on our prosecutor who was being conspicuously bored by an elderly alderman. 'That young Hearthstoke seems a pretty able sort of fellow,' he said.

'Totally ruthless,' I told him. 'He'd stop at nothing to win a case.'

'Nothing?'

'Absolutely nothing.'

Guthrie took the decanter and started to pour wine into his own glass. His hand was trembling slightly and he was staring at Hearthstoke in a haunted way.

'Horace,' he started confidentially, 'you've been practising at the Old Bailey for a considerable number of years.'

'Almost since the dawn of time.'

'And you can see nothing wrong with a judge, impressed by the hard work of a court official, say a shorthand writer, for instance, sending that official some little token of gratitude?'

'What sort of token are you speaking of, Judge?'

'Something like' — he gulped down wine — 'a pot plant.'

'A plant?'

'In a pot. With pink blossoms.'

'Pink blossoms, eh?' I thought it over. 'That sounds quite appropriate.'

'You can see nothing in any way improper in such a gift, Horace?' The Judge was deeply grateful.

'Nothing improper at all. A "Busy Lizzie"?'

'I think her name's Lorraine.'

'Nothing wrong with that.'

'You reassure me, Horace. You comfort me very much.' He took another swig of the claret and looked fearfully at Hearthstoke. Poor old Guthrie Featherstone, he spent most of his judicial life painfully perched between the horns of various dilemmas.

'In the car after we arrested him, driving away from the off licence, Tony Timson said, "You got me this time, then," ' This was the evidence of that hammer of the Timsons, Detective Inspector Brush. When he had given it, Hearthstoke looked hard at the Jury to emphasize the point, thanked the officer profusely and I rose to cross-examine.

'Detective Inspector. Do you know a near neighbour of the Timsons named Peter, better known as "Peanuts", Molloy?'

'Mr Peter Molloy is known to the police, yes,' the Inspector answered cautiously.

'He and his brother Greg are leading lights of the Molloy firm? Fairly violent criminals?'

'Yes, my Lord,' Brush told the Judge.

'Have you known both Peanuts and his brother to use coshes like this one in the course of crime?'

'Well. Yes, possibly . . .'

'My Lord, I really must object!' Hearthstoke was on his feet and Guthrie said, 'Mr Rumpole. Your client's own character . . .'

'He is a petty thief, my Lord.' I was quick to put Tony's character before the Jury. 'Tape-recorders and freezer-packs. No violence in his

221

record, is there, Inspector?'

'Not up to now, my Lord,' Brush agreed reluctantly.

'Very well. Did you think he had been guilty of that attempted murder charge, after he and his wife quarrelled in the bathroom?'

'I thought so, yes.'

'You were called to the scene very quickly when the quarrel began.'

'A neighbour called us.'

'Was that neighbour a member of the Molloy family?'

'Mr Rumpole, I prefer not to answer that question.'

'I won't press it.' I left the Jury to speculate. 'But you think he got off lightly at his first trial?' I was reading the note Tony Timson had scribbled in the dock while listening to the evidence as D.I. Brush answered, 'I thought so, yes.'

'What he actually said in the car was "I suppose you think you got me this time, then?" '

'No.' Brush looked at his notebook. 'He just said, "You got me this time, then." '

'You left out the words "I suppose you think" because you don't want him to get off lightly this time?'

'Now would I do a thing like that, sir?' Brush gave us his most honestly pained expression.

'That, Inspector Brush, is a matter for this Jury to decide.' And the Jury looked, by now, as though they were prepared to consider all the possibilities.

Lord Justice MacWhitty's wife, it seems, met Marigold Featherstone in Harrods, and told her she was sorry that Guthrie had such a terrible attitude to women. There was one old judge, apparently, who made his wife walk behind him when he went on circuit, carrying the luggage, and Lady MacWhitty said she felt that poor Marigold was married to just such a tyrant. When we finally discussed the whole history of the Tony Timson case at the Chambers party, Guthrie told me that Marigold had said that she was sick and tired of women coming up to her and feeling sorry for her in Harrods.

'You see,' Guthrie had said to his wife, 'if Timson gets off, the Lord Cnancellor and all the women of England will be down on me like a ton of bricks. But the evidence isn't entirely satisfactory. It's just possible he's innocent. It's hard to tell where a fellow's duty lies.'

'Your duty, Guthrie, lies in keeping your nose clean!' Marigold had no doubt about it.

'My nose?'

'Clean. For the sake of your family. And if this Timson has to go inside for a few years, well, I've no doubt he richly deserves it.'

'Nothing but decisions!'

'I really don't know what else you expected when you became a judge.' Marigold poured herself a drink. Seeking some comfort after a hard day, the Judge went off to soak in a hot bath. In doing so, I believe Lady Featherstone made it clear to him, he was entirely on his own.

Things were no easier in the Rumpole household. I was awakened at some unearthly hour by the wireless booming in the living-room and I climbed out of bed to see Hilda, clad in a dressing-gown and hairnet, listening to the device with her pencil and notebook poised whilst it greeted her brightly with 'Good morning, students. This is first-year Criminal Law on the Open University. I am Richard Snellgrove, law teacher at Hollowfield Polytechnic, to help you on this issue. . . . Can a wife give evidence against her husband?'

'Good God!' I asked her, 'what time does the Open University open?'

'For many years a wife could not give evidence against her husband,' Snellgrove told us. 'See *R.* v. *Boucher* 1952. Now, since the Police and Criminal Evidence Act 1984, a wife can be called to give such evidence.'

'You see, Rumpole.' Hilda took a note. 'You'd better watch out!' I found and lit the first small cigar of the day and coughed gratefully. Snellgrove continued to teach me law. 'But she can't be compelled to. She has been a competent witness for the defence of her husband since the Criminal Evidence Act 1898. But a judgment in the House of Lords suggests she's not compellable . . .'

'What's that mean, Rumpole?' She asked me.

'Well, we could ask April Timson to give evidence for Tony. But we couldn't make her,' I began to explain, and then, perhaps because I

224

was in a state of shock from being awoken so early, I had an idea of more than usual brilliance. 'April Timson!' I told Hilda, 'she won't know she's not compellable. I don't suppose she tunes into the "Open at Dawn University". Now I wonder . . .'

'What, Rumpole. What do you wonder?'

'Quarter to six.' I looked at the clock on the mantelpiece. 'High time to wake up Bernard.' I went to the phone and started to dial my instructing solicitor's number.

'You see how useful I'll be to you' — Hilda looked extremely pleased with herself — 'when I come to work in your Chambers.'

'Oh, Bernard,' I said to the telephone, 'wake you up, did I? Well, it's time to get moving. The Open University's been open for hours. Look, an idea has just crossed my mind . . .'

'It crossed *my* mind, Rumpole,' Hilda corrected me. 'And I was kind enough to hand it on to you.'

When Mr Bernard called on April Timson an hour later, there was no need for him to go into the nice legal question of whether she was a compellable witness or not. Since she had seen Peanuts and her friend Chrissie come out of the 'offey' she was, she made it clear, ready and willing to come to Court and tell her whole story.

'Mrs April Timson,' I asked Tony's wife when, to the surprise of most people in Court including my client, she entered the witness-box, as a wit-

225

ness for the defence, 'some while ago you had a quarrel with your husband in a bathtub. What was that quarrel about?'

'Peanuts Molloy.'

'About a man called Peter "Peanuts" Molloy. What did you tell your husband about Peanuts?'

'About him as a man, like. . . . ?'

'Did you compare the virility of these two gentlemen?'

'Yes, I did.' April was able to cope with this part of the evidence without embarrassment.

'And who got the better of the comparison?'

'Peanuts.' Tony, lowering his head, got his first look of sympathy from the Jury.

'Was there a scuffle in your bath then?'

'Yes.'

'Mrs April Timson, did your husband ever try to drown you?'

'No. He never.' Her answer caused a buzz in Court. Guthrie stared at her, incredulous.

'Why did you suggest he did?' I asked. 'My Lord. I object. What possible relevance?' Hearthrug tried to interrupt but I and everyone else ignored him. 'Why did you suggest he tried to murder you?' I repeated.

'I was angry with him, I reckon,' April told us calmly, and the Prosecutor lost heart and subsided. The Judge, however, pursued the matter with a pained expression. 'Do I understand,' he asked, 'you made an entirely false accusation against your husband?'

226

'Yes.' April didn't seem to think it an unusual thing to do.

'Don't you realize, madam,' the Judge said, 'the suffering that accusation has brought to innocent people?' 'Such as you, old cock,' I muttered to Mizz Liz.

'What was that, Rumpole?' the Judge asked me. 'Such as the man in the dock, my Lord,' I repeated.

'And other innocent, innocent people.' His Lordship shook his head sadly and made a note.

'After your husband's trial did you continue to see Mr Peanuts Molloy?' I went on with my questions to the uncompellable witness.

'We went out together. Yes.'

'Where did you meet?'

'We met round the offey in Morrison Avenue. Then we went out in his car.'

'Did you meet him at the off licence on the night this robbery took place?'

'I never.' April was sure of it.

'Your husband says that your neighbour Chrissie came round and told him that you and Peanuts Molloy were going to meet at the off licence at nine thirty that evening. So he went up there to put a stop to your affair.'

'Well, Chrissie was well in with Peanuts by then, wasn't she?' April smiled cynically. 'I reckon he sent her to tell Tony that.'

'Why do you reckon he sent her?'

Hearthstoke rose again, determined. 'My Lord, I must object,' he said. 'What this witness "reckons" is entirely inadmissible.' When he had finished, I asked the Judge if I might have a word with my learned friend in order to save time. I then moved along our row and whispered to him vehemently, 'One more peep out of you, Hearthrug, and I lay a formal complaint on your conduct!'

'What conduct?' he whispered back.

'Trying to blackmail a learned judge on the matter of a pot plant sent to a shorthand writer.' I looked across at Lorraine. 'Not in the best traditions of the Bar, that!' I left him thinking hard and went back to my place. After due consideration he said, 'My Lord. On second thoughts, I withdraw my objection.'

Hearthstoke resumed his seat. I smiled at him cheerfully and continued with April's evidence. 'So why do you think Peanuts wanted to get your husband up to the off licence that evening?'

'Pretty obvious, innit?'

'Explain it to us.'

'So he could put him in the frame. Make it look like Tony done Ruby up, like.'

'So he could put him in the frame. An innocent man!' I looked at the Jury. 'Had Peanuts said anything to make you think he might do such a thing?'

'After the first trial.'

'After Mr Timson was bound over?'

'Yes. Peanuts said he reckoned Tony needed a bit of justice, like. He said he was going to see he got put inside. 'Course, Peanuts didn't mind making a bit hisself, out of robbing the offey.'

'One more thing, Mrs Timson. Have you ever seen a weapon like that before?'

I held up the cosh. The Usher came and took it to the witness.

'I saw that one. I think I did.'

'Where?'

'In Peanuts' car. That's where he kept it.'

'Did your husband ever own anything like that?'

'What, Tony?' April weighed the cosh in her hand and clearly found the idea ridiculous. 'Not him. He wouldn't have known what to do with it.'

When the evidence was complete and we had made our speeches, Guthrie had to sum up the case of *R.* v. *Timson* to the Jury. As he turned his chair towards them, and they prepared to give him their full attention, a distinguished visitor slipped unobtrusively into the back of the Court. He was none other than old Keith from the Lord Chancellor's office. The Judge must have seen him, but he made no apology for his previous lenient treatment of Tony Timson.

'Members of the Jury,' he began. 'You have heard of the false accusation of attempted murder that Mrs Timson made against an innocent man. Can you imagine, Members of the Jury, what misery that poor man has been made to suffer? Devoted to ladies as he may be, he has been called a heartless "male chauvinist". Gentle and

harmless by nature, he has been thought to con-
nive at crimes of violence. Perhaps it was even
suggested that he was the sort of fellow who would
make his wife carry heavy luggage! He may well
have been shunned in the streets, hooted at from
the pavements, and the wife he truly loves has
perhaps been unwilling to enter a warm, domestic bath with him. And then, consider,'
Guthrie went on, 'if the unhappy Timson may
not have also been falsely accused in relation to
the robbery with violence of his local "offey".
Justice must be done, Members of the Jury. We
must do justice even if it means we do nothing
else for the rest of our lives but compete in croquet
competitions.' The Judge was looking straight at
Keith from the Lord Chancellor's office as he
said this. I relaxed, lay back and closed my eyes.
I knew, after all his troubles, how his Lordship
would feel about a man falsely accused, and I
had no further worries about the fate of Tony
Timson.

When I got home, Hilda was reading the result
of the trial in the *Evening Sentinel.* 'I suppose
you're cock-a-hoop, Rumpole,' she said.
'Hearthrug routed!' I told ber. 'The women
of England back on our side and old Keith from
the Lord Chancellor's office looking extremely
foolish. And a miraculous change came over
Guthrie.'
'What?'
'He suddenly found courage. It's something you

can't do without, not if you concern yourself with justice.'

'That April Timson!' Hilda looked down at her evening paper. 'Making it all up about being drowned in the bathwater.'

'When lovely woman stoops to folly' — I went to the sideboard and poured a celebratory glass of Château Thames Embankment — 'And finds too late that men betray,/What charm can soothe her melancholy . . .'

'I'm not going to the Bar to protect people like her, Rumpole.' Hilda announced her decision. 'She's put me to a great deal of trouble. Getting up at a quarter to six every morning for the Open University.'

' "What art can wash her guilt away?" *What* did you say, Hilda?'

'I'm not going to all that trouble, learning Real Property and Company Law and eating dinners and buying a wig, not for the likes of April Timson.'

'Oh, Hilda! Everyone in Chambers will be extremely disappointed.'

'Well, I'm sorry.' She had clearly made up her mind. 'They'll just have to do without me. I've really got better things to do, Rumpole, than come home cock-a-hoop just because April Timson changes her mind and decides to tell the truth.'

'Of course you have, Hilda.' I drank gratefully. 'What sort of better things?'

'Keeping you in order for one, Rumpole. Seeing you wash up properly.' And then she spoke with considerable feeling. 'It's disgusting!'

'The washing up?'

'No. People having baths together.'

'Married people?' I reminded her.

'I don't see that makes it any better. Don't you ever ask me to do that, Rumpole.'

'Never, Hilda. I promise faithfully.' To hear, of course, was to obey.

That night's *Sentinel* contained a leading article which appeared under the encouraging headline BATHTUB JUDGE PROVED RIGHT. *Mrs April Timson, it read, has admitted that her husband never tried to drown her and the Jury have acquitted Tony Timson on a second trumped-up charge. It took a Judge of Mr Justice Featherstone's perception and experience to see through this woman's inventions and exaggerations and to uphold the law without fear or favour. Now and again the British legal system produces a Judge of exceptional wisdom and integrity who refuses to yield to pressure groups and does justice though the heavens fall. Such a one is Sir Guthrie Featherstone.*

Sir Guthrie told me later that he read these comforting words whilst lying in a warm bath in his flat near Harrods. I have no doubt at all that Lady Featherstone was with him on that occasion, seated at the tap end.

# Rumpole and the Chambers Party

Christmas comes but once a year. Once a year I receive a gift of socks from She Who Must Be Obeyed; each year I add to her cellar of bottles of lavender water, which she now seems to use mainly for the purpose of 'laying down' in the bedroom cupboard (I suspect she has only just started on the 1980 vintage).

Tinselled cards and sprigs of holly appear at the entrance to the cells under the Old Bailey and a constantly repeated tape of 'God Rest Ye Merry Gentlemen' adds little zest to my two eggs, bacon and sausage on a fried slice in the Taste-Ee-Bite, Fleet Street; and once a year the Great Debate takes place at our December meeting. Should we invite solicitors to our Chambers party?

'No doubt at the season of our Saviour's birth we should offer hospitality to all sorts and conditions of men . . .' 'Soapy' Sam Ballard, Q.C., our devout Head of Chambers, opened the proceedings in his usual manner, that of a somewhat backward bishop addressing Synod on the wisdom of offering the rites of baptism to non-practising, gay Anglican converts of riper years.

'All conditions of men and *women.*' Phillida Erskine-Brown, Q.C., née Trant, the Portia of our Chambers, was looking particularly fetching in a well-fitting black jacket and an only slightly flippant version of a male collar and tie. As she looked doe-eyed at him, Ballard, who hides a ridiculously susceptible heart beneath his monkish exterior, conceded her point. 'The question before us is, does all sorts and conditions of men, and women too, of course, include members of the junior branch of the legal profession?'

'I'm against it!' Claude Erskine-Brown had remained an ageing junior whilst his wife Phillida fluttered into silk, and he was never in favour of radical change. 'The party is very much a family thing for the chaps in Chambers, and the clerk's room, of course. If we ask solicitors it looks very much as though we're touting for briefs.'

'I'm very much in favour of touting for briefs.' Up spake the somewhat grey barrister, Hoskins. 'Speaking as a man with four daughters to educate. For heaven's sake, let's ask as many solicitors as we know, which, in my case, I'm afraid, is not many.'

'Do you have a view, Rumpole?' Ballard felt bound to ask me, just as a formality.

'Well, yes, nothing wrong with a bit of touting, I agree with Hoskins. But I'm in favour of asking the people who really provide us with work.'

'You mean solicitors?'

'I mean the criminals of England. Fine conservative fellows who should appeal to you, Ballard. Greatly in favour of free enterprise and against the closed shop. I propose we invite a few of the better-class crooks who have no previous engagements as guests of Her Majesty, and show our gratitude.'

A somewhat glazed look came over the assembly at this suggestion and then Mrs Erskine-Brown broke the silence with 'Claude's really being awfully stuffy and old-fashioned about this. I propose we invite a smattering of solicitors, from the better-class firms.'

Our Portia's proposal was carried *nem con*, such was the disarming nature of her sudden smile on everyone, including her husband, who may have had some reason to fear it. Rumpole's suggestion, to nobody's surprise, received no support whatsoever.

Our clerk, Henry, invariably arranged the Chambers party for the night on which his wife put on the Nativity play in the Bexley Heath Comprehensive at which she was a teacher. This gave him more scope for kissing Dianne, our plucky but some what hit-and-miss typist, beneath the mistletoe which swung from the dim, religious light in the entrance hall of number three, Equity Court.

Paper streamers dangled from the bookcase full of All England Law Reports in Ballard's room and were hooked up to his views of the major English cathedrals. Barristers' wives were invited, and Mrs Hilda Rumpole, known to me only as She Who Must Be Obeyed, was downing sherry and telling Soapy Sam all about the golden days when her Daddy, C. H. Wystan, ran Chambers. There were also six or seven solicitors among those present.

One, however, seemed superior to all the rest, a solicitor of the class we seldom see around Equity Court. He had come in with one hand outstretched to Ballard, saying, 'Daintry Naismith, Happy Christmas. Awfully kind of you fellows to invite one of the junior branch.' Now he stood propped up against the mantelpiece, warming his undoubtedly Savile Row trousers at Ballard's gas fire and receiving the homage of barristers in urgent need of briefs.

He appeared to be in his well-preserved fifties, with grey wings of hair above his ears and a clean-shaven, pink and still single chin poised above what I took to be an old Etonian tie. Whatever he might have on offer it wouldn't, I was sure, be a charge of nicking a frozen chicken from Safeways. Even his murders, I thought, as he sized us up from over the top of his gold-rimmed half glasses, would take place among the landed gentry.

He accepted a measure of Pommeroy's very ordinary white plonk from Portia and drank it bravely, as though he hadn't been used to sipping Chassagne-Montrachet all his adult life.

'Mrs Erskine-Brown,' he purred at her, 'I'm looking for a hard-hitting silk to brief in the Family Division. I suppose you're tremendously booked up.'

'The pressure of my work,' Phillida said modestly, 'is enormous.'

'I've got the Geoffrey Twyford divorce coming. Pretty hairy bit of in-fighting over the estate and the custody of young Lord Shiplake. I thought you'd be just right for it.'

'Is that the Duke of Twyford?' Claude Erskine-Brown looked suitably awestruck. In spite of his other affectations Erskine-Brown's snobbery is completely genuine.

'Well, if you have a word with Henry, my clerk' — Mrs Erskine-Brown gave the solicitor a look of cool availability — 'he might find a few spare dates.'

'Well, that is good of you. And you, Mr Erskine-Brown, mainly civil work now, I suppose?'

'Oh, yes. Mainly civil.' Erskine-Brown lied cheerfully; he's not above taking on the odd indecent assault when tort gets a little thin on the ground. 'I do find crime so sordid.'

'Oh, I agree. Look here. I'm stumped for a man to take on our insurance business, but I suppose you'd be far too busy.'

'Oh, no. I've got plenty of time.' Erskine-Brown lacked his wife's laid-back approach to solicitors. 'That is to say, I'm sure I could make time. One gets used to extremely long hours, you know.' I thought that the longest hours Erskine-Brown put in were when he sat, in grim earnest, through the *Ring* at Covent Garden, being a man who submits himself to Wagner rather as others enjoy walking from Land's End to John O'Groats.

And then I saw Naismith staring at me and waited for him to announce that the Marquess of Something or Other had stabbed his butler in the library and could I possibly make myself available for the trial. Instead he muttered, 'Frightfully good party,' and wandered off in the general direction of Soapy Sam Ballard.

'What's the matter with you, Rumpole?' She Who Must Be Obeyed was at my elbow and not sounding best pleased. 'Why didn't you push yourself forward?' Erskine-Brown had also moved off by this time to join the throng.

'I don't care for divorce,' I told her. 'It's too bloodthirsty for me. Now if he'd offered me a nice gentle murder . . .'

'Go after him, Rumpole,' she urged me, 'and make yourself known. I'll go and ask Phillida what her plans are for the Harrods sale.' Perhaps it was the mention of the sales which spurted me towards that undoubted source of income, Mr Daintry Naismith. I found him talking to Ballard in a way which showed, in my view, a gross over-estimation of that old darling's forensic powers. 'Of course the client would have to understand that the golden tongue of Samuel Ballard, Q.C., can't be hired on the cheap,' Naismith was saying. I thought that to refer to our Head of Chambers, whose voice in Court could best be compared to a rusty saw, as 'golden-tongued' was a bit of an exaggeration.

'I'll have to think it over.' Ballard was flattered but cautious. 'One does have certain principles about' — he gulped, rather in the manner of a fish struggling with its conscience — 'encouraging the publication of explicitly sexual material.'

'Think it over, Mr Ballard. I'll be in touch

with your clerk.' And then, as Naismith saw me approach, he said, 'Perhaps I'll have a word with him now.' So this legal Santa Claus moved away in the general direction of Henry and once more Rumpole was left with nothing in his stocking.

'By the way,' I asked Ballard. 'Did you invite that extremely smooth solicitor?'

'No, I think Henry did.' Our Head of Chambers spoke as a man whose thoughts are on knottier problems. 'Charming chap, though, isn't he?'

Later in the course of the party I found myself next to Henry. 'Good work inviting Mr Daintry Naismith,' I said to our clerk. 'He seems set on providing briefs for everyone except me.'

'I don't really know the gentleman,' Henry admitted. 'I think he must be a friend of Mr Ballard's. Of course we hope to see a lot of him in the future.'

Much later, in search of a small cigar, I remembered the box, still in its special Christmas reindeer-patterned wrapping, that I had left in my brief tray. I opened the door of the clerk's room and found the lights off and Henry's desk palely lit by the old gas lamp outside in Equity Court.

There was a dark-suited figure standing beside the desk who seemed to be trying the locked drawers rather in the casual way that suspicious-looking youths test car handles. I switched on the light and found myself staring at our star solicitor guest. And as I looked at him, the years rolled away and I was in Court defending a bent house agent. Beside him in the dock had been an equally curved solicitor's clerk who had joined my client as a guest of Her Majesty.

'Derek Newton,' I said. 'Inner London Sessions. Raising mortgages on deserted houses that you didn't own. Two years.'

'I knew you'd recognize me, Mr Rumpole. Sooner or later.'

'What the hell do you think you are doing?'

'I'm afraid . . . well, barristers' chambers are about the only place where you can find a bit of petty cash lying about at Christmas.' The man seemed resolved to have no secrets from Rumpole.

'You admit it?'

'Things aren't too easy when you're knocking sixty, and the business world's full of wide boys up to all the tricks. You can't get far on one good suit and the Old Etonian tie nowadays. You always defend, don't you, Rumpole? That's what I've heard. Well, I can only appeal to you for leniency.'

'But coming to our party,' I said, staggered by this most confident of tricksters, 'promising briefs to all the learned friends . . .'

'I always wanted to be admitted as a solicitor.' He smiled a little wistfully. 'I usually walk through the Temple at Christmas time. Sometimes I drop in to the parties. And I always make a point of offering work. It's a pleasure to see so many grateful faces. This is, after all, Mr Rumpole, the season of giving.'

What could I do? All he had got out of us,

240

after all, was a couple of glasses of Pommeroy's Fleet Street white; that and the five pound note he 'borrowed' from me for his cab fare home. I went back to the party and explained to Ballard that Mr Daintry Naismith had made a phone call and had to leave on urgent business.

'He's offered me a highly remunerative brief, Rumpole, defending a publisher of dubious books. It's against my principles, but even the greatest sinner has a right to have his case put before the Court . . .'

'And put by your golden tongue, old darling,' I flattered him. 'If you take my advice you'll go for it.'

It was, after all, the season of goodwill, and I couldn't find it in my heart to spoil Soapy Sam Ballard's Christmas.

# Rumpole and Portia

This is a story of family life, of parents and children, and, like many such stories, it began with a quarrel. There was I, ensconced one evening in a quiet corner of Pommeroy's Wine Bar consuming a lonely glass of Château Thames Embankment at the end of a day's labours, when the voices of a couple in dispute came drifting over from the other side of one of Jack Pommeroy's high-backed pews which give such an ecclesiastical air to his distinguished legal watering-hole. The voices I heard were well known to me, being those of my learned friend, Claude Erskine-Brown, and of his spouse, Mrs Phillida Erskine-Brown, née Trant, the Portia of our Chambers, whom I befriended and advised when she was a white-wig, and who, no doubt taking advantage of that advice, rose to take silk and become a Queen's Counsel when Claude was denied that honour, and thus had his nose put seriously out of joint. The union of Claude and Phillida has been blessed with a girl and a boy named, because of Claude's almost masochistic addiction to the lengthier operas of Richard Wagner (and an opera isn't by Richard Wagner if it's not lengthy), Tristan and Isolde. It was the subject of young Tristan which was causing dissension between his parents that evening.

'Tristan was still in bed at quarter to eight this morning,' Claude was complaining. 'He won't be able to do that when he goes away to Bogstead.'

'Please, Claude' — Phillida sounded terminally bored — 'don't go on about it.'

'You know when I was at Bogstead' — no Englishman can possibly resist talking about his boarding-school — 'we used to be woken up at half past six for early class, and we had to break the ice in the dormy wash-basins.'

'You have told me that, Claude, quite often.'

'We had to run three times round Tug's Patch before early church on saints' days.'

'Did you enjoy that?'

'Of course not! I absolutely hated it.' Claude was looking back, apparently on golden memories.

'Why do you imagine Tristan would enjoy it then?'

'You don't *enjoy* Bogstead,' Claude was pointing out patiently. 'You're not meant to enjoy it. But if I hadn't gone there I wouldn't have got into Winchester and if I hadn't got into Winchester I'd never have been to New College. And I'll tell you something, Philly. If I hadn't been to Bogstead, Winchester and New College, I'd never be what I am.'

'Which might be just as well.' Our Portia sounded cynical.

'Whatever do you mean by that?' Claude was nettled. I strained my ears to listen; things were obviously getting nasty.

'It might be just as well if you weren't the

man you are,' Claude's wife told him. 'If you hadn't been at Bogstead you might not make such a terrible fuss about losing that gross indecency today. I mean, the way you carried on about that, you must still be in the fourth form at Boggers. I notice you don't talk about sending Isolde to that dump.'

'Bogstead is not a dump,' Claude said proudly. 'And you may not have noticed this, Philly, but Isolde is a girl. They don't *have* girls there.'

'Oh, I see. It's a boy's world, is it?'

'I didn't say that.'

'Poor old Isolde. She's going to miss all the fun of breaking the ice at six thirty in the morning and running three times round Tug's Patch on saints' days. Poor deprived child. She might even grow up to be a Queen's Counsel.'

'Come on, Philly. Isn't that a bit . . . ?'

'A bit what?' I had taught Phillida to be dead sharp on her cross-examination.

'Well, not quite the thing to say. Of course I'm terrifically glad you've been made a Q.C. I think you've done jolly well.'

'For a woman!' A short, somewhat bitter laugh from Mrs Erskine-Brown emphasized her point.

'But it's just not "the thing" to crow about it.' Erskine-Brown spoke with the full moral authority of his prep school and Winchester.

'Sorry, Claude! I don't know what "the thing" is. Such a pity I never went to Boggers. Anyway, I don't see the point of having children if you're going to send them away to boarding-school.'

At that point, and much to my regret, the somewhat grey and tedious barrister named Hoskins of our Chambers, a man weighed down with the responsibility of four daughters, sat down at my table in order to complain about the extortionate price of coffee in our clerk's room, and I lost the rest of the Erskine-Brown family dispute. However, I have given you enough of it to show the nature of their disagreement and Phillida's reluctance to part with her young hopeful. These were matters which were to assume great importance in the defence of Stanley Culp on a charge of illicit arms dealing, for Stanley was a father who would have found our Portia's views entirely sympathetic.

In most other respects, the home life of the Culps and the Erskine-Browns was as different as chalk and cheese. Stanley Culp was a plump, remorselessly cheerful, disorganized dealer in second-hand furniture — bits of junk and dubious antiques — in a jumbled shop near Notting Hill Gate. Unlike the Erskine-Browns, the Culps were a one-parent family, for Stanley was in sole charge of his son, Matthew, a scholarly, bespectacled little boy of about Tristan's age. Some three and a half years before, Mrs Culp, so Stanley informed me when we met in Brixton prison, had told her husband that he had 'nothing romantic in his nature whatever'. 'So she took off with the Manager of Tesco's, twenty years older than me if he was a day. Can you understand that, Mr Rumpole?'

I have long given up trying to understand the inscrutable ways of women in love, but I did come to understand Stanley Culp's attachment to his son. My son Nicky and I enjoyed a similar rapport when we used to walk in the park together and I would tell him the Sherlock Holmes stories in the days before he took up the mysterious study of sociology and went to teach in Florida. It was for young Matthew's sake, Stanley Culp told me, that he preferred to work at home in his antique business. 'We are good companions, Mr Rumpole. And I have to be there when he comes home from school. I don't approve of these latch-key children, left alone to do their homework until Mum and Dad come back from the office.'

The events which drew me and Stanley Culp together took place early one morning, not long before I heard the Erskine-Browns arguing in Pommeroy's. Young Matthew, a better cook and housekeeper than his father, was making the breakfast in the kitchen upstairs whilst Stanley was engaged in some business with an early caller in the shop below. Matthew put bread in the antique electric toaster, heard a car door slam, and then looked out of the window. What he saw was an unmarked car which in fact contained three officers of the Special Branch in plain clothes. A fourth man, wearing slightly tinted gold-rimmed glasses, who will have some importance in this account, was walking away from the car and paused to look up at the shop. Then the toast popped up and Matthew transferred it to a tarnished 'Georgian' rack and went to the top of the staircase which led down to the shop to call his father up for breakfast.

From his viewpoint at the top of the stairs Matthew saw the familiar jumble of piled tables, chairs and other furniture, and he saw Stanley talking to a thick-set, ginger-haired man who was carrying a brief-case. Matthew said, 'Breakfast, Dad!', at which moment the shop door was kicked open and two of the men from the car, Superintendent Rodney and Detective Inspector Blake, were among the junk and informing Stanley that they were officers of the Special Branch who had come to arrest him. As they said this, the thick-set ginger-haired man, whose name turned out to be MacRobert, made a bolt for the back door and was out in the untidy patch of walled garden behind the building. He was there pursued by a third officer from the car, Detective Sergeant Trump, and shot dead in what Trump took to be the act of pulling out a gun. MacRobert, it transpired at the trial, was an important figure in a Protestant paramilitary group dedicated to open warfare in Northern Ireland.

Stanley was removed in the car and a subsequent search revealed, in a large storeroom behind his shop, a number of packing-cases filled with repeating rifles of a forbidden category. Matthew didn't go to school that day, but a woman police constable and a social worker arrived for him and he was taken into the care of the local council. His fate was that which Phillida feared for young Tristan; he was sent away from home to be brought up by strangers.

Unhappiness, you see, was getting in every-where, not only *à côté de chez* Erskine-Brown, but also among the Culps. And things had also taken an unfortunate turn in the Rumpole house-hold. I came back one evening to the mansion flat in the Gloucester Road, and, as I unlocked the front door, I heard the usual cry of 'Is that you, Rumpole?'

'Good heavens, no!' I called back. 'It's the Lord High Chancellor of England just dropped in to read the meter. What're you talking about, Hilda?'

'Ssh, Rumpole,' Hilda said mysteriously. 'It's Boxey!'

'Is it? Just a little fresh, I noticed, coming out of the Underground.'

'No. It's Boxey Horne. You must have heard me speak of my second cousin. Cousin Nancy's youngest.' We had spent many hours discussing the complexities of Hilda's family tree, but I couldn't immediately recollect the name. 'We were so close when we were youngsters but Boxey felt the call of Africa. He rang up this afternoon from Paddington Station.'

A masculine voice called through the open sit-ting-room door, 'Is that old Horace, back from the treadmill?'

'Boxey?' I was perplexed. 'Yes, of course.' And Hilda warned me, 'You will try and behave yourself, won't you, Rumpole?'

With that she led me into our sitting-room where a skinny, elderly and, I thought, cunning-looking cove was sitting in my chair nursing a glass of my Château Fleet Street and smiling at me in the slightly lopsided manner which I was to know as characteristic of Mr Boxey Horne. He wore a travel-stained tropical suiting, scuffed suede shoes and an M.C.C. tie which had seen better days. When Hilda introduced me, he rose and gripped me quite painfully by the hand. 'Good old Horace,' he said. 'Back from the office same time every evening. I bet you can set your watch by the old fellow, can't you, Hilda?'

'Well. Not exactly,' Hilda told him.

'Your wife gave me some of this plonk of yours, Horace.' Boxey raised his glass to me. 'We'd have been glad of this back on the farm in Kenya. We might have run a couple of tractors on it!'

'Get Boxey a whisky, Rumpole,' Hilda instructed me. 'I expect you'd like a nice strong one, wouldn't you? Boxey couldn't get into the Travellers' Club.'

'Blackballed?' I asked on my way to the sideboard.

'Full up.' Boxey grinned cheerfully. 'Hilda was good enough to say I might camp here for a couple of weeks.' It seemed an infinity. I poured a very small whisky, hoping the bottle would last him out, and drowned it in soda.

'I've been knocking around the world, Horace,' Boxey told me. 'While you were off on your nine to five in a lawyers' office.'

'Not office,' I corrected him as I handed him his pale drink, 'Chambers.'

'That sort of life would never have suited old Boxey,' he told me, and I wondered if his name might be short for anything. 'Oh no,' Hilda laughed at my ignorance. 'We called him that because of the beautiful brass-bound box he had when he set off to Darkest Africa.'

'Always been a rover, Horace.' Boxey was in a reminiscing mood. 'All my worldly goods were in that old box. Tropical kit. Mosquito net. Dinner-jacket to impress the natives. Family photographs, including one of cousin Hilda looking young and alluring.' He drank and looked suitably disappointed, but Hilda, clearly entranced, said, 'You took me to Kenya? In your box?'

'Many a time I've sat alone,' he assured her, 'listening to the strange sounds of an African night and gazing at your photograph. You have been looking after Cousin Hilda, haven't you, Horace?'

'Looking after her?' I poured myself a bracing Pommeroy's plonk and confessed myself puzzled. 'Hilda's in charge.'

'A sweet, sweet girl, cousin Hilda. I always thought she needed looking after but I suppose I had itchy feet and couldn't resist the call of Africa.' He propelled himself to the sideboard then, and with his back towards us, poured himself a straight whisky and then made a slight hissing noise imitating a siphon.

'What were you doing in Africa?' I asked him. 'Something like discovering the source of the Zambesi?'

'Well, not exactly. I was in coffee.'

'All your life?'

'Most of it.' Boxey returned to my chair to enjoy his drink.

'Working for the same firm?'

'Well, one has certain loyalties. You've never seen dawn over Kilimanjaro, Horry? Pink light on the snow. Zebra stampeding.'

'What time did you start work?' I was pursuing my own line of cross-examination.

'Well,' Boxey remembered, 'after my boy had got my bacon and eggs, coffee and Oxford marmalade . . . then I'd ride round the plantation.'

'Starting at nine o'clock?'

'About then, I suppose.'

'And knocking off?'

'Around sundown. Get a chair on the verandah and shout for a whisky.'

'At about five o'clock?'

'Why do you ask?'

'The old routine!' I muttered and the Defence rested.

'What was that?'

'What a rover you've been,' I said without envy.

'Well, I had itchy feet.' Boxey slapped my knee. 'But thank God for chaps like you who're prepared to slog it out in the old country, and look

251

after girls like Hilda.' Then he leant back in his chair, took a sizeable swig and prepared to give us another chapter of his memories. 'Ever been tiger-shooting, Horace?'

'Not unless you could call my frequent appearances before Judge Bullingham tiger-shooting,' I assured him.

'Best sport in the world! Tie an old goat to a tree and lie doggo. Your loader says, "Bwana. Tiger coming." There she is, eyes glittering through the undergrowth. She starts to eat the goat and . . .' — he raised an imaginary rifle — 'aim just above the shoulder. Pow!'

'What do you think of that, Rumpole?' Hilda was starry-eyed.

'I think it sounds bad luck on the goat.' We had a short silence while Boxey renewed his whisky. Then he said, 'I suppose it's another long day in Court for you tomorrow.'

'Oh, yes,' I agreed, 'dusty old law.'

'I don't know how you put up with it!'

'Tedious case about an Ulster terrorist shot by the police in Notting Hill,' I told him — by then I had received the brief for the defence in *R. v. Culp* — 'an inefficient gun-runner who acts as mother and father to his twelve-year-old son, and the curious activities of the Special Branch. Not nearly so exciting as nine to five on the old coffee plantation.'

That night, Hilda lay for a long time with the light on, when I was in dire need of sleep, staring into space. She was also in a reminiscing mood.

'I remember when we used to go to dances at Uncle Jacko's,' she said. 'Boxey was quite young, then. He brought his dancing pumps along in a paper bag. He was simply marvellous at the valeta.'

'It's a wonder he didn't join the Royal Ballet.'

'Rumpole. You *are* jealous!'

'I just thought he might've found *Casse Noisette* a good deal more interesting than coffee.'

'In those days I got the feeling that Boxey had taken a bit of a shine to me.' It wasn't, I thought, much to boast about, but Hilda seemed delighted. 'A definite shine! How different my life might have been if I'd married Boxey and gone to Africa!'

'My life would have been a bit different too,' I told her. 'With no one to make sure I didn't linger too long in Pommeroy's after work. No one to make sure I didn't take a second helping of mashed potatoes. And,' I added, *sotto voce,* 'magical!'

'What did you say, Rumpole?'

'Tragical, of course. Is there any chance of turning out the light?'

Mr Bernard, my favourite instructing solicitor, had briefed me in the Culp case, and we went together to Brixton, where, in the cheerfully painted interview room with its pot plants and reasonably tolerant screws, I made the acquaintance of Stanley. His first request was to get him out of confinement so that he could be with his son, to which I made not very encouraging noises, reminding him that he'd been charged with delivering automatic rifles to a known Irish terrorist and that my name was Rumpole and not Houdini.

The story he told me went roughly as follows. He dealt, he said, in bric à brac, *objets d'art,* old furniture — anything he could make a few bob out of. Asked where this property came from, he said we'd find it wise not to ask too many questions. (Well, I sometimes feel the same about my practice at the Bar.) He had a certain amount of space at the back of his shop and he put an advertisement in the local newsagent's window offering to store people's furniture for a modest fee. Some months previously a man had telephoned Stanley saying he was a Mr Banks, from the Loyalist League of Welfare and Succour for Victims of Terrorist Attack, and he wanted storage space for a number of packing-cases which contained medical supplies for his organization in Northern Ireland. As a result, he received a visit from Mr Banks who paid him three months' rent in advance, a sum of money which Stanley found extremely welcome. Asked to describe this mysterious Banks he could only remember a man of average age and height, wearing a dark business suit and a white shirt. His sole distinguishing mark was apparently a large pair of gold-rimmed, slightly tinted spectacles. Stanley never saw Mr Banks again, but in due course a lorry arrived with the packing-cases which it took a couple of blokes to lift. When I put the point to him he said they did seem heavy for sticking plaster and bandages.

Later Mr Banks telephoned and said that a man called MacRobert, a name which Stanley assured me meant nothing to him, would be calling to arrange the collection of the cases. MacRobert called whilst Matthew was preparing the breakfast and had wanted to see the goods inside, but before he could do so their conversation was interrupted by the Special Branch in the way I have described. Stanley was arrested and, while trying to escape across the garden wall, MacRobert was shot, so he was not in a position to tell us anything about the mysterious Mr Banks.

When he had finished his account Stanley looked at me beseechingly. 'You've got to get me out, Mr Rumpole,' he said. 'It's where they've put my Matthew.'

'Don't worry,' Bernard tried to console the client. 'He's being well looked after, Mr Culp. He's been put into care.'

'Me too. We're both in care.' Stanley managed a smile. 'That's it, isn't it? And it won't suit either of us. As I say, we've always been used to looking after each other.'

I looked at him, wondering what sort of a client I'd got hold of. If Stanley wasn't innocent, he was a tender-hearted gun-runner, so keen to be at home with Master Matthew that he flogged automatic rifles to political terrorists to fire off at other people's sons. It didn't make sense, but then not very much did in crime or politics.

Whilst I exercised my legal skills on a bit of gun-running in Notting Hill Gate, Portia's practice went on among the jet-setters. Cy Stratton, it seems — I have to confess his name was unknown to me — was an international film star for whom Hilda, who pays more attention to the television than I can manage, has a soft spot. He had been detected, as well-known film stars too often are, carrying exotic smoking materials through the customs at London Airport. In the consequent proceedings he hired, at a suitable fee, Mrs Phillida Erskine-Brown to make his apologies for him. She was ably assisted in this task by Mizz Liz Probert, to whom I am grateful for an account of the proceedings. Picture then the West Middlesex Magistrates Court, unusually filled with reporters and spectators. On the bench sat three serious-minded amateurs: a grey-haired schoolmaster chairman, a forbidding-looking woman in a hat, and a stout party with a toothbrush moustache and a Trades Union badge. In the dock, Mr Cy Stratton, a carefully suntanned specimen, whose curls were now greying, sat wearing a contrite expression and a suit and tie in place of his usual open-necked shirt and gold chain. On his behalf, our Portia, sincere and irresistible, spoke words which, when Liz Probert reported them to me, seemed to come straight out of Rumpole's first lesson on getting round to the soft side of the West Middlesex Magistrates as taught by me to Mrs Erskine-Brown in her white-wigged years.

'Cy Stratton is, of course,' she ended, 'a household name, known throughout the world from a string of successful films.' The star in the dock looked gratified. 'The Bench won't, I'm sure, punish him for his fame. He is entitled to be treated as anyone else found at London Airport with a small amount of cannabis for his own personal use. At the time he was under considerable personal strain, having just completed a new film, *Galaxy Wives*.' The Trades Union official, clearly a fan, nodded wisely. 'And, may I say this, Mr Stratton is absolutely opposed to hard drugs. He is a prominent member of the Presidential "Say No to Coke" Committee of Los Angeles. In these circumstances, I do most earnestly appeal to you, sir, and to your colleagues. You will do justice to Cy Stratton.' And here Portia used a gambit which even I have long since rejected as being over-ripe ham. 'But let it be justice tempered with that mercy which is the hallmark of the West Middlesex Magistrates Court!'

Well, sometimes the old ones work best. Much moved, Cy Stratton looked as though he were about to applaud; even the lady in the hat seemed mollified. The Chairman smiled his thanks at Phillida and, after a short retirement and a warning to Cy to set a good example to his huge army of fans, imposed a fine of three hundred pounds.

'And I had that,' said Cy to his learned Counsel and Liz outside the Court, 'in my pants pocket.'

257

'They might have given you two months,' Phillida told him, 'and you wouldn't have had *that* in your pants pocket.'

On that occasion Cy told Phillida he had a proposition to put to her and invited her to share a celebratory bottle of Dom Perignon with him in some private place. However, she declined politely, gathered her legal team about her, and saying, 'We do have to work, you know, at the Bar,' drove back to the Temple, doing so, Liz thought, in a sort of reverie brought on by an impulsive kiss from her grateful client.

I was in our clerk's room a few days later, with Claude and Phillida, sorting out our business affairs when a messenger arrived with a huge cellophane-wrapped bouquet and called out, 'Flowers for Erskine-Brown!' I asked Claude if he had an admirer, but they appeared to be for his wife and he asked, somewhat nervously, I thought, as she read the card attached, if they were from anyone in particular.

'Oh, no. Flowers just drop on me by accident, from the sky.' Phillida sounded testy. 'Do try not to be silly, Claude.'

'Perhaps they're from a satisfied client,' I suggested.

'Yes, they are!'

'Really, Portia? Who was that?'

'Oh, someone I kept out of prison. Nothing tremendously important.' She sounded casual, and Uncle Tom, our oldest inhabitant, who was as usual practising approach shots at the waste-paper basket, began to reminisce. 'I've never had a present from a satisfied client,' he told us. 'Not that I've had many clients at all, come to that, satisfied or not. I suppose it's better to have no clients than those that aren't satisfied. Damn! I seem to be in a bunker.' His golf ball had taken refuge behind Dianne's desk.

'What've I got this afternoon, Henry?' Phillida asked. And when he told her she had a three-thirty conference she supposed, after some thought, that she could be back in time. Meanwhile Uncle Tom was off down Memory Lane in pursuit of presents from satisfied clients. 'Old Dickie Duckworth once had a satisfied client,' he told us. 'Some sort of a Middle-Eastern Prince who was supposed to have got a Nippy from Lyons Corner House in pod and Dickie turned up at Bow Street and got him off. So you know what this fellow sent as a token of his appreciation? An Arab stallion! Well, Dickie Duckworth only had a small flat in Lincoln's Inn. No one ever sent me an Arab stallion. Chip shot out of the bunker!'

At that moment, Superintendent Rodney of the Special Branch, together with an official from the prosecution service, entered our clerk's room. Soapy Sam Ballard, Q.C., the Head of our Chambers, had been briefed to prosecute Stanley Culp and they were to see him in conference. Unfortunately Uncle Tom's chip shot was rather too successful; his golf ball rose into the air and struck the Superintendent smartly on the knee-cap, producing a cry of pain and dire consequences for Uncle Tom.

The note on Phillida's bouquet was a pressing invitation to meet Cy Stratton for lunch at the Savoy Hotel. I suppose the suntanned and ageing Adonis had figured too largely in her thoughts since the trial for her to pass up the invitation, and when they met he surprised her by suggesting that they share a bottle of champagne and a surprise packet from the delicatessen on a bench in the Embankment Gardens. So Phillida found herself eating pastrami on rye and drinking Dom Perignon out of a plastic cup, both excited by the adventure and nervous at the amount of public exposure she was receiving. I learnt, long after the event, and when certain decisions had been made, the gist of Cy's conversation on that occasion from my confiding ex-pupil. It seems that after complimenting her on looking great — 'Great hair, great shape. Classy nose. Great legal mind' — Cy informed her that their 'vibes' were good and that they should spend more time together. He had, he said, 'A proposition to put'.

'Perhaps you shouldn't.' Phillida was flattered but nervous.

'What?'

'You shouldn't put a proposition to me.'

'Can't a guy ask?'

'It might be a great deal better if a guy didn't.'

'I need you, Phillida.' The actor was at his most intense, and he moved himself and the sandwiches closer to her.

'You may think you do.'

'I know I do. Desperately.'

'Don't exaggerate.' There has always been a strong streak of common sense in our Portia.

'I swear to you. I can't find anyone to do what I'd expect of you.'

'You can't?'

'Not a soul. They haven't the versatility.'

'What would you expect of me exactly?' Phillida was still nervous, but interested. His answer, she confessed, came as something of a surprise. 'Only, to take over the entire legal side of Cy Stratton Enterprises. Real estate. Audio-visual exploitations. Cable promotions. I want your cool head, Phillida, and your legal know-how.'

'Oh, is that what you want?' She tried not to sound in the least disappointed.

'Come to the sunshine. I'll find you a house on the beach.'

'I *have* got two children,' she told him.

'The kids'll love it.'

'And a husband,' she admitted. 'He's a lawyer too.'

'Maybe we could use him, as your assistant?'

'You don't send children away from home in California?' The idea was beginning to appeal to Portia.

'Summer camps, maybe. Think about it, Phillida. Our vibes are such we should spend more time together.'

'I'll think about it. Can I have another sandwich?' She put out her hand and Cy held it and

261

looked into her eyes. And then Liz Probert, walking through the Gardens, stopped in front of them as Cy was saying, 'Find our own space together. That's all it takes!'

'Good afternoon. Having a picnic?' Liz's greeting was somewhat cold. Phillida quickly released her hand. 'Oh, Probert,' she greeted her colleague formally. 'You remember Cy Stratton?'

'Of course. Illegal possession.' Liz looked at Phillida. 'A satisfied client?'

The Erskine-Browns' private life was, you see, not exactly private — either they were spied on by Liz Probert or overheard by Rumpole. A few evenings later I was at my corner table in Pommeroy's trying to raise my alcohol level from the dangerous low to which it had sunk, when I heard their raised voices once again from the pew behind me. 'Haven't we been getting into a bit of a rut lately, Claude?' was the far from original remark which collared my attention.

'It's hardly fair to say that.' Claude sounded pained. 'When I got us tickets for *Tannhäuser*.'

'It's like Tristan's education. You want him to go to Bogstead and Winchester and New College. Because you went to Winchester and New College and your father went to Winchester . . .'

'And Balliol. There was an unconventional streak in Daddy.'

'Claude. Don't you ever long to go to work in an open-necked shirt and cotton trousers?'

'Of course not, Philly.' The man was shocked. 'In an open-necked shirt and cotton trousers, the

Judges at the Old Bailey can't even hear you. You'd be quite inaudible and sent up to the public gallery.'

'Oh, I don't mean that, Claude. Don't you ever long for the sun?'

'You want me to book up for Viareggio again?' Claude clearly thought he'd solved it, but his wife disillusioned him.

'Not just a holiday, Claude. I mean a change in our lives. It's only fair I should tell you this. There's someone I might want to spend time with in, well, a different sort of life. It's not that I'm in love in the least. Nothing to do with that. I just want a complete change. I sometimes feel I never want to go back to Chambers.'

This fascinating dialogue was interrupted again by the arrival of Ballard at their table. He had come to report the disgraceful occurrence of a superintendent of the Special Branch smitten by a golf ball, a blow from which, it seemed, he didn't think Chambers would ever recover. I didn't know then how the differences of the Erskine-Browns were to be resolved, but Phillida did come into Chambers the next morning, and there found an official-looking letter from the Lord Chancellor which was to have some considerable effect on the case of *R. v. Culp*.

In due course, Miss Sturt, his social worker, brought young Matthew Culp to visit his father in Brixton prison. A special room was set aside for visits by prisoners' children, and the two Culps

263

sat together trying to cheer each other up, Matthew being, by all accounts, the more decisive of the two. He told his father that he was determined to help him and that he meant to see to it that they were soon able to renew their contented domestic life together. He also asked Stanley to pass on certain information to me, his brief, as a consequence of which Mr Bernard made another appointment for me to visit the alleged gun-runner.

'My Matthew saw him, Mr Rumpole,' Stanley told me as soon as we were ensconced in the interview room. 'He says he saw that Mr Banks you were so interested in.'

'He did?'

'Oh, yes. Once when he came about leaving the packing-cases, what he said were medical supplies for his charitable organization. Matthew can tell them all about it. And that last morning, my Matthew'll say, he saw the same man in gold-rimmed glasses get out of the police car.'

'So that's the trap you walked into?' If Stanley were a criminal, he was clearly incompetent.

'Trap?' He looked at me, puzzled.

'Oh, yes. Isn't that the way they shoot tigers? Tie a goat to a tree, wait for the tiger to come hunting and then shoot. In this case, Mr Culp, you were the bait. Possibly innocent. The only question is . . .' I looked thoughtfully at Stanley. 'How much did the goat know?'

'I didn't know anything, Mr Rumpole,' he protested. 'Medical supplies they were, as far as I was concerned. But Matthew will tell you all about it.'

'Your boy's prepared to give evidence?' Mr Bernard looked encouraged.

'Ready and willing. He wants to help all he can.'

'And you want me to put him in the witness-box? How old is he? Twelve?'

'But such an old head on his shoulders, Mr Rumpole. I told you how he masters his geometry.'

'He may be a demon on equilateral triangles, but he's a bit young for a starring role, down the Old Bailey.'

'Please, Mr Rumpole,' my client begged me. 'He'd never forgive me if we didn't let him have his say. We make it a rule, you see, to look after each other.'

The man was so eager, and obviously proud of the son he trusted to save him. But I was still not convinced of the wisdom of calling young Matthew to give evidence in the daunting atmosphere of the Central Criminal Court.

When Phillida had opened her official-looking envelope she spread the news it contained around Chambers. Ballard then called a meeting, and opened the agenda in his usual ponderous, not to say, pompous, fashion.

'The first business today,' he began, 'is to congratulate Phillida Erskine-Brown, who has received gratifying news from the Lord Chancellor's office. She has been made a Recorder and so will sit in as a criminal judge from time to time, in the intervals of her busy practice.'

'A Daniel come to justice!' I saluted her.

'How do you feel about having your wife sit in judgment, Claude?' Hoskins asked.

'I'd say, used to it by now,' Claude gave him the reply jocular.

'Thank you very much.' Phillida looked becomingly modest. 'Quite honestly, it's come as a bit of a shock.'

'Of course, we all know that the Lord Chancellor is anxious to promote women, so perhaps, Phillida, you've found the way to the Bench a little easier than it's been for some of us.' Ballard was never of a generous nature and he found congratulating other learned friends very hard.

'I suppose we'd see you Lord Chancellor by now, Bollard, if only you'd been born Samantha and not Sam,' was my comment.

'My second duty is a less pleasant one.' Soapy Sam ignored me. 'Which is why I have asked Uncle Tom not to join this meeting. Something quite inexcusable in a respectable barristers' Chambers has occurred. An officer of the Special Branch arrived to see me in conference. Rather a big matter. Gun-running to Ulster. You may have read about *R.* v. *Culp* in the newspapers? Terrorist got shot in Notting Hill Gate . . . Well, you can see it's an extremely heavy case.'

'Oh, I'm in that,' I told him casually. 'Storm in a teacup, I think you'll find.'

'Superintendent Rodney came here for a consultation with myself,' Ballard continued with great seriousness. 'He walked into the clerk's room and was struck on the knee by a golf ball! I need hardly say who was responsible.'

'Uncle Tom!' Hoskins guessed the answer.

'He's been playing golf in there as long as I can remember.' Erskine-Brown was querulous.

'It wasn't Uncle Tom's fault,' I told them. 'I clearly heard him shouting, "Fore!"'

'He shouldn't have been shouting "fore" or anything else.' Ballard showed a very judicial irritation. 'A clerk's room is for collecting briefs, and discussing a chap's availability with Henry. A clerk's room isn't for shouting "fore" and driving off into superintendents' knee-caps!'

'He wasn't driving off,' I insisted.

'Oh. What was he doing then, Rumpole?'

'He was getting out of a bunker.'

'Sometimes you defeat me! I have no idea what you're talking about; there are no bunkers in our clerk's room!' Ballard seemed to think that decided the matter.

'It was an imaginary bunker.'

'I don't understand.'

'That's because you have no imagination.'

'Perhaps I haven't. In any event I can't see why Uncle Tom has to play golf in our clerk's room. It's quite unnecessary.'

'Of course it is,' I agreed.

'I'm glad you admit it, Rumpole.'

'Just as poetry is unnecessary,' I pointed out. 'You can't eat it. It doesn't make you money. I suppose people like you, Bollard, can get through life without Wordsworth's sonnet "Upon Westminster Bridge". What we are discussing is the quality of life. Uncle Tom adds an imaginative touch to what would otherwise be a fairly dreary, dusty little clerk's room, littered with biscuits, briefs and barristers.'

'Personally I don't understand why Uncle Tom comes into Chambers every day; he never gets any work.' Now Erskine-Brown showed his lack of imagination. If he lived with Uncle Tom's sister he'd come into Chambers every day whether there was any work for him there or not. Not that there was anything wrong with Uncle Tom's sister, she'd just worked her way through the entire medical directory without having had a day's illness in her life. Uncle Tom also, strange as it may have seemed, enjoyed our company.

Ballard now proceeded to judgment. 'Uncle Tom and his golf balls are,' he said, 'in my considered opinion, a quite unnecessary health hazard in Chambers. I intend to ask him to make his room available to us.'

'You're going to ask him to leave?' I wanted to get the situation perfectly clear.

'Exactly that.' Ballard made it perfectly clear, so I stood up.

'If Uncle Tom goes, I go,' I told him.

'That would seem to make the departure of

Uncle Tom even more desirable,' Soapy Sam was saying with a faint smile as I left the room.

So that was how I decided, after so many years enduring the splendours and miseries of an Old Bailey hack, to leave our Chambers in Equity Court and perhaps quit the Bar for ever. The decision was one which I couldn't wait to tell that lately reunited couple of lovebirds, She Who Must Be Obeyed and Boxey Horne. As I entered the mansion flat that evening I was singing 'You take the High Road and I'll take the Low Road, and I'll be in Zimbabwe before you!' I entered our sitting-room and I spotted Hilda pouring Boxey a generous whisky. 'I have news for you both,' I told them. 'My feet itch!'

'What do you mean by that, Rumpole?' My wife seemed puzzled.

'I can smell the hot wind of Africa,' I told them. 'I hear the cry of the parrot in the jungle and the chatter of monkeys. I wish to see the elephant and the gazelle troop shyly up to the waterhole at night. You have inspired me, Boxey, my old darling. I'm leaving the Bar.'

'Don't talk nonsense!' Hilda was somewhat rattled.

'I have handed in my resignation.'

'You've *what?*'

'I have informed our learned Head of Chambers, Soapy Sam Ballard, Queen's Counsel, that I no longer wish to be part of an organization which can't tolerate golf in the clerk's room.'

'Uncle Tom!' Hilda got my drift.

'Of course.'

'I've never understood why he had to play golf in the clerk's room.'

'Because no one sends him any briefs,' I enlightened her. 'Do you think he wants to be seen doing nothing? Anyway. I've handed in my resignation. One more case — I intend to defeat Soapy Sam over a spot of illicit arms dealing — and then travels Rumpole East away!'

'You're not serious?' Boxey also looked alarmed.

'Farewell to dusty old law! No more nine to five in the office. Ask for me in the Nairobi Club in five years' time and the fellows might have news of me. Up country.'

'He's joking,' Hilda told her childhood sweetheart. 'Definitely joking.' But then she sounded uncertain. 'Aren't you, Rumpole?'

'I wish I could come back with you,' Boxey told me. 'But . . .'

'Oh, you can't do that, Boxey. Of course not. Somebody's got to stay here and look after Hilda.' I was gratified to see that they looked at each other with a wild surmise. They wanted to talk further, but I refused to discuss the matter until my Swan Song, the Queen against Stanley Culp, was safely over and, I hoped, won.

Some days later I invited Phillida for a drink in Pommeroy's. When we were safely seated with glasses in our hands, she asked me if I were really thinking of leaving Chambers. I told her that my future depended on Ballard, and Hilda's long-lost cousin, who rejoiced in the name of Boxey Horne. She Who Must Be Obeyed, I explained, said she might have married Boxey.

'And I might not have married Claude.' Our Portia stared thoughtfully into her vodka and tonic. As Shelley would probably have said, in the circumstances, 'We look before and after; We pine for what is not.' 'I might,' she added, 'have had a husband full of energy, and jokes, with a taste for adventure. Someone unconventional. A rebel who hadn't been to Bogstead and Winchester.'

'Portia. You're flattering me.' I smiled modestly.

'What do you mean?'

'But mightn't I have been a little old for you?'

'Why did you ask me for this drink?' Portia looked at me and asked sharply. It was time for me to put my master plan into practice. I began, I hope, as tactfully as possible with: 'There's a bit of an east wind blowing between you and Claude on the subject of young Tristan's education . . .'

'I don't see why the family has to be split up.' She was quite clear on the subject.

'Exactly. A boy needs his father.'

'And his mother, don't forget.'

'Worst thing that can happen,' I argued profoundly, 'for families is to be separated, torn apart by society's unnatural laws and customs.'

'You understand that?' She looked at me with more than usual sympathy.

'Handing a small boy over for other people to bring up has to be avoided at all costs.'

'You ought to tell Claude that.'

'Oh, I certainly shall,' I promised her as I raised my glass. 'Family togetherness. Here's to it, Portia, and I hope you support it, whenever you sit in judgment.'

Mizz Liz Probert had her own, somewhat uncomfortable, standards of honesty, which were usually calculated to cause trouble to others. It will be recalled that when Claude had incautiously invited her to a night *à deux* at the Opera, she immediately told Phillida of the invitation, thus causing prolonged domestic disharmony.* It was therefore predictable that she should tell Claude that she had seen Phillida on a bench in the Embankment Gardens, drinking champagne and holding hands with a famous film star. My learned friend, Mr Erskine-Brown, gave me an account of this conversation at a later date. It seems that Mizz Probert had her own explanation for this event, one hard to understand by anyone not intimately connected with the North Islington Women's Movement. 'You drove her to it, Claude,' Liz said. 'If a woman does that sort of thing, it's always the man's fault, isn't it?'

'And if a man does that sort of thing?'

* See 'Rumpole and the Official Secret' in *Rumpole's Last Case*, Penguin, 1987.

'Well, it's always his fault. Don't you understand? Phillida's just rebelling against your enormous power and sexual domination.'

'Oh?' Claude tried to reason with Mizz Probert. 'Phillida is a Queen's Counsel. She wears a silk gown. She's about to sit as a Recorder. In judgment at the Old Bailey. I'm still a junior barrister. With a rough old gown made of some inferior material. How can I possibly dominate her?'

'Because you're a man, Claude,' Liz told him. 'You were born for domination!'

'Oh, really? Do you honestly think so?' At the time, Claude was not entirely displeased by this view. Later, in the privacy of his home, Phillida told me, he apologized to his wife for his terrible habit of domination. 'I suppose I can't help it; it's a bit of a curse really. Men just don't know their own strength.'

'Claude' — Phillida tried to keep a straight face — 'I have to decide on the shirts you want to buy. When we went out to dinner with the Arthurian Daybells you asked me to remind you whether you like smoked mackerel!'

'Do I?' her husband asked seriously.

'Not very much.'

'Ah. That's right.'

'You seem to suffer from terminal exhaustion directly your head hits the pillow. Can you please tell me exactly how you are exercising this terrible power over me? Could you give me one single instance of your ruthless domination?'

'I suppose it's just the male role. I'll try not

to play it, Philly. I honestly will.'

'Oh, Claude!' Portia could no longer contain her laughter. 'Do you think I ought to stay here and look after you?'

'Well, you'll have to stay here now, won't you, anyway?' Claude told his wife.

'Because you tell me to?' She was still laughing.

'No. Because you're a Recorder.'

Portia had become a part-time judge and Portia was devoted to the idea of keeping children within the family circle. There was only one element of my equation left to supply, and to do so I entered our clerk's room with the intention of having a confidential chat with Henry. As good luck would have it, I found him patiently addressing Dianne, who sat with a book on her typewriter. ' "I knew that suddenly, when we were dancing," ' Henry told her, ' "an enchantment swept over me. An enchantment that I've never known before and shall never know again. My heart's bumping. I'm trembling like a fool." '

' "Thumping",' Dianne insisted.

'What's that?'

' "My heart's thumping." Otherwise very good.'

'The late Sir Noël Coward, Henry?' I guessed.

'Oh, yes, Mr Rumpole. The Bexley Thespians. We're putting on *Tonight at 8.30*, sir. We likes his stuff. I do happen to have the starring role.'

'With your usual co-star?' Fate was giving me unusual help with *R. v. Stanley Culp*.

'I shall be playing opposite Miss Osgood from the Old Bailey List Office. As per always.'

'Miss Osgood, who fixes the hearings and the Judges. A talented actress, of course?'

'Sarah Osgood has a certain magic on stage, Mr Rumpole.'

'And considerable powers in the List Office also, Henry. Remind me to send her a large bouquet on the first night. And for our Portia's debut on the Old Bailey Bench, I thought it would be nice if Miss Osgood gave her something worthy of her talents.'

'No doubt you had something in mind, sir?' Our clerk wasn't born yesterday.

'R. v. *Culp*.' I told him what I had in mind. 'A drama of gun-dealing in Notting Hill Gate. Likely to run and run. It might be Portia's way to stardom. Mention it to your fellow Thespian during a break in rehearsals, why don't you?' My hint dropped, I moved out of the room past our ever-putting oldest inhabitant. 'Still golfing, Uncle Tom?'

'Ballard wants to see me,' he said, almost proudly.

'Oh, yes. When?'

'Any time at my convenience before the end of the month. Do you think he's fixed me up with a junior brief?'

'Would you like that?'

'I'm not sure. I haven't kept my hand in at the law.'

'Never mind, Uncle Tom. Your putting's com-

275

ing on splendidly!' And I left him to it.

And so it came about that fate spun its wheel and, with a little help from my good self and Miss Osgood at the List Office, the Queen against Culp was selected as the case to be tried by Mrs Recorder Erskine-Brown when she made her first appearance on the Old Bailey Bench. She sat there, severely attractive, a large pair of horn-rimmed glasses balanced on that delicate nose which has sent the fantasies whirling in the heads of many barristers, distinguished and otherwise. I thought how I had advised and trained her up, from white-wig to judge's wig, to lean to the Defence, particularly when the defendant has a twelve-year-old son who is the apple of his eye. I also thought that there was no judge in England better suited to try the case against Stanley Culp.

As I rose to cross-examine the Special Branch superintendent, Portia selected a freshly sharpened pencil and prepared to make a note. This was in great contrast to such as Judge Bullingham who merely yawns, examines his nails or explores his ear with a little finger during cross-examination by the Defence, that is, if he's not actively heckling.

'Superintendent Rodney,' I began. 'Have you, as a Special Branch officer, ever heard of the Loyalist League of Welfare and Succour for Victims of Terrorist Attack?'

'Not till your client told us they sent him those packing-cases.'

'Or of a Mr Banks, who apparently runs that philanthropic organization?'

'Not till your client told us his story.'

'A story you believed?'

'If I had we wouldn't be here, would we, Mr Rumpole?' Rodney smiled as though he'd won a point, but the Judge interrupted for the first time.

'Mr Rumpole. What does it matter what this officer believes? It's what the Jury believes that matters, isn't it?'

'Your Ladyship is, of course, perfectly right. A Daniel come to judgment,' I whispered to Mizz Probert. 'Yea, a Daniel!' I then asked, 'Did my client Mr Culp give you a description of Banks, the man who had asked him to store the packing-cases for him?'

'Superintendent,' her Ladyship said quite properly, 'you may refresh your memory from your notes, if you wish to.'

'Thank you, my Lady.' He turned a page or two in his notebook. 'Yes. Culp said, "Mr Banks called on me and asked me to store some . . . medical supplies. He was a man of average height, he had gold-rimmed glasses with . . ." '

'Slightly tinted lenses?' I suggested.

'Tinted lenses. Yes.'

'Well. You know perfectly well who that is, don't you?' I asked, looking at the Jury.

'Excuse me, Mr Rumpole' — the superintendent rather overacted complete bewilderment — 'I have absolutely no idea.'

'Really?' And I asked, 'Have the Special Branch made any effort whatsoever to find this elusive Banks? Have you sought him here, Superintendent? Have you sought him there?'

'My Lady' — Soapy Sam arose with awful solemnity — 'it is my duty to object to this line of questioning.'

'*Your duty*, Mr Bollard?' I thought his duty was to sit still and let me get on with it.

'My patriotic duty!' The fellow seemed about to salute and run up a small Union Jack. 'My Lady. This is a case in which the security of the realm is involved. The activities of the Special Branch necessarily take place in secret. The inquiries they have made cannot be questioned by Mr Rumpole.'

'What do you say, Mr Rumpole?' Portia was ever anxious to know both sides of the question.

'What do I say?' I came to the defence of the legal system against the Secret Police. 'I say quite simply that contrary to what Mr Ballard seems to believe, this trial is not taking place behind the Iron Curtain. We are in England, my Lady, breathing English air. The Special Branch is not the K.G.B. They are merely a widely travelled department of our dear Old Bill.' This got me a little refreshing laughter from the jury box. 'I should be much obliged for an answer to my question.'

'Is the whereabouts of this man Banks vital to your defence?' Portia asked judicially.

'My Lady, they are.'

'And you wish me to make a ruling on this matter?'

'The first, I'm sure, of many wise judgments your Ladyship will make in many cases.'

'Then in my judgment . . .' I whispered to Liz to keep her fingers crossed, but happily justice triumphed and her Ladyship ruled, '. . . Mr Rumpole may ask his question.' A wise and upright judge, a Daniel come to judgment, but Superintendent Rodney stonewalled our efforts by saying, 'We have not been able to trace Mr Banks or the Loyalist League of Welfare.'

'Much good did that do you!' Ballard muttered to me, and I muttered back, 'Wait for it. I'm not finished yet, Comrade Bollardski!' I said to the witness, 'Superintendent. You arrived at breakfast time on the 4th of May outside the shop in Notting Hill Gate to arrest my client. Who was in the car with you?'

'Detective Inspector Blake and Detective Sergeant Trump, my Lady.'

'And who had told you that a transaction in arms was likely to take place in Mr Culp's shop that morning?'

'My Lady . . .' the Superintendent appealed to the Judge, who ruled with a smile I found quite charming, 'I don't think the officer can be compelled to give the name of his informer, Mr Rumpole.' I accepted her decision gratefully and asked, 'Was your informer, let's call him Mr X, in the car with you and the other officers when you arrived at the shop?'

'My Lady.' Ballard rose again to maintain secrecy. 'The Court no doubt understands that any information about a police informer on terrorist activities would place the man's life in immediate danger.'

'Very well.' Portia saw the point. 'I don't think you can take the matter further, can you, Mr Rumpole?'

I could and did with my next question. 'Let me just ask this, with your Ladyship's permission. Did a man wearing gold-rimmed spectacles and tinted lenses get out of the police car in front of the shop that morning and walk away before the arrest took place?'

'I'm not prepared to answer that, my Lady,' the Superintendent stonewalled again.

'And was that man "Mr Banks"?' I pressed on.

'I have already told you, sir. We don't know Mr Banks.'

'But you do know whoever it was, an officer of your Special Branch, perhaps, who stored the packing-cases in Mr Culp's shop, who told Mr Culp they were medical supplies, and arranged for this man MacRobert, who wanted to buy arms for his Ulster terrorists, to walk into your trap?'

'All I can tell you is that the cases of arms were in the shop and MacRobert called for them.' The Superintendent sighed, as though my defence were no more than a waste of his precious time.

'Had MacRobert met Mr Banks?'

'I can't say.'

'And the Jury will never know because MacRobert has been silenced forever.'

'Detective Inspector Blake saw him in the act of pulling out a weapon. He fired in self defence.'

'No doubt he did. But it leaves us, doesn't it, a little short of evidence?'

We weren't entirely bereft of evidence, of course. All through my cross-examination I had been aware of a small, solemn, spectacled boy sitting outside the Court with his social worker, longing to help his father. I had hoped to get enough out of the Superintendent to avoid having to put young Matthew through the rigours of the witness-box, but I hadn't succeeded. Now, Bernard whispered to me, 'The little lad's just longing to go in. Are you going to call him?' The business of being a barrister involves the hard task of making decisions, instantly and on your feet. You may make the right decision, you may often get it wrong. The one luxury not open to you is that of not making up your mind. I stood silent as long as I dared and then committed myself.

'Fortunately,' I told the Superintendent, 'I am in a position to call a witness who might be able to tell us a little more about the damned elusive Banks.'

'Oh, please, Mr Rumpole' — Sam Ballard's whispered disapproval echoed through the court — 'don't swear, particularly in front of a lady Judge.'

Dressed in his best brown suit, a white shirt and a red bow-tie, in the dock Stanley somehow looked more crumpled and less impressive than ever. He sat slumped like a sack of potatoes; the Court seemed too hot for him and he frequently dabbed his forehead with a folded handkerchief. However, when his son, a more alert figure, stepped into the witness-box and had the nature of the oath gently explained to him by Portia, Stanley pulled himself together. He sat up straight, his eyes shone with pride and he looked like a devoted parent whose son has just stood up to collect the best all-rounder prize at the school Speech Day. His pride only seemed to increase as I led young Matthew through his examination-in-chief.

'Matthew. Do you remember a man coming to ask your father to store some boxes?'

'I was in the shop.'

'You were in the shop when he arrived?'

'Yes. He said he was Mr Banks and I went and fetched Dad from the back. He was mending something.' The boy answered clearly, without hesitation.

The Jury seemed to like him and I felt encouraged to ask for further details.

'Can you remember what Mr Banks looked like?'

'He had these gold-rimmed glasses. And they were coloured.'

'What was coloured?'

'The glass in them.'

'Did your father talk to Mr Banks?'

'Yes. I went upstairs. To finish my homework.' Portia was listening carefully and noting down the evidence. Matthew was doing well and his ordeal, I hoped, was almost over. I asked him, 'Did you see Mr Banks again?'

'Oh, yes.'

'When?'

'When the policemen arrived for Dad. Mr Banks got out of the police car.'

I looked at the Jury and repeated slowly, 'Mr Banks got out of the police car. What did he do then?'

'He walked away.' I smiled at Matthew, who didn't smile back, but remained standing seriously at attention. 'Yes. Thank you, Matthew. Oh, just wait there a minute, will you?' I had to sit down then, and leave him to the mercy of Ballard. I had no particular fear, for Soapy Sam had never been a great cross-examiner. His first question, however, was not badly chosen. 'Matthew. Are you very fond of your father?'

'We look after each other.' For the first time Matthew looked, unsmiling, at the dock. His father beamed back at him.

'Oh, yes. I'm sure you do.' Ballard tried the approach cynical. 'And you want to help him, don't you? You want to look after him in this case?'

'I'd like him to come home.' I was pleased to see Portia give Matthew a small smile before busying herself with her notes.

'I'm sure you would. And have you and your father discussed this business of Mr Banks getting out of the police car?' Ballard asked an apparently innocent question.

'I told Dad what I saw.'

'And did he tell you it was going to be his story that the police had set up this deal, through Mr Banks?'

'He said something like that. Yes.' It wasn't exactly the best answer we could have expected.

'So does it come to this? You'd say anything to help your father's defence?'

'My Lady. That was a completely uncalled for —' I rose with not entirely simulated rage, anxious to give the boy a little respite.

'Yes, Mr Rumpole,' Portia agreed and then turned to the young witness. 'Matthew. Are you sure you saw a man with glasses get out of the police car?'

I subsided. My interruption had been a mistake. I had changed a poor and unsympathetic cross-examiner for a humane and understanding one who might put our case in far more damage. 'Yes, I am. Quite sure.'

'Apart from the fact that he had gold-rimmed glasses with tinted lenses, can you be sure it was the same man who came to your father's shop and said he was Mr Banks?' Portia probed gently and Ballard got on the band-wagon with a sharp 'You can't be *sure*, can you?'

'Please, Mr Ballard.' Unhappily, Phillida didn't

284

let Soapy Sam show himself at his worst. 'Just think, Matthew,' she said. 'There's absolutely no hurry.'

There was a long silence then. Matthew was frowning and worried.

'I *think* it was the same man,' he said, and my heart sank.

'You think it was.' The Judge made a perfectly fair note and Ballard's voice rose triumphantly as he repeated. 'You *think* it was! But you can't be sure.'

'Well . . . Well, he looked the same. He *was* the same!' And then Matthew turned from a carefully controlled, grown-up witness to a child again. He called across to his father in the dock, 'He was, Dad? Wasn't he?'

And Stanley looked at him helplessly, unable to speak. The Jury looked embarrassed, fiddled with their papers or stared at their feet. The blushing, confused child in the witness-box stood beyond the reach of all of us until the Judge mercifully released him. 'I don't think we should keep Matthew here a moment longer,' she said. 'Have either of you gentlemen any further questions?'

Ballard had done his worst and there was no way in which I could repair the damage. Phillida said, 'Thank you, Matthew. You can go now.' And the boy walked down from the witness-box and towards the door of the Court. His social worker rose to follow him. As he got to the dock he looked at his father and said quietly, 'Did I let you down, Dad?'

I could hear him, but Stanley couldn't. All the same his father raised his thumb in a hopeful, encouraging signal as Matthew left us to be taken back into care.

Henry told me that, whilst we were on our way back from Court, the world-famous film star called at our clerk's room in search of Phillida. When he was told that she had been sitting as a judge down at the Old Bailey, he looked somewhat daunted.

'Isn't she too pretty to be a judge?'

'I don't think the Lord Chancellor considered that, sir' — Henry was at his most dignified — 'when he made Mrs Erskine-Brown a Recorder.'

'A judge, ugh!' Cy seemed to think this new position of Phillida's was something of a bar to romance. 'Anyway. Tell her I called by, will you? I'm getting the red-eye back to the Coast tonight. Say, that's a great gimmick!' This came as a direct result of seeing Uncle Tom putting in the corner of the room. 'What a great selling-point for your legal business.'

On his way downstairs, Cy met Soapy Sam Ballard and engaged him in some conversation which our Head of Chambers later reported to me. It seems that Cy had asked Ballard if he worked with Phillida and, on being told that Sam was Head of our Chambers, said, 'You run the shop! What a great gimmick you got, having an old guy playing golf in reception.' When Ballard explained he meant to put an end to it, Cy said, 'Are you crazy? Wait till I let them know on the Coast. There's a British lawyers' office, I'll tell them, where they keep an old guy to play golf in reception. Kind of traditional. I tell you. You'll get so much business from American lawyers! They'll all want to come in here and they won't *believe* it!'

'You think Uncle Tom'll bring us business?' Ballard was puzzled.

'You wait till I spread the word. You won't be able to handle it.'

In due course we made our final speeches and I sat back, my duty done, to hear her Ladyship sum up. 'Members of the Jury,' she concluded, 'the defence case is that this arms sale was staged by the police to trap the man, MacRobert. Mr Rumpole has said that the arms were deposited in the shop by a Mr Banks, who was a police officer in plain clothes, and that Mr Culp was simply told they were medical supplies. He was a quite innocent man, used as bait to trap the terrorist MacRobert. Are you sure that Mr Culp knew what was in those packing cases. They must have been extremely heavy for medical supplies. Do you accept young Matthew's identification of Mr Banks as the man in the police car? He *thinks* it was Banks but, you remember, he couldn't be sure. Members of the Jury, the decision on the facts is entirely for you. If there's a doubt, Mr Culp is entitled to the benefit of that doubt.

287

Now, please, take all the time you need and, when you're quite ready, come back and tell me what you have decided. Thank you.'

So the Usher swore to conduct the Jury to their room and not to communicate with them until they had reached a verdict. As I said to my learned friend Mizz Liz Probert, it had been an utterly fair summing up by a completely unbiased judge — always a terrible danger to the Defence.

The Jury were out for almost three hours and then returned with a unanimous verdict of guilty. Of course, an Old Bailey hack should take such results as part of the fair wear and tear of legal life. 'Win a few, lose a few', should be the attitude. I have never managed to do this, but I still hoped, by an argument which I thought might be extremely sympathetic to our particular judge, to keep Stanley out of prison.

Accordingly, when the time came for my speech in mitigation, I aimed straight for our Portia's maternal instincts. 'Whoever may be guilty in this case,' I ended, 'one person is entirely innocent. Young Matthew Culp has broken no laws, committed no offence. He is a hardworking, decent little boy and his only fault may be that he loves his father and wanted to help him. But if you sentence his father to prison, you send Matthew also. You sentence him to years in council care. You sentence him to years as an orphan, because his mother has long gone out of his life. You sentence him to being cut off from his only family, from the father he needs and who needs him. You sentence this small boy to a lonely life in a crowd of strangers. I ask your Ladyship to consider that and on behalf of Matthew Culp I ask you to say . . . no prison for this foolish father!'

Phillida looked somewhat moved. She said quietly, 'Yes. Thank you, Mr Rumpole. Thank you for all your help.'

'If your Ladyship pleases.' I sat and then Stanley Culp was told to stand for sentence. The fact that the Judge was an extremely pretty woman in no way softened the awesome nature of the occasion. 'Culp,' she began, 'I have listened most carefully to all your learned Counsel has said, and said most eloquently, on your behalf.' So far so good. 'Unhappily, all the crimes we commit, all the mistakes we make, affect our innocent children. I am very conscious of the effect any prison sentence would have on your son, to whom I accept that you are devoted.' So far so hopeful, but this wasn't the end. 'However, I have to protect society. And I have to remember that you were prepared to deal in murderous weapons which might have left orphans in Northern Ireland.' This was not encouraging, and Portia then concluded, 'The most lenient sentence I can impose on you is one of four years' imprisonment. Take him down.'

Stanley Culp was looking hopelessly round the Court as though searching for his son Matthew before the Dock Officer touched his arm and removed him from our sight.

Pommeroy's was the place to attempt to drown the memory of my failure, and Stanley's four years. I sat alone at my corner table and there my old pupil, her day of judging done, sought me out. 'I'm sorry about Culp,' Portia said.

'Never plead guilty,' I advised her.

'I was only . . .'

'Doing your job?'

'Well, yes.'

'It is your job, isn't it, Portia?' I told her. 'Deciding what's going to happen to people. Judging them. Condemning them. Sending them downstairs. Not a very nice job, perhaps. Not as agreeable as cleaning out the drains or holding down a responsible position as a pox doctor's clerk. Every day I thank heaven I don't have to do it.'

'Shouldn't I have become a Recorder? Is that what you're saying?'

'Oh, no. No. Of course you should. Someone's got to do it. I just thank God it's not me.'

'You're lucky.' She looked at me and I think she meant it.

'I enjoy the luxury of defending people, protecting them where I can, keeping them out of chokey by the skin of my teeth. I've said a good many hard words in my time but "take him down" is an expression I've never used.'

'Rumpole!' She was hurt. 'Do you imagine I enjoyed it?'

'No, Portia. No, of course not. I never imagined that. You had to do your job and you did it so bloody fairly that my fellow got convicted. He was caught in a trap. Like the rest of us.'

'Cheer up, Rumpole.' Then she smiled. 'I'll buy you a large Pommeroy's plonk.'

'I am greatly obliged to your Ladyship.' I drank up. 'And what about young Tristan? Is he to pay his debt to society?'

'I don't know what you mean. He's going to Bogstead.' She announced another verdict.

'Your Ladyship passed judgment in favour of my learned friend Mr Claude Erskine-Brown?' I couldn't believe it.

'Well. Not exactly. As a matter of fact Tristan passed judgment on himself.'

What had happened, it seemed, was that, saying good-night to her son, Phillida had been amazed to hear him say that he was eagerly looking forward to Bogstead. 'But don't you want to stay with us?' his mother asked, and Tristan confessed that being in the bosom of his family all the time was a bit of a strain on his nerves as his father was forever listening to operas and his mother always had her nose inside some brief or other. It was difficult to talk to either of them.

'I told him I'd talk to him whenever he wanted, that I'd tell him what I'd been doing, being a judge, and all that sort of thing.'

'And what did young Tristan say to that?' I asked her.

'He thought he'd find more to talk about with the chaps at Boggers,' Phillida said more than a little sadly.

I went back to Chambers to collect a brief for the next day, and there I met Sam Ballard, who was still unusually excited by his conversation with Cy Stratton, and had decided not to fire Uncle Tom, which made it unnecessary for me to set out for darkest Africa. I bought some flowers for Hilda at the Temple underground station, and when I got home and presented them to her I noticed our so-called 'mansion' flat was strangely silent.

'Boxey's gone.' Hilda spoke in a businesslike tone, concealing whatever emotion she may have felt. 'And what are *they* for?'

'Oh, to stick in a vase somewhere.' I restrained myself, with difficulty, from dancing with joy.

'He must have gone when I was out buying chops for our supper and he didn't even say goodbye. Why would Boxey do a thing like that?'

'Certainly not running away from the prospect of looking after you, Hilda. Never mind.' We went into the sitting-room and I poured her a large gin and tonic and myself a celebratory Pommeroy's. 'He was always such *fun* as a young man was Boxey, Hilda said.

'We look before and after;
We pine for what is not;
Our sincerest laughter

With some pain is fraught,'

I told her.

'Quite honestly, Rumpole' — Hilda was becoming daring — 'did you think Boxey had become a bit of a bore in his old age?'

' "Our sweetest songs are those that tell of saddest thought." I'm not going to Africa, Hilda.'

'I didn't think you were.'

'I shall never see the elephant and gazelle gathering at the waterhole. I shall never see zebra stampeding in the dawn. I shall get no nearer Africa than Boxey did.'

'What on earth do you mean, Rumpole?'

'All that talk about evening-dress to impress the natives. I bet he got that straight out of H. Rider Haggard. And didn't it occur to you, Hilda? There are absolutely no tigers in Kenya!'

There was a long silence, and then Hilda said with a rueful smile, 'Boxey asked me for a thousand pounds to start a smallholding, with battery hens.'

'I don't believe he's been further East than Bognor. You didn't give him anything?'

'Out of the overdraft? Don't be foolish, Rumpole. So you're staying here.'

'Soapy Sam Ballard told Uncle Tom to carry on golfing; he thinks it'll bring us a great deal of business with American lawyers.' I poured myself another comforting glass. 'You know, I lost the case against Ballard.'

'I thought so. You're not so unbearable when

you lose.' She thought the situation over and then said, 'So we'll have to get along without Boxey.'

'How on earth shall we manage?'

'As we always do, I suppose. Just you and I together.'

'Nothing changes, does it, Hilda?' The day had given me an appetite and I was looking forward to Boxey's chops. 'Nothing changes very much at all.'

# Rumpole and the Quality of Life

It's impossible to hack away for getting on for half a century in the Criminal Courts, rising to your feet, bending low to say 'If Your Lordship pleases' to ignorant white-wigs, or stooping to lick the boots of the Uxbridge Magistrates, without feeling a little out of sorts, occasionally. The truth of the matter is that I was suffering an attack of Bullinghamitis, a condition of which the symptoms are exhaustion and bouts of nervous depression and nausea brought about by frequent appearances before Judge Bullingham down the Bailey. 'You're feeling seedy, Rumpole. You'd better go to Dr MacClintock for a check-up.' She Who Must Be Obeyed said this not once, but three or four times a day, over a period of months. It was as effective as the Chinese water torture and it was to escape the merciless persistence of Hilda's advice that I was driven to an appointment with our friendly neighbourhood quack. 'And whatever Hector MacClintock tells you to do,' were Hilda's orders, 'you do it.'

Dr MacClintock was a small, lightweight, puritanical Scot who looked as though he existed on a glass of cold water and a handful of Quaker Oats a day. Once in his power, he had me stripped to the waist, braces hanging useless in the breeze, as he plied his stethoscope and asked me about my daily intake of calories. 'For instance,' he murmured as though receiving my confession, 'tell me about breakfast.'

'Taken at the Taste-Ee-Bite in Fleet Street if I'm busy. A fairly light affair.'

'Good.' He nodded approval.

'Couple of eggs on a fried slice.'

'Fried sliced?' I might have admitted a taste for hard drugs with my morning tea; the good Doctor was clearly shaken.

'Three or four rashers . . .'

'That's all, I hope?'

'Apart from the sausages. Rounds of toast. Marmalade.'

The Doctor put away his stethoscope nervously and said, 'Let's have you up on the scales, then. And for luncheon?'

'We only get an hour. It's a bit of a snack as it so happens.' I stood on the fatally revealing platform.

'A salad, perhaps?' MacClintock tried to sound hopeful as he arranged the weights.

'Who am I to take food from the mouths of starving rabbits?' I denied salad. 'A quick steak and kidney pud in the pub opposite the Bailey. A few boiled potatoes. Serving of cabbage. I find a pint of draught Guinness keeps the strength up at lunch-time.' The Doctor forced himself to look at the scales, and sighed heavily. 'Then I take nothing at all until dinner.'

'Nothing? Well, I'm glad of that at least. Oh,

do put your shirt back on.' He sat at his desk and started to write voluminous notes.

'Unless you count a small crumpet at tea-time.' I had to be honest.

'There have been times,' the Doctor said mournfully, 'when I have known indulgence in a small crumpet at tea-time to make the difference between life and death. Dinner?'

'Hilda usually grills a few chops with two veg, and I confess to a weakness for a touch of jam roly-poly.' I was restoring the shirt.

'Drink?'

'Oh, thank you very much.' Dr MacClintock was getting out the blood-pressure apparatus.

'No. *Do* you drink? Apart from non-alcoholic beverages.'

'Oh, I hardly touch them.'

'Very good. Just roll up the sleeve.'

'I hardly touch non-alcoholic beverages. Pommeroy's Very Ordinary claret, in my medical experience, keeps you astonishingly regular. Of course, I'm extremely modest in my consumption.'

'Modest?' The Doctor was pumping. 'Good.'

'Château Thames Embankment. About all I can afford nowadays.'

'And how much? Shall we say a bottle?'

'Oh, a couple. Maybe a little more when I'm before Judge Bullingham or Graves.'

'Two bottles a week?' He looked at the blood-pressure gauge and sighed again.

'A day. I haven't signed the pledge,' I told him.

'Smoke. A lot?'

'Do you, really?' I was glad to hear the man had some weaknesses, and getting out a packet of small cigars, I offered one to the Doctor.

'Let's face the fact' — he shook his head — 'there is a great deal too much of you, Mr Rumpole.'

'Oh, I don't know.' I tried to sound modest. 'If a fellow's a decent barrister, knows a thing or two about bloodstains, sharp cross-examiner, makes an effective final speech, how can there possibly be too much of a good thing?'

'The question is,' the Doctor asked with great seriousness, 'do you want to drop dead?'

It was an interesting question, and I gave it due attention. When I'm doing a hopeless rape, say, under the icy stare of Judge Gerald Graves, I might. On the other hand, when I've got the Jury on my side I feel I could live forever. As it happened, I had just received the brief in *R. v. Derwent,* one of the most fascinating cases of homicide I have encountered since the great days of the Penge Bungalow Murders. So I told the Doctor, quite frankly, 'No. I don't think I'd like to do that.'

'Then you must go on the diet I'm giving you at once. No wine. No meat. No fish, eggs, bread, butter, milk . . .'

'Ugh. Milk!' I agreed.

'Bread or pastry of any sort.'

'How do I manage without food?'

'Thin-O-Vite.' Dr MacClintock produced a name I was to learn to dread. 'Mix it with water and eat as much of it as you like. Make a pig of yourself. I hope to see less of you in about a month's time.'

'Meanwhile, "I eat the air, promise-crammed. You cannot feed capons so." '

'Who said that?'

'Hamlet. A Dane who'd no doubt have been a great deal less gloomy with a square meal inside him. Good day, Doctor.'

Is not being dead really enough, even if you have to keep alive on Thin-O-Vite? Battery hens aren't dead. Chained-up fattening pigs aren't dead. Even Judge Graves down the Bailey appears to be still breathing, if you watch him very closely. Life is not enough, in my opinion, *per se*. It's the quality of life that matters, and a fellow has to have something to live *for*. Some fine, ennobling, enriching experience. And that essential was supplied for me, in the absence of steak and kidney pud, by my engagement to defend in the case of *R.* v. *Derwent*. So, I was induced by that, and the insistence of She Who Must Be Obeyed, to follow the Doctor's Spartan regime. And now I must tell you something of that strange and, in many ways, pathetic case which had tempted me to go on living.

Sir Daniel Derwent, C.H., R.A., was a painter of the old school. He had a head like an elderly, bearded lion; he was given to wearing capes, wide-brimmed hats or the occasional beret. His portraits of important men and beautiful women were always competent, often charming, but never stunning. It might be said that Sir Daniel looked too much like a great artist to be one entirely. All the same, his work was greatly admired by many people including himself. He had, in his life, two great loves, painting and beautiful women.

Perdita, Derwent's wife at the time he died, was extremely beautiful and less than half his age. She had been a student at St Matthew's School of Art, where her husband was the Professor of Painting. He took her to live with him in his Chelsea house and subsequently married her. His household there consisted of his old mother, Barbara, always known as Bunty, Derwent, and Helen, his daughter by a previous marriage, who had run his life and continued to do so and make his new young wife extremely unwelcome.

The story begins on an evening which was described in detail in the evidence given at the Old Bailey. In the old-fashioned studio which was a feature of the house, Lady Derwent was seated on a model's throne, wearing a long skirt and no top. Sir Daniel was painting a three-quarter-length portrait of his wife. Bunty Derwent, a large, spreading and cheerful woman, was knitting by the stove, and Helen Derwent was making trouble because her new step-mother had forgotten to order the fish for supper.

'I'm terribly sorry, Helen.' Perdita opened her blue eyes wide, in a sort of panic. 'Did I really forget?'

'Don't move,' Daniel growled from behind his canvas.

'It's too bad of you!' Helen was unforgiving. 'You know how Daddy looks forward to his fish pie. It's really not much to ask of anyone, just to ring up and order the fish.'

'Don't make such a fuss about it, Helen.' Bunty was always the peacemaker. 'It's really not important. We'll have eggs.'

Perdita gave a small, grateful smile, being very careful not to move. And then, so the evidence told us, Daniel's brush-bearing hand started to tremble as it approached the canvas, misfired and made a long smear across Perdita's portrait. He threw down his brush in a fury and clasped his hand to his forehead.

'Hell and *death!*' he was heard to say.

That night Miss Helen Derwent couldn't sleep. She got up at about four o'clock and, going downstairs to make herself a cup of tea, she saw a light under the studio door. She opened it and found her father lying, fully dressed, on the studio couch. His eyes were open but she closed them. He was quite dead.

Later that morning, the youngish, spectacled and earnest Doctor Harman, who had been treating Sir Daniel, returned to the Chelsea house and was closeted with his late patient's wife and mother. He had been surprised by the sudden

301

onset of death, and he had established that Nurse Gregson, who helped care for the painter, had been called and visited at tea-time on the previous afternoon to give an injection. I must here deal with the medication given to relieve the pain caused by the cancer from which Sir Daniel was suffering. He regularly took morphine in the form of syrup, but, to cope with the 'breakthrough' of severe pain, he received booster injections of diamorphine which were administered by the visiting nurse. She gave him the usual supplementary dose when she called the previous afternoon, and then she went off duty. On checking her medical bag the next morning, Nurse Gregson found that a number of additional ampoules, containing what would have been a fatal dose of diamorphine, had been removed. She remembered leaving the bag, for a while, unwatched in the hall of the Derwent household.

'You're sure he didn't take anything after the nurse left?' the Doctor asked the young widow.

'I don't think so.' Because of his illness, the Derwents had been occupying separate bedrooms, each one with a bathroom attached. As Perdita gave this answer, her step-daughter Helen came into the room, holding, almost triumphantly, some articles which later became important exhibits in the case.

'Don't you think you ought to tell Doctor Harman about these, Perdita? I found them in your bedroom.' What she had found was a number of empty ampoules which had once contained diamorphine, a hypodermic syringe and a pamphlet which I was to get to know almost by heart, advocating euthanasia for those suffering from terminal illness.

This discovery led to investigations by the police, instigated by Doctor Harman. It was not until another breakfast-time, about three weeks later, that I was telephoned by my old friend and instructing solicitor, Mr Bernard. He told me that Lady Derwent had been taken to Chelsea police station and charged with the murder of her husband, by poison. 'Haven't had a poison case through my hands, oh, since the Bride of Orpington in 1958. That was chocolates, if you recollect. And this is an overdose of what? We'll go into that when we meet in Holloway.'

'Poison, Hilda,' I said as I put down the telephone. 'Something to live for at last.'

'If you want to live,' she told me, 'you'd better go straight round and see Hector MacClintock.' So I did, with what results you already know.

The conference at Holloway was fixed for a week after my visit to the Doctor, and before it took place an event occurred which removed most of the gilt from the gingerbread of my most recent murder case. I was leaving the Temple underground station on my way to Chambers, a little weakened by the sole intake of Thin-O-Vite, when I heard a familiar voice issue some kind of military command behind me.

303

'Pick 'em up, Rumpole!'

'Pick what up?'

Soapy Sam Ballard, Q.C., his umbrella shouldered and his brief-case swinging, marched up beside me. 'Pick up your feet. One . . . two . . . One . . . two . . .' he intoned. 'I have just walked the entire way from Liverpool Street station, along the river. Chin up, now. Swing the arms!'

'What's the matter with you, Bollard? The war's over.'

'The war may be over, Rumpole, but the battle for fitness goes on. I mean to introduce a new scheme of health education in Chambers. You know what I've got in this brief-case?'

'Astonish me.'

'I have a device in here for expanding the chest,' he said proudly. 'I intend to use it, during the odd free moment. Keep the chest open! Keep the lungs free! It's my duty as your Head of Chambers to prolong my life, as much as possible.'

'Why should you want to do that?'

'Can't let you fellows down.'

'We wouldn't want to put you to any trouble,' I assured him.

'Anyway, I can't let *you* down, Rumpole, now that I'm leading you.'

'You're doing *what?*' I felt a cold thrill of horror. Was my precious poisoning case to be taken out of my hands?

'Haven't you heard? Terrible business. Murder of Sir Daniel Derwent, R.A. Well-known painter, so they tell me. I know nothing of these things. Oh, yes. I'm leading you.'

'I hope you'll be able to keep up with me!' was all I could say, extremely ungraciously. But Ballard only quickened his pace and marched away. 'One . . . two! One . . . two!' he called as he went.

'I shall be leading you from behind,' I threatened him.

'It's you that's going to have to keep up, Rumpole,' he said as the distance between us grew. 'I just hope you're fit enough for it!' I'm afraid I was no longer audible as I said, 'Don't bother about prolonging your life, old darling. Not on my account.'

When I arrived in our clerk's room, things were much as usual. Dianne was making coffee, Henry was telephoning, Uncle Tom was trying to get his putts into the waste-paper basket and Mizz Liz Probert, looking slightly better groomed than usual, was getting a brief from her tray. My learned friend, Claude Erskine-Brown, arrived out of breath. 'Terrible traffic jam in Islington today, and you know what caused it?' He laughed mirthlessly. 'A procession of gay and lesbian demonstrators, demanding more services off the rates.'

'Why's that funny?' Mizz Probert pricked up her ears.

'I say!' Erskine-Brown looked at her with sudden admiration. 'Is that a new hairdo?'

'I don't see that it's at all funny. And what's my hair got to do with it?'

'It looks jolly nice, actually.' Claude became somewhat inarticulate. 'Much softer and . . . well, more feminine. Congratulations!'

'Oh, for God's sake, Claude!' Liz was losing patience with the man. 'Give us a break. And why shouldn't the Islington Council provide gay and lesbian counselling? Think of what they save you on education and . . .'

'Radiant!' Claude continued to stare. 'Quite honestly, you're looking radiant.'

'Of course, I'd expect *you* to be against it. I'd expect discrimination from you, Claude.'

'Discrimination?' He looked hurt.

'Oh, yes. How many gay and lesbian members have we got in these Chambers?'

'None, I hope. I mean, none, I think. No, I'm sure . . .'

'There you are, then! Discrimination.'

'Perhaps it's just because we don't get many gay and lesbian applications.' Claude was trying to be reasonable.

'Well, I'd like to see what'd happen if you got one. Just one! I can imagine your middle-class, middle-aged, male attitudes bristling.'

'Middle-aged, Liz? Did you say middle-aged?' He was clearly wounded.

'Sexual discrimination comes in a packet, Claude. With middle-aged spread.'

'Radiant!' He avoided the subject of the Erskine-Brown figure. 'You look absolutely radiant. Come for a coffee later? I'll let you pay for yourself,' he promised.

'Improve your attitudes, Claude. That's all you need.' Liz removed herself and her brief in a rapid and businesslike fashion, and Erskine-Brown was left staring after her. 'Miss Probert's got a new hairdo, Henry,' he said, entranced.

'Really, sir? I can't say I noticed. Got the ginger biscuits there, have you, Dianne?' Dianne put a number of biscuits on a plate by Henry's coffee, thus presenting the staring Rumpole with a terrible temptation. I protested to Henry about Bernard's insanity in taking in Soapy Sam to lead me, and he started on a long story about how Bernard got the case from Jones, the Derwent family solicitor, who didn't do crime, and Ballard had done a bit of insurance work for Jones's firm and they had been greatly impressed.

'This is poisoning, Henry,' I told him. 'Not fooling around with some piffling insurance.'

So I left him and heard, as I made it to the door, Henry's pained cry, 'You're not going to believe this, Dianne! Mr Rumpole's just nicked two of my biscuits.'

So, in due course, I rolled up at Holloway prison to play an ill-tempered second fiddle to Ballard, Q.C., and act as his far older and wiser 'Junior' in our first conference with Lady Derwent. Mr Bernard, who was no longer in my good books, was also of the party. Ballard started off in the voice of a most hostile prosecutor and said to the beautiful young woman we were meant to be defending, 'Lady Derwent. The extremely serious allegation in this case is that you deliberately administered a massive overdose of diamorphine to your husband, who had recently made a will in your favour. It is further suggested that you took the morphine ampoules from the bag of a Nurse Gregson who had called at the house that afternoon. Now the question is, did you administer that fatal dose, Lady Derwent?'

'Be careful,' I muttered a warning to my learned leader, but Ballard paid no attention and continued to attack our client.

'I'd advise you to be perfectly frank with your legal advisers, madam,' he said. 'Well, did you?'

'Just a minute, Ballard,' I interrupted before Perdita had a chance to answer. 'If I may make so bold. As your mere Junior.'

'Well, what is it, Rumpole?'

'A word, if I may, over here.' I got up and went to a corner of the room. Ballard followed me reluctantly. 'Don't ask her that!' I whispered.

'What?'

'Don't ask if she pumped her husband full of morphine so she could get her fingers on a bit of ready cash. Of all the tactless questions!'

'But isn't that what this case is all about?'

'Of course it's what it's all about. That's why you don't ask.'

'Why not?'

'In case she says "yes",' I hissed.

Bernard and Lady Derwent sat at the table, no doubt curious about the *sotto voce* dialogue taking place in the corner of the room. 'Then we'd know, for certain.' Ballard seemed to think that would be no bad thing.

'Exactly. And I'd be sitting in Chambers un-employed, having fantasies about steak and kidney pudding, and you'd be back to motor insurance. First lesson in murder, old darling. Never ask the customer if she did it. She might tell you.'

'Really, Rumpole!' Ballard seemed shocked. 'What do you suggest I ask her?'

'Ask her about the weather. Ask her if she's seen any good films lately. Murder conferences aren't for asking awkward questions, Bollard. Save those for the Prosecution. All we need now is to give the client a little confidence.'

'Confidence, Rumpole . . . ?' It seemed a quality Ballard didn't know how to impart. 'Watch care-fully,' I said, 'and you might learn something.' I led him back to the table, sat, smiled at Perdita and began to conduct the conference in my own way, starting with an entirely harmless question. 'Lady Derwent. You met your husband when he was a professor at St Matthew's?'

'Yes. I was a student.'

'And he fell in love with you? Quite under-standably.'

'I don't know about that.' She rewarded me with a faint smile. 'I fell in love with him.'

'Then he got a divorce and married you. I think you were twenty-four at the time.'

'Twenty-three.'

'And his daughter Helen continued to live with you. She was about fifteen years older?'

'I'm afraid Helen always resented me. She thought I'd taken Daniel away from her mother. It wasn't like that at all.'

'Of course not.' I looked understanding. 'They'd separated before you met, hadn't they?'

'They used to separate and come together. It was never happy. But when it finally ended, well, Daniel's wife was very bitter.'

'Helen was bitter too?' I could imagine the jealousy an older daughter felt towards the younger beauty who she thought had ensnared her father.

'I think she worshipped Daniel. She didn't make it particularly easy for me.' Then Ballard couldn't resist what he clearly considered an awkward question for Perdita. 'So did you resent your husband having his daughter to live with you? Were there quarrels about that? Were there, Lady Derwent?'

'Daniel hated quarrels. I did my best not to have them,' she said, and I believed her. In my role as the nice policeman I asked gently, 'I suppose Helen wanted to go on running the house. Just as her mother had for so many years?'

'You understand!' She looked at me gratefully.

'I'd better understand Helen Derwent,' I told her, 'if I'm going to cross-examine her.' Bernard cleared his throat in an embarrassed manner and Ballard protested, 'I imagine *I* will be cross-examining Miss Helen Derwent, Rumpole. It will fall to *me*, as *leading* Counsel for the Defence.'

'But if you happen to be feeling tired. When

we get to that stage,' I suggested hopefully.

'I don't anticipate feeling in the least tired, Rumpole. At any stage.'

'Don't let's look on the black side.'

And then, desperate to make peace between his barristers, Mr Bernard was ill-advised enough to say, 'Mr Rumpole. Mr Ballard is briefed as leading Counsel in this case. On our client's previous solicitor's instructions.'

'Mr Bernard!' I interrupted him with some force. 'Perhaps I should remind you. There is a trial which has gone down to history as the Penge Bungalow Murders. If you happen to consult the relevant volume of Notable British Trials you will find that I brought home victory in that case alone *and without a leader*. That is my last word to you on the subject. Now, Lady Derwent.' I smiled at Perdita and took over control of the conference again. 'You also lived with your mother-in-law, Mrs Barbara Derwent. How did you get on with her?'

'I've always loved Bunty,' Perdita told us. 'She never criticized me, or made me feel a fool about the house or anything. And she was so pleased when Daniel and I got married. She said Imogen . . .'

'That's the first Lady Derwent,' Mr Bernard explained to Soapy Sam, who was looking a little lost.

'Yes. Bunty said Imogen was the most terrible snob. Bunty wasn't a snob at all. She'd been a dancer when she was young. In the chorus. Of course, you'd never guess that now. She's got so fat. Funny, isn't it?'

'We all change, Lady Derwent, over the years, and we can't all get many laughs out of it. I suppose you don't have a biscuit about you, by any chance? No? Of course not.' I had been stopped in my tracks by pangs of hunger and Ballard, seizing his chance, took over again with 'Lady Derwent. We've had the *post mortem* results on your husband.'

'The medical evidence.' I put it more attractively.

'He was clearly suffering from an illness which gave him only a short time to live.'

'It doesn't make any sense,' I said thoughtfully, and Perdita, with whom I had set up a certain rapport, nodded. 'I've been trying to work it out. Danny loved life so much. Everything about it. He loved his work. I think he loved me.'

'What doesn't make sense,' I suggested, 'is the idea of anyone killing Sir Daniel for his money when he was going to die anyway. No doubt that's a point that's even occurred to you, Ballard.'

Ballard, however, was busy getting out of his papers a copy of a pamphlet to which he obviously attached great importance. 'We also have seen,' he told our client, 'copies of this booklet found among the clothes in your bedroom, Lady Derwent. It's a work entitled "Helping the Loved One Across the River".'

'I honestly don't know how it got there. I'd

never seen it before.' Perdita looked at us anxiously.

'It seems to advocate euthanasia . . .'

'Ballard!' It was my duty to warn him.

*'The troubled soul in a state of acute pain or terminal illness . . .'* Soapy Sam started to read, and there was nothing else for it. I rose to my feet. 'Well, now, Lady Derwent,' I said. 'It's been most useful for us to have this little chat with you.'

But Ballard went on reading remorselessly from the work in his hand: *'Relatives or dear friends may provide a loved one with a bridge or at least a little raft on which to float gently away to a happier land. All that is needed is a rudimentary knowledge of medical science and the effects of various drugs on the unnecessary prolongation of life. Join Across the River, 19A Goshawk Street, Kentish Town for full details . . .'*

'Must be getting along now.' I managed a realistic stagger and grasped the back of my chair. 'The truth of the matter is, I'm not feeling absolutely up to snuff.'

'Rumpole! You look decidedly unfit, sir.' Mr Bernard was easily persuaded. 'What is it?'

'The prolongation of life, Bernard! It usually proves fatal in the end.'

'Mr Rumpole . . . ?' Perdita was touchingly concerned. 'I shall be all right, Lady Derwent,' I reassured her. 'You and I will probably be all right. Mr Bernard, how about running us back to the Temple in your sturdy little motor?' At that moment I would have dropped dead rather than let Ballard ask the idiotic question he had in mind.

Some time later I was having breakfast in the Taste-Ee-Bite tearoom in Fleet Street, loading my tray with nothing but a cup of black coffee, a glass of orange juice and *The Times*, when I saw Mizz Probert in front of me in the queue. She looked at my iron rations and I explained that some dotty doctor wanted to keep me alive, although I supposed she held the view that when men get to a certain age they should be bagged up and put out with the dustbins. She didn't deny the charge but went off to breakfast with a pleasant-looking young man who I judged to be an embryo barrister. When she had gone I weakened and added a sugar bun to my purchases; this I secreted in my pocket for use only in an emergency. Then I went to a table near Mizz Probert and hid behind my *Times*. From this point of vantage I was able to hear Liz making what I thought was a rather rash promise to her companion.

'I'll get you into our Chambers I promise you, Dave. It just needs a little organization. There's a man called Claude Erskine-Brown in charge of admission. To be honest, he reckons he fancies me.'

'Liz' — the young man was clearly of a pure and moral disposition — 'you don't mean to say you'd use sexual manipulation?'

314

'It's all in a good cause, Dave.' She put out her hand and held his across the table. 'We can work together on the rent inquiry in Tower Hamlets. You wouldn't mind going for an interview with Claude, would you?'

'For you, Liz,' young Dave spoke with a certain amount of passion, 'I'd go for an interview with the Lord Chancellor.'

'Oh, don't worry. Claude's not a bit like the Lord Chancellor. For one thing he can't seem to keep his mind off sex.'

After this meeting, Mizz Probert went to her admirer Claude Erskine-Brown and again accused him of discrimination against gay and lesbian persons. When he hotly denied all such prejudices she challenged him with 'I bet you don't let Dave Inchcape into Chambers. He's coming to see you next week.' From this, Erskine-Brown made certain deductions about young Inchcape. His subsequent interview with the new applicant took, as he told me much later, a somewhat unusual course.

'Inchcape?' Claude asked nervously when the young man entered his room.

'Yes. Dave Inchcape.'

'Dave. Of course.' Claude raised a hand. 'Hi! Why don't you sit down?' He pointed to a distant chair. 'Over there.' He sat himself safely behind his desk and seemed to have difficulty in starting the conversation. 'Well . . . Dave. Fact is, Liz Probert's had a long talk to me about you. Great

315

girl, Liz. She's tremendously keen that we shouldn't have any kind of . . . discrimination in Chambers. I mean, we shouldn't be against you simply because you are what you are.'

'What am I?'

'Well. What you are. Entirely through no fault of your own.' Claude was unable to make himself completely clear.

'You mean, young?' Inchcape was puzzled.

'Well. Yes. Young, I suppose. And . . . well, these things are no doubt decided for us at a very early age.'

'You mean, wanting to be a barrister?' The young man was doing his best to follow Claude's drift.

'Well, that. And . . . I mean, it's a matter of the sort of genes you get born with. Biologically speaking.'

'You think I got born with a barrister's genes?' Inchcape asked seriously.

'Oh, very good that!' Claude laughed appreciatively. 'Very funny. Of course, you lot always have a marvellous sense of humour and, we always noticed at Winchester, a great aptitude for the violin.'

'I can't do it,' Inchcape said after a thoughtful silence.

'What?'

'Play the violin.'

'Well, you can rest assured, Dave,' Claude said generously, 'we're not going to hold that against you.'

'Well, thanks.' And after another somewhat embarrassed pause Inchcape added, 'I expect you want to know about my experience.'

'Good heavens, no!' quick as a flash, Claude answered.

'You don't?'

'I take the view, Dave, that your experiences are entirely a matter between you and . . . well, whoever you've had the experiences with.'

'Tomkins. In Testament Buildings.' Inchcape mentioned the name of the elderly barrister whose pupil he'd been.

'Please. Don't tell me! It's absolutely none of my business!' Claude was incredulous, but couldn't help asking, 'You mean Tommy Tomkins?'

'Yes. I was with him for about a year.'

'But I thought Tommy was married to a lady magistrate?' Claude was shocked.

'So he is. Does that make any difference?'

'Well. Not nowadays, I suppose.' Liz, Claude thought, would condemn his attitude as ridiculously old-fashioned. 'The way I look at it is this, Dave. My attitude is . . . There's no real difference between us!'

'Except you've had a great deal more experience than I have,' Inchcape suggested.

'I wouldn't say that,' Claude denied hastily. 'But of course I do have the children. Young Tristan and Isolde. A perpetual joy. Named after Wagner's star-crossed lovers, of course. You don't know what it's like having little ones around you.'

'No, I'm sorry,' the young bachelor apologized, but Claude reassured him, 'No one's going to blame you. And think what you save us on the rates.'

'What do you mean?' Now Inchcape was completely lost.

'By not having children. In my view you're absolutely entitled to counselling services.' Claude stood up, conscious of a duty well done. 'I'll be reporting to Ballard. I'm sure we'll be able to squeeze you in.'

'I don't mind sharing a room . . .' Inchcape stood and advanced on Claude Erskine-Brown who backed away, saying, 'Not with me, I'm afraid. That would hardly do, would it? Perhaps we can put you in with Liz Probert. Then you wouldn't have any . . . distractions!'

'Well, thank you, Claude. Thanks very much.' Inchcape seemed to like the idea.

'Not at all. That way out, Dave.'

> It was about the noon
> Of a glorious day in June
> When our General rode along us
> For to form us for to fight . . .

The battle was an exciting and exhilarating occasion, the trial of Lady Derwent on a charge of poisoning her husband. It was the General who let the side down, for I had been landed with a commanding officer with about as much talent for Old Bailey warfare as a sheep in Holy Orders.

He was interested in body-building, which wouldn't do a thing except unnecessarily prolong the life of Ballard, but courage-building was what he needed — the talent to draw the sabre and charge into the gun-fire of Judge Gerald Graves. Into the mouth of hell! I couldn't see Ballard doing it. Cannon to right of him, cannon to left of him, and Ballard would sneak off home and exercise with his chest-expander. However, there was little I could do about it.

'Mine not to reason why, Mine but to do or die,' I murmured to myself as I arrived short of breath, but fully wigged and gowned for the fight ahead, in front of Judge Graves's Court. 'Mine though I damn well know Bernard has blundered . . . Briefing Bollard to lead *me!*' And then a resonant contralto voice interrupted my thoughts with 'Your big case today, isn't it? I just saw Sam Ballard going up to the robing-room.'

'That must have been a treat for you, Matron,' I said, for the speaker was none other than the Old Bailey medical supremo, Mrs Marguerite Plumstead, a powerfully built, still handsome woman who could deal in a swift and determined manner with fainting jurors or malingering criminals.

'I suppose it's a case of follow my leader for you today, isn't it, Mr Rumpole?' I winced. 'And our Sam was looking wonderfully well.' She gave me a quick look over and put me in the C.3 category. 'Aren't we letting that naughty tummy of ours get a little out of hand?'

'I'm melting into thin air, thank you, Matron.' I went on about my business and she called after me, 'That's all right, my dear. I like to keep an eye on all my barristers.'

The Court was full and the press benches crowded for the Derwent murder. That cold fish, Judge Gerald Graves, promoted above his station to try the case, decorated the Bench like something lifeless on a marble slab. Perdita was looking beautiful in the dock, but as though her thoughts were far away. Bunty was sitting largely in the public seats; she smiled at Perdita, who smiled faintly back. Marcus Griffin, the Senior Treasury Counsel, was prosecuting. Griffin is a perfectly nice, rather fair prosecutor, whom I like to treat as though he were some particularly ruthless Grand Inquisitor. His Junior, Arthurian Daybell, was seated behind him, and I, God save the mark, was seated behind Soapy Sam Ballard, Q.C. Such was the scene in which Marcus Griffin rose to his feet to open his case to the Jury.

'Members of the Jury,' prosecuting Counsel began. 'This case concerns the death, from a massive overdose of diamorphine, of Sir Daniel Derwent, R.A., the well-known portrait painter. He had made a will leaving his entire estate, a considerable sum of money, Members of the Jury — something well over two million pounds — to his wife Perdita, the defendant in this case. He made no provision for his mother, Mrs Barbara Derwent, or his daughter by a previous marriage,

Helen, although the two ladies lived with him at number one, Ruskin Street, Chelsea, as members of his family.'

'He settled money on them during his lifetime,' I whispered urgently to the back of my not-so-learned leader. 'It's quite unfair to suggest that our client scooped the pool.'

'Horace, I do know.' He tried to quieten me. 'It *is* my brief.'

'The Jury haven't read your brief! Get up and tell them.'

'Horace.' He only wanted to be left in peace.

'Don't "Horace" me! Get up on your hind legs, why don't you? Make your presence felt.'

'Mr Ballard.' The Judge sounded his most sepulchral note. 'I think your Junior is trying to tell you something.'

'I'm extremely sorry, my Lord.' Ballard rose sycophantically. 'I must apologize most sincerely for any interruption.'

'No need to apologize. Sit down, Bollard.' I couldn't resist rising to address the Court. 'I was trying to communicate vital information to the Jury, my Lord. Sir Daniel Derwent made a generous financial settlement on his mother and daughter during his life-time.'

'My Lord. That would appear to be correct,' Griffin conceded after a brief word with his Junior.

'Of course it's correct!' I continued somewhat to my leader's chagrin. 'It would also be correct if the Prosecution were to present the facts in a full and unbiased way to the Jury at this stage, and not try to colour the evidence by a one-sided account.'

'My Lord. I assure the Court that any mistake I may have made was quite unintentional,' Griffin protested. I had got him on the defensive and followed on with 'Provided it's agreed that this Prosecution is capable of mistakes.'

'Mr Rumpole!' I had succeeded in provoking a sort of frozen fury in his Lordship. 'My understanding is that you appear here as Junior Counsel to your learned and very experienced leader, Mr Samuel Ballard.'

'Strange things happen down the Old Bailey,' I muttered to no one in particular and my leader chimed in with 'My Lord. That is perfectly correct.'

'Thank you, Mr Ballard. I'm grateful for your assistance.' When the Judge said that, Ballard bowed humbly and sat down. I was left standing on my own. 'Then, no doubt, Mr Rumpole,' Graves continued, 'you can safely leave any further objections and interruptions in the skillful hands of Mr Samuel Ballard.'

'You must be joking,' I muttered again.

'I find difficulty in hearing you, Mr Rumpole.'

'You can rest assured I shall only interrupt again when the interests of justice demand it, my Lord.' I said it very loudly and then sat down to give way to Griffin, who outlined the facts of Sir Daniel's death and showed the Jury the incriminating articles — the used ampoules, the pamphlet and the hypodermic — he undertook to prove were found in our client's bedroom. Then he told them, 'It will be our case that Lady Derwent, knowing exactly what she was doing because she had read this pamphlet, administered that massive overdose to her husband. She may have deluded herself into thinking that she was helping him to a peaceful and painless death, but of course that would be no defence to a charge of murder. Her true motive, the Prosecution will suggest, is money. The freehold of the Chelsea house and Sir Daniel's considerable investments would be hers on his death. Members of the Jury. You will hear evidence about the matrimonial relationship of this couple. I have told you that they occupied separate bedrooms . . .'

'Because he couldn't *sleep*.' I tried to stir my leader into some sort of activity.

'Do you wish to interrupt *again*, Mr Rumpole?' the judge was asking.

'No, my Lord.' I rose as impressively as I could manage to my feet and stared at the Jury. 'I am quite content to let my learned friend Mr Griffin continue with his inaccuracies. Our time will come!'

An early prosecution witness was Nurse Gregson, a thin, wiry, grey-haired lady who ministered to the sick and dying around Chelsea and took, I imagined, no nonsense from them. In answer to Marcus Griffin, she remembered calling at the house about four P.M. on the day Sir Daniel died to give him his injection. Miss Helen and Mrs Barbara Derwent, the deceased's mother, were there, and, of course, Lady Derwent. Nurse Gregson glanced disapprovingly at the dock and said, 'I couldn't help noticing her.'

'Why not?' Griffin asked innocently.

'She was sitting on a chair, my Lord, stripped to the waist.'

'Am I to understand that this young lady was sitting among the family with her bosoms unclothed?' His Lordship sounded incredulous.

'That is right, my Lord.'

'Is that a criminal offence?' I whispered to my leader, loudly enough for the Jury to hear. 'Mr Rumpole?' the Judge inquired, and I rose to address him. 'I only ask for a legal direction, my Lord. At the moment this evidence seems utterly irrelevant.'

At which point I sat down and the Judge spoke despairingly to my leader. 'Mr Ballard. Is there any way in which you can discourage further interruptions by your learned Junior?'

'I can only say I will do my best, my Lord.' Soapy Sam rose humbly.

'Thank *you*, Mr Ballard.' The Judge was very much obliged and Marcus Griffin went back to work. 'And you saw Sir Daniel Derwent?'

'Oh, yes. He was there. He was painting his wife's portrait.'

'Painting unclothed bosoms,' I whispered again for the benefit of the Jury. 'An unfortunate habit of artists throughout the centuries!'

'Mr Ballard, I think Mr Rumpole spoke again.'
The Judge was on to it, quick as a shot. Ballard
rose sadly to admit, 'That may very well be so,
my Lord.'

'See to it, Mr Ballard.' Those were his
Lordship's orders. So Ballard said, 'Ssh, Horace!'
and I told him to keep quiet because I was trying
to listen to the evidence, which now reached a
vital point. Nurse Gregson described giving Sir
Daniel the injection of diamorphine. 'I understand,' Griffin said, 'this was a top-up injection,
as he was in considerable pain?'

'Yes, it was. They always got me to give the
injections. They had acquired a hypodermic but
none of the family could use it, so I always did
the job for them.'

'*This* was the hypodermic they kept but didn't
normally use?' My learned friend lifted the exhibit
he said was found in Perdita's bedroom.

'I imagine so.'

'Was the diamorphine you injected in ampoules?'

'Yes.'

'Did you have other ampoules of morphine in
your medical bag?'

'Yes, I did. I had other patients, of course.'
Nurse Gregson went on to give evidence of the
number of missing ampoules and the milli-
grammes they contained. Griffin said, 'We have
heard such a dose might prove fatal.' He had
called an expert who had testified to that; it was
evidence that Ballard had not felt able to

challenge. 'Did you use any of the other ampoules when you gave Sir Daniel Derwent his injection?'

'No.'

'Were the ampoules and their wrappings similar to these?' Griffin held up more of the treasure trove found in Perdita's bedroom.

'Yes, they were.'

'After you had given the injection, what did you do?'

'I went out into the hall, with my bag, and I was putting on my coat when Mrs Derwent . . .'

'The deceased's mother?'

'Yes. She asked if I'd like to stay for a cup of tea. I said I would and I went back into the studio. I left my bag in the hall.'

'Unattended?'

'Yes. Mrs Derwent went out to make the tea and Lady Derwent was given a break from sitting. She put on some kind of a wrap and went out to help her mother-in-law.'

'What about you?'

'Oh, I stayed in the studio.'

'Did Sir Daniel leave the studio at all, while you were there?'

'I couldn't be certain. If he did, it was only for a few minutes.'

'Did Miss Helen Derwent leave it?'

'No. I'm sure she didn't.'

'Why do you say that?'

'We were talking about the garden she looked after. We're both keen gardeners.'

'And how did your visit end?'

'We all had tea and I collected my bag and left. I went off duty then and didn't check the contents of my bag until next morning. I discovered that a large number of diamorphine ampoules were missing from my bag. These were to be used in the treatment of other patients, my Lord. I also heard on the radio that Sir Daniel had died during the night. I immediately telephoned the Derwent household. Dr Harman was there and I told him the whole thing.'

'Nurse Gregson,' Griffin ended, 'are you quite sure that you didn't administer a massive overdose of diamorphine on that afternoon to your patient, Sir Daniel Derwent?'

'I am a state registered nurse with twenty-five years' experience, my Lord. I am quite certain that I did not.'

' "I am quite certain that I did not." ' Graves was delighted to make that note. Griffin sat and Ballard rose slowly; it was, as I whispered to him, his great moment. He stood in silence for a while and then turned to whisper for my help. 'Is there any particular question?'

'Couldn't Sir Daniel have administered the overdose to himself? If he had the diamorphine and a hypodermic syringe.' I loaded him with my best ammunition.

'Ah, yes.' Ballard tried to look as though he'd thought of it himself. 'If Sir Daniel had been in possession of that syringe, and a large number of diamorphine ampoules, could he not have administered an overdose to himself?'

'I suppose it's possible,' Nurse Gregson answered reluctantly.

'And might he not have left the studio when your bag was unattended in the hall?' I filled Ballard with another round. He turned to the witness, appeared to think the matter over carefully and said, 'And let me ask you this. Sir Daniel might have left the studio when tea was being prepared. And your bag was in the hall and he might have taken the diamorphine from it?'

'I have said he might have gone out for a few minutes. That's all.'

Our work was done, but still Ballard lingered on his feet. I whispered some words of command. 'Sit down and shut up. Don't spoil it now.'

'And you admit that Sir Daniel *could* have injected himself?' Soapy Sam couldn't take orders.

'He *could* have. But I don't think he did,' the witness told him.

'Leave it alone, Bollard!' The situation was desperate, but my leader went on, delighted with himself. 'Tell the Members of the Jury, Nurse Gregson. *Why* don't you think so?' It was, of course, the one question that shouldn't have been asked, and the witness was delighted to answer it.

'Sir Daniel had a horror of hypodermic needles,' she told the Jury. 'I'm quite sure he could not have done such a thing on his own.'

My learned leader had scored an own goal, and it was four o'clock, crumpet-time, although I wasn't allowed crumpets. Marcus Griffin said he thought it was too late to embark on the evidence of Miss Helen Derwent, which might take a little time, and the Judge told the Members of the Jury that they would meet again at ten thirty the next morning when 'we shall hope to proceed without further interruptions from Mr Rumpole'.

When the Court rose, Ballard retired to the Q.C.s' robing-room on the top floor of the Old Bailey. He was delighted to find the room empty, as he had some sort of work-out in mind. He removed his wig and gown, tailed Court coat and waistcoat, and then opened his brief-case and removed his much-loved chest-expander. This particular instrument of torture had two wooden handles, which Ballard gripped, and he proceeded to haul away at the steel spring, expanding his chest and shouting orders to himself, 'One . . . two! One . . . two!' This is what he was doing when I opened the door and put my head round it, having had a few ideas on the cross-examination of Miss Helen Derwent.

'One . . . two! In . . . out!' chanted my leader, who didn't seem to have heard me. He had the chest-expander pulled out to its fullest possible extent when I called out sharply, 'Bollard!'

At that, he turned suddenly, loosing his grip on one of the handles, which flew inwards, propelled by the spring, and having struck him smartly on the side of the head felled him to the ground. I was left standing, looking down at an unconscious leader. I suppose I should have warned him that exercise is likely to prove fatal. I crossed to the telephone and asked the operator to put out an urgent call for Matron on the Tannoy.

Soon the great Palais de Justice was ringing with the call of 'Matron to the Q.C.s' robing-room at once, please!' They heard it in the canteen, in the Judge's corridors and in the cells. In no time at all, Mrs Marguerite Plumstead was kneeling beside the fallen figure who had been stunned by his own chest-expander. Ballard opened his eyes, focused on the concerned face peering down at him, and whispered, 'Matey!'

'*You* are to carry on, Mr Rumpole?' Judge Graves looked at me in some horror as I rose in Court the next morning to announce the unfortunate indisposition of my learned leader. I had met Matron in the corridor and she had told me that Ballard was suffering from the after-effects of concussion, a back muscle was strained and he had been severely shocked. The Doctor, it seemed, had ordered him to take two days' complete rest. 'He's being so wonderfully brave about it.' Matron looked a little misty-eyed. 'Never a thought of "self". Well, isn't that our lovely Sam all over? Almost his last words as we got him into the ambulance were "Of course Rumpole will ask for an adjournment." '

'Delirious, no doubt,' I said, and went into Court to announce that I was prepared to act without the inestimable advantage of Mr Ballard's inspired leadership. 'My client,' I assured Judge Graves, 'is most anxious there should be no further delays. She has waited too long to be cleared of these monstrous allegations.' He sighed heavily, but came to the conclusion that he had no choice but to continue with the case if I weren't asking for an adjournment until the recovery of Ballard. 'I hope your client realizes the risk she is taking,' he said in a voice of terrible warning, 'in depriving herself of her leading Counsel's wisdom and *moderation*.'

I bowed and resumed my seat. Happily, the time for moderation was over and I meant to launch an immoderate attack on the principal witness against us. Whilst Griffin was taking Miss Helen Derwent gently through her evidence-in-chief, I whispered a few vital instructions to Bernard. I wanted him to issue a subpoena on the organization Across the River or use any other means at his disposal to get a list of their members. Then I leaned back to look at my client's stepdaughter.

Helen was dark and Perdita fair. Helen was intense, serious and capable, I thought, of bearing long grudges. Perdita was gentle, smiled easily and was, I judged, forgiving. No doubt, Helen was like her mother, Derwent's first wife, and if that were so, I could imagine with what relief he embraced his second marriage. He would have been like a man enjoying a late summer holiday. As I watched her, Helen told the Jury, in quiet, unemotional tones, that she had found the empty ampoules and the pamphlet in Perdita's chest-of-drawers and the hypodermic in her bedroom cupboard, although it was usually kept in the cupboard in her late father's bathroom.

This was the witness I rose to cross-examine in the welcome absence of my learned leader. I decided to go right to the heart of her evidence and waste no time on polite persiflage. 'Miss Derwent. You didn't approve of your father's second wife?'

'She was very young and feckless. I suppose he was besotted with her, in a way.' She looked at Perdita in the dock, and the young woman lowered her eyes, avoiding a confrontation.

'I suppose some men enjoy being besotted?' I suggested.

'Perhaps.'

'By "feckless" you mean incompetent?'

'Totally incompetent! On the very night my father died, for instance, she had forgotten to order the fish.'

'How terrible!' I looked at the Jury.

'It may not sound much but Daddy looked forward to his fish pie on a Friday night. Of course, Perdita had forgotten to order it so we had to have omelettes.'

'Did Lady Derwent cook them?'

'Perdita?' The witness smiled scornfully. 'Of course not. She was just about up to boiling water. I think Granny cooked them.'

'Just omelettes for dinner?'

'I think we had some mulligatawny soup

Granny had made the day before. Oh, and treacle tart. Is that what you wanted to know?'

It wasn't really. I just couldn't keep off the subject of food. I forced myself to another topic. 'His painting meant a great deal to your father?'

'It was his whole life.'

'His increasing illness meant that a time was coming when he would no longer be able to paint. That night he'd spoiled a picture, didn't he?'

'I remember that.'

'That was a terrible prospect for an artist who loved his work?'

'Yes.'

'So might he not have felt he had nothing left to live for and taken his own life? Have you considered that possibility?' I turned and asked the Jury to consider it, but Helen said quickly, 'Daddy never mentioned suicide!'

'Never mentioned it to you, perhaps.'

'Or to anyone, as far as I know. Besides, he still had a lot to live for.'

'You mean he had his happiness with a beautiful young wife?'

'No.' She looked at me with intense dislike. 'I didn't mean that.'

'Miss Derwent.' I leant forward and kept my eyes on her face. We were coming to the vital part of her testimony. 'You found your father dead in his studio?'

'I couldn't sleep so I went downstairs. I found him then. On the couch . . .' She put her hand over her face and trembled a little, but I don't think she was crying.

'Please' — Judge Graves looked almost human — 'don't distress yourself, Miss Derwent.'

'Then you telephoned Doctor Harman. He called and arranged for the removal of your father's body. He called again later, and spoke to your mother and your step-mother. While he was doing that, do you say you searched Lady Derwent's bedroom?'

'I took a look round in there. Yes.'

'You took a look round? In the hope of finding something that would incriminate your step-mother?'

'No . . .'

'Then *why?*'

Helen was silent then, thinking. At last she said, 'I never thought Perdita would be able to face looking after Daddy through his final illness. She was just too young and . . .'

' "Feckless". Is that the word you'd use?'

'Exactly! So it often occurred to me that she might try and well . . . help Daddy out of this world. And,' she added coldly, 'especially if it would be so much to her financial advantage.'

'Did Daddy tell you he was leaving all his money to his young wife?'

'He said that. Yes.'

'Having previously settled comfortable incomes on you and his mother.'

'That's been agreed by the Prosecution,' the Judge thought fit to remind me. 'We needn't waste time on that.'

'Your Lordship is always helpful.' I smiled sweetly at the old darling and asked the witness, 'You know something, I expect, about the law of wills?'

'I know a little.'

'Do you know that if Lady Derwent is found guilty of her husband's murder she will inherit nothing?'

"We all know *that*, Mr Rumpole.' The Judge's patience, never in lavish supply, was running out.

'Oh, I'm sorry, my Lord,' I apologized. 'I'd forgotten that the Members of the Jury had all passed their Bar exams.' I got a little laughter from the Jury, quickly silenced by an angry 'Mr Rumpole!' from the Judge. I turned hurriedly back to the witness. 'Very well, Miss Derwent. Did you know that or didn't you?'

'I suppose I may have had some idea that that was the law. It would only be fair.'

'So that this two-million-pound estate would then be divided between you and your grand-mother.'

'Yes, I suppose it would.'

'An extremely satisfactory result so far as you're concerned?'

For the first time the Jury looked at Helen Derwent with suspicion, so the Judge thought it time to interrupt my flow. 'Mr Rumpole,' he asked, 'are you suggesting that these exhibits, the used ampoules, the syringe and the pamphlet, were never in your client's bedroom at all?'

'Your Lordship sees the point so quickly.' I

gave him the retort courteous, and then turned on the witness. 'You found these used ampoules didn't you, near your father's body. Probably the syringe was there too. And the pamphlet, was that his?'

Helen Derwent no longer disliked me, she hated me. But her voice was still controlled as she asked, 'What are you accusing me of?'

'Mr Rumpole.' The Judge came to her rescue. 'May I remind you of the evidence Nurse Gregson gave. This witness remained in the studio with the nurse during the whole time the medical bag was left unattended. She had no chance at all of removing the diamorphine ampoules.'

'Oh, I agree with that, my Lord.' I was Rumpole respectful. 'I'm not suggesting for a moment that Miss Helen Derwent killed her father.'

'Well, what are you suggesting, may I ask?'

'That she put those exhibits in my client's bedroom in the hope that some gullible jury might convict her of murder, my Lord.'

'Oh, really.' Helen was still fighting. 'And how do you say my father died?'

'I say what the Jury is going to say, when they have considered all the evidence,' I answered her with all the confidence I could muster. 'He killed himself when his painter's hand would no longer obey his orders.'

That night, as I was ingesting Thin-O-Vite, Mr Bernard telephoned and told me he had managed to get a membership list of the Across the

River society at last. So I learned something that I should, perhaps, have thought of before. Now I had learnt it too late. My defence had been firmly planted in the minds of the Jury and it would be dangerous to change horses in mid-stream, particularly as the other horse was so dark and so uncertain a runner. I lay awake thinking of my final speech to the Jury, my last opportunity to convince them of the possibility of Daniel Derwent's suicide.

By morning I had decided not to put Perdita in the witness-box. More customers sink themselves by their own evidence than ever get scuppered by the prosecution witnesses. I saw no point in calling my client so that Marcus Griffin could try to squeeze some admission out of her to boost his tottering case. I had all the facts I wanted; now was the time for some gentle persuasion. I thought of another cogent argument for going straight to final speeches and not calling Perdita. If I did so, there was a decent chance of getting the case over before Ballard got back to ruin it all.

'No accused person can be forced into the witness-box,' I told the Jury. 'Lady Derwent has been accused of the abominable crime of murdering the husband she loved. She is fully entitled, as you or I would be, were we accused, to say to this blundering Prosecution "All right. Prove it. Don't expect any help in your unsavoury work from me." And at the end of the day, to say to you now that nothing,

337

nothing at all, has been proved beyond reasonable doubt. A successful painter, who loves his art, finds that, through illness, he can paint no longer. Can you not understand, can't we all understand, his deciding to end his life? Nurse Gregson leaves her bag in the hall. Sir Daniel Derwent leaves the studio for just long enough, perhaps only a few minutes, to take those diamorphine ampoules. Later that night he injects himself with a massive overdose. Nurse Gregson tells us he didn't like needles; not many of us do, Members of the Jury, but if we are desperate enough we can all use them. The desperate addict forces himself to use them when longing for his fix. The desperately ill artist was also forced to inject himself when longing for death. So what remains of this pathetic prosecution? Merely Helen Derwent's evidence of what she says she found after her father's death. Why did she, cold and calculating as she is, go up to her step-mother's bedroom on that terrible morning after she had found her father dead, when any normal woman would be too overcome with grief to do anything? Was it to find evidence? Or to *plant* evidence? Of course, these things were in the house, her father had used them. Did she lie and say she had found them in Perdita's bedroom to feed her spite and to satisfy her greed for money? Members of the Jury . . . I suggest that you wouldn't convict in a case of non-renewed dog licence on the evidence of Miss Helen Derwent!'

One of the happier moments in a barrister's life is when he sits down at the end of his final speech. A huge weight seems to have been lifted from his shoulders. He has done all he can and his work is over. The Jury has to decide the case, and in that decision he can take no further part.

Judge Graves summed up in a manner as hostile to the Defence as he could manage, without giving a free run to the Court of Appeal. His delivery, however, was so lugubrious and monotone that even the eagerest juror could be seen closing his eyes occasionally and I doubted if the subtle insertions of his boot would have much effect.

When the Jury had gone, my anxiety returned. I have never paced a Court corridor smoking too many cigars, or sat in the canteen drinking too many cups of coffee, waiting for a verdict, without a dry mouth and sweaty palms, as though it was Rumpole and not his client who stood in danger of the nick. The stakes were perhaps higher in this case, as I had taken the great gamble of not calling my client. If she were convicted I would never be sure I had made the right decision. And had I fought the whole case on a false assumption? Now I knew the truth, or thought I did, should I have taken the desperate step of trying to start again? I lit another small cigar and told myself that the game was over, the judicial croupier had called *'rien n'va plus!'* and there was nothing to do except wait for the roulette wheel to stop spinning.

As these thoughts were going through my mind I saw a spreading figure in a black dress sitting alone on a distant bench. As I sat down beside Bunty Derwent, she looked at me and asked, 'She'll get off, won't she?' Although she was a fat old woman she had, I thought, the calm and trusting face of a child.

'I suppose you think anyone should get off,' I told her. 'I mean, anyone who killed him, speaking as a member of the Across the River Society. You are a member, aren't you? It was your pamphlet?'

There was a silence and then she said, 'He couldn't paint any more. He wouldn't want to live if he couldn't paint.'

'Are you sure?' That had been my defence, but I was an advocate; I wasn't necessarily convinced by it.

'Oh, yes. Perfectly sure. It was for the best.'

'Individual omelettes?' I asked her. 'And the soup, served out in the kitchen, was it? Mulligatawny. I suppose that would hide the taste of the diamorphine.'

'What are you trying to say, Mr Rumpole?' She was like a child, I thought again, and determined not to understand difficult questions.

'Nothing very complicated,' I assured her. 'Only that you pinched the ampoules from the nurse's bag. You knew exactly what they looked like. You got the contents of those ampoules into your son's food somehow. I suppose you left them somewhere in the kitchen where Helen found them and used them to put all the blame on the step-mother she hated. What I'd like to know is this . . .'

'There's something you want to know? I thought you had *all* the answers!' The old woman was almost laughing at me.

'Did you discuss this sudden decision to end his life with your son at all? What were his views on the subject?'

'Oh, there was no need for a discussion,' she explained carefully, as though I were the child. 'A mother knows, Mr Rumpole. A mother always knows.'

'And you let Perdita go through this trial . . .' It was hard to forgive her.

'Oh, you'll get her off.' I found her confidence in my powers a little chilling. 'I've got absolutely no doubt about that. She's quite innocent.'

'I wish I had your simple faith in British justice,' I told her, but then the Usher came out of the door of the Court and called to us. The Jury was coming back and Perdita's fate had been decided.

The formalities, as always, seemed to take for ever. The Jury had to answer to their names; the foreman had to be asked to stand, and then to be asked if they had reached a verdict upon which they were all agreed. When that had been done, the Court door opened and Ballard was

suddenly among us like a wounded soldier, un-
expectedly back from the wars, his head bandaged
under his wig and walking with the aid of a stick
and Matron. He settled into the row in front
of me just as the final question was asked. 'Do
you find the defendant Perdita Derwent guilty
or not guilty of murder?'

The answer, as always, seemed to take for ever,
and I held my breath until it came.

'Not guilty, my Lord.'

I saw Perdita in the dock, her eyes filled with
tears of sorrow and relief, which, now that it
was over, she was finding it hard to control. I
saw Bunty, the mother who knew best, smiling
as though there had never been any doubt about
the verdict. Then Ballard had the nerve to stand
and ask if our client could be released, just as
though he'd done all the work.

'Lady Derwent,' Ballard said to Perdita when
they sprang her from the dock. 'I'm so very glad
we were able to pull it off for you.'

'It's a wonderful victory for Sam, isn't it?' Matron was looking as pleased as Punch. 'Considering
he was away so much of the time.'

'Matron was a ministering angel, Rumpole,' Ballard confided in me. 'She practically
camped out in the hospital. She wouldn't let me
come back until she was quite sure I was out
of danger.'

'Well, I suppose we should all be grateful for
that,' I said, and then took my leave of Perdita.
'Mr Rumpole,' she said as Ballard looked on,

'how can I thank you?'

'Oh, I don't know. Just go on living,' I suggested. 'You've got a great deal of it left to do.' We parted then, and I hoped she'd find another husband and never set her foot in a Law Court again.

Not long after his self-proclaimed triumph in the Derwent murder case, Ballard called a Chambers meeting. There were two items on the agenda, the admission of a new tenant and what our Head had advertised as a 'big surprise' — the exact nature of which he didn't propose to tell us until we met. Claude Erskine-Brown proposed a new member for our gallant band of legal hacks in Equity Court. 'I just think it'd be jolly bad if this Chambers got the reputation for any sort of discrimination,' he told us.

'I'm with you there, Claude.' Ballard nodded wisely. 'Entirely with you.'

'Which is why I'm particularly keen on the admission of young David, "Dave".' Claude looked serious. 'He prefers the style "Dave" Inchcape.'

'Is Inchcape black?' Uncle Tom muttered.

'No, Uncle Tom,' Claude told him. 'Dave is not black.'

'Pity.' Uncle Tom searched for a precedent. 'They had a little black chap in old Batty Jackson's Chambers. Let him in after a great deal of soul-searching. And then this little chap went off and became Prime Minister of Limpopo-

343

land or whatever, and he made old Batty Lord Chief Justice. Other fellows in Chambers got Attorney-General and all sorts of rich pickings. Would you like to go off to Limpopoland, Rumpole?'

'Anywhere where they don't have Chambers meetings.'

'It seems that Liz Probert and Dave are prepared to share a room, so there should be no problems accommodation-wise.' Claude then moved to a subject which caused him only minor embarrassment. 'As I say, I have met Dave and he has been extremely frank with me. "Out of the closet", as we would say.'

'Out of what closet?' Uncle Tom was puzzled. 'Are they going to put this black fellow in the closet?'

It seemed that Ballard wanted to get on to the next item on the agenda. He dealt with the matter shortly. 'So, if no one has any objections to Inchcape . . . Rumpole?'

'Is he keen on exercise?' I wanted to know.

'I don't think people like Dave usually are, are they?' Claude smiled tolerantly.

'Then I don't mind him in the least.'

'Good. That's settled then.' Here Ballard took a deep breath and looked around us with a certain pride. It was the moment to divulge his great secret. 'Now I have an announcement to make of a purely personal and private nature,' he began. 'You will all know Mrs Marguerite Plumstead, the Matron down at the Old Bailey. She is respected and, may I say, loved by so many barristers.'

'A formidable lady!' I agreed.

'During my recent indisposition,' he went on undeterred, "Matey", as I shall always think of her, was a ministering angel to me. She was at my bedside in hospital. She saw me through my convalescence. We have been thrown together as a result of my accident. I am now happy to tell you that I shall no longer be living a bachelor existence in Waltham Cross. Mrs Plumstead has consented to become my wife!'

If I didn't know what a stunned silence was like, I discovered then. We had all imagined that Soapy Sam Ballard was settled in his ways and resigned to solitude, and if he had been smitten by a final irresistible passion, the masterful figure of the Old Bailey Matron seemed an unlikely love object. However, it was useless to speculate on the mysterious chemistry which had drawn these two together and I only had one question for our Head of Chambers.

'Have you consulted *Mr* Plumstead at all?'

'Mr Plumstead, after long service in the Department of the Environment, has, I regret to say, passed over.'

'Oh, I see. Across the river!'

'Of course, you will all be invited to attend the celebrations, with your wives.'

'And in the case of Dave Inchcape, no doubt'
— Claude widened the invitation in the interests

of tolerance — 'live-in companions.'

Ballard was as good as his word and in due course we all hired toppers and tailed coats from Moss Bros and were invited to guzzle and sluice in a handsome marquee erected for the purpose, after the unlikely union had been celebrated in the Temple Church. There was a large cake on which the tiny figures of a gowned and wigged Ballard and a uniformed Matron stood over a scrawled message in pink icing which read BEST OF LUCK TO SAM AND MARGUERITE. Matron cut the cake to general applause and then approached Hilda with a minute segment on a plate. I watched the scene moodily, eating a few peanuts, whilst the barristers around me were stuck into the salmon and champagne. 'Won't you have a wee slice of cake, Mrs Rumpole,' Matron asked, 'as it's *such* a special occasion?' 'Of course I will. Why ever not?' Hilda found the offering with some difficulty.

'I thought you might be watching that naughty tummy. Like your husband.'

'Rumpole and I are both perfectly fit, thank you, Matron.' No one can say 'Thank you' with such bitter irony as She Who Must Be Obeyed.

'Oh, I know. Sam says your husband was such a help to him in the big murder. I'm so glad old Rumpole can still lend a hand as a *junior* barrister.'

'Old Rumpole, as you call him, seems to

have done the big murder largely on his own.' Hilda was displeased. 'As he did the Penge Bungalow Murders. You must have heard of that case.'

'I'm not sure I have . . .'

'I really envy you, Matron' — Hilda smiled sweetly — 'having so much to learn about the law.'

I wandered off then to have a look at more food I couldn't participate in and found Henry depressed. 'It's happened, Mr Rumpole,' he told me. 'My wife's turn has come. She is no longer a Chair.'

'What now?'

'My year has started. I am now Mayoress of Bexley Heath.'

'Henry! My heart bleeds for you.'

'Dianne is being extremely brave about it.'

I had hardly had time to give our clerk my full sympathy when Hoskins, the grey barrister much concerned with the education of his daughters, came up with some more extraordinary news. 'Rumpole! Terribly sad, isn't it?'

'Oh, I don't know. I suppose if you want to prolong your life you've got no alternative but to marry "Matey".'

'No. Sad about Hector MacClintock. He was your doctor too, wasn't he?'

'What's happened?'

'Dropped dead. And he must have been considerably younger than you.'

'Oh, dear! I *am* sorry. Poor Dr MacClintock.

I'm very sorry. And he took all those precautions . . .' It was of course a blow, but one fact stood out a mile. Unlike the careful doctor, I was still alive. I took a large dinner plate and began to fill it methodically, decorating cold beef, a chicken drumstick and fish with a generous dollop of potato salad. Looking up from this work for a moment I saw a young couple, clearly in love, embracing behind a palm in a corner of the tent. They were Mizz Liz Probert and our new entrant David or 'Dave' Inchcape, and watching them like a man who has been totally deceived and is feeling particularly bitter about it was my learned friend, Claude Erskine-Brown.

'Look at that, Rumpole.' The man was clearly outraged. 'The ice-cold cheek of it. The fellow's a raving heterosexual!'

'That Inchcape.' Uncle Tom joined us, apparently puzzled. 'Remarkably fair skin for an African prime minister. Do you think we've been led up the garden?'

I took my plate over to where Hilda was sitting and told her why I now felt free to scoff at will, filling our glasses with Ballard's bubbly. She might have had a few words to say on the subject, but Claude had gone to the centre of the tent and embarked on a speech.

'A big welcome to you all,' he said. 'Ladies and gentlemen. Fellow members of Chambers. As Sam Ballard's best man, and as his learned leader in the field of matrimony' — there was a smidgin of laughter at this and Phillida sighed — 'it's my pleasure to wish the happy couple health . . .'

'Not too much health . . .' I was refilling my champagne glass. 'Just enough health to stand up in Court and lift a glass to your lips. It's the quality of life that matters, isn't it? The quality of life. And the hell with Thin-O-Vite.'